FIERCE HEART

FIERCE HEART

ELVEN ALLIANCE BOOK ONE

TARA GRAYCE

Sword & Cross
Publishing

Published by Sword & Cross Publishing
Grand Rapids, MI

Sword & Cross Publishing and the Sword & Cross Publishing
logo are trademarks. Absence of ™ in connection with Sword &
Cross Publishing does not indicate an absence of trademark
protection of those marks.

Cover by Savannah Jezowski of Dragonpenpress.com
Map by Amythyst_art on Fiverr

To God, my King and Father. Soli Deo Gloria

LCCN: 2019920747
ISBN: 978-1-943442-09-6

BOOKS BY TARA GRAYCE

ELVEN ALLIANCE
Fierce Heart
War Bound

PRINCESS BY NIGHT
Lost in Averell

CHAPTER ONE

The two dead elves laid out on tables in the town morgue were young. At least, Essie guessed they were young. It was hard to tell with elves, since they didn't start showing their age until they were at least eight or nine hundred years old. But elves were considered young if they were less than a hundred, and there was something about the slimness of their faces, the lankiness of their bodies, that reminded Essie of teenage boys, like her older brothers had been a few years ago.

And their actions were the actions of the young. Just two boys sneaking across the border, causing trouble. Much like that of the four teenage boys who had sneaked across the border into Tarenhiel two weeks ago. Only one of the boys returned home to Escarland.

"Essie." Her brother Averett's voice came from the doorway behind her. "You shouldn't be here."

"Why not? I'm a part of this diplomatic mission too. I needed to see…" Essie didn't turn around. She wasn't yet ready to leave. Something in her ached, seeing the blood covering the chests and stomachs of these two young elf males. One had been shot in the chest, and the musket ball had killed him instantly. The other had been stabbed after a lengthy fight to take him down, according to the townsfolk.

Yes, definitely young. Too young to fully come into their magic and defend themselves.

Too much blood shed on both sides. Again.

Averett halted next to her. The sunlight slanting through the cracks between the building's board slat siding glinted on the crown he wore on hair that had the good taste to be auburn instead of her indecorous, flame-red hair. "Still, you shouldn't have to see this. I can't believe you talked me into letting you come."

"This is a peaceful diplomatic meeting, and my presence will help reassure the elven king of our intentions." Essie forced herself to turn away from the bodies laid out on the tables. This was the reason they were traveling to the border their country of Escarland shared with the elven forest kingdom of Tarenhiel. To stop the escalating incidents and deaths at the border from inciting another war.

She suppressed a shudder. No one wanted another war. She'd only been three when the last war between Escarland and Tarenhiel broke out. She'd been five when it ended. But that didn't mean she couldn't remember.

A girl didn't forget the moment she learned her father

had been killed.

If there was anything in her power she could do to stop another young daughter from feeling the pain she had back then, she would do it.

She let a smile cross her face, as she had done so many times in the fifteen years since her father had been killed. Smile and carry on. So many others carried on with frowns or constant melancholy, but she chose to smile and keep smiling no matter what. "I'm twenty years old, Avie. If all of you hadn't spoiled me so much, you probably would've already married me off to form some alliance."

Averett grimaced, as if what she'd said pained him. "I may be the king, but I'm first and foremost your big brother. I'm not going to sacrifice my little sister to some other king-dom just for political gain. I wouldn't ever do that to you."

Did he have to take everything so seriously? Probably. He had become king at twelve, though Mother had been his regent until he turned eighteen. He hadn't had a lot to smile about growing up.

Essie patted his arm. "I know you won't. But I also know it's the way of things. I've accepted my marriage will probably have some political end, and that's all right. That's part of being a princess. But I'll let you know which match is acceptable to me when the time comes." Better she picked which marriage of alliance she wanted than have Parliament try to pressure Avie into making one for her.

"Essie…" Averett looked like he was about to argue more, but one of their guards, a lieutenant based on his shoulder stripes, stuck his head into the morgue.

The lieutenant glanced at the dead elves, grimaced, then bowed as much as he could to Averett while still standing half in and half out of the doorway. "Your Majesty. Your High-ness. The train's water and coal has been resupplied. We are ready to depart when you are."

"Thank you. Please have your squad transport the bodies to the train car we set aside for them. And see to it that the bodies are properly wrapped and cared for. I don't want the elves to believe we handled their dead with anything less than dignity."

"Yes, sir." The lieutenant bowed and saluted before he popped back out the door.

Averett glanced one more time at the dead elves before he held out an arm to Essie. "If only our problem with the elves could be solved as simply as arranging a marriage alliance."

As his words sank in, Essie nearly forgot to take his arm. Or move. That wasn't a marriage alliance she'd ever considered. She'd always thought she'd marry into one of the other human nations around Escarland. Maybe Mongalia to the east since they had access to the ocean, and it would benefit trade to be more closely aligned with them.

But if she could secure an alliance with the elves…that would be an alliance few human countries could attain.

"Do you think they would agree to a marriage alliance?"

Averett halted so fast Essie's hand slipped from his arm. "You can't be serious. You'd actually marry an elf?"

Essie drew her chin up higher. Once she'd been old enough, she'd taken to studying whatever she could find on elves, their culture, and their language. At first it had been a child's way of dealing with the grief, telling herself that if she simply learned enough, she could stop the tragedy of the war happening again.

But after a while, the studying had turned into a grudging respect. "Yes, I would. Though, I highly doubt the elves would accept, even if you made the offer. They see humans as beneath them and, while sometimes elves do marry humans, I highly doubt an elf among the royal family would deign to do so."

Averett held out his arm again and started walking once she took it. He remained silent as they left the morgue, waved to the townsfolk one more time, and climbed into their train car, the second car after the steam locomotive and a car full of guards.

Once they were seated across from each other on one of the padded benches, alone in the car as they waited for the lieutenant and his men to load the bodies of the elves, Averett turned to her, something speculative in his gaze. "You know, it might not hurt to offer a marriage alliance. It would be a good way to show that I'm serious about peace if I'm offering my own sister for an alliance. When they refuse, I can ask what elven gesture of peace they would suggest since they rejected the gesture of peace my people deem culturally appropriate. It would force them to make an effort in this negotiation. Too often elves just sit back and let us humans squirm and make all the concessions. I'll run it by Master Wendee once the train gets moving to the border."

"Good idea." Master Wendee, their chief diplomat and negotiator for situations like this, would know if that was a good opening gambit or not. Essie leaned back in the seat and studied her brother's face. "You're really worried about this, aren't you?"

"Yes. Escarland can't afford another war with the elves. Not now when we're finally getting back on our feet after the devastation of the last war." Averett stared out the window at the rolling cornfields, though Essie doubted he was really seeing them. "I didn't realize it back then, but our soldiers only survived the war as long as they did because the elves' chief warrior was kept busy with an invasion by the trolls from the north."

"Laesornysh." Essie hadn't meant to, but the name came out as a whisper. It was the sort of name one didn't just blithely say out loud. It wasn't so much a name but a title, meaning *Death on the Wind*.

"Yes. The elves ended the war last time only because Laesornysh had been captured by the trolls, and they wanted to concentrate on rescuing him and defeating the trolls." Averett shivered and looked away from the window long enough to meet her gaze. "It's said he can take out whole packs of trolls single-handedly. We can't afford a war against the elves if Laesornysh is fighting with them."

A shiver raced down Essie's back. She'd learned a respect and appreciation for most elves, but the stories she'd heard about Laesornysh...he was an assassin. A killer. He had slipped into the trolls' capital city and killed their king. When he fought the troll armies, it wasn't a battle. It was slaughter.

No, whatever happened, Averett needed to avoid that same slaughter for Escarland.

Even if Essie had to marry an elf to do it.

Linder Island had been chosen as the meeting place for its position roughly in the center of the Hydalla River, the border between Escarland and Tarenhiel.

Convenience was the only thing the island had going for it. *Island* was a generous word, considering it wasn't much more than a rock with a gravelly beach and a few sprigs of vegetation gamely growing between the cracks in the stone. That was probably why neither Escarland or Tarenhiel had bothered to officially claim it, since it wasn't even big enough to bother building a decent watchtower or guard post.

Essie stepped from the dinghy that had rowed them from the steamboat, since Linder Island didn't have anything as fancy as a jetty. She had to hold her wide, puffy skirts high to keep from dipping them in the brown river water.

Her fancy slippers didn't have enough sole to protect her feet properly from the sharp rocks of the beach. She was probably going to ungracefully twist an ankle right in front of the elven king at this rate. That would make him reject the marriage alliance proposal in half a second instead of a full second.

Across the barren rock of an island, the elven contingent was disembarking from their own small boat, though theirs appeared to have been pushed across the river by magic instead of anything as mundane as oars.

What would it be like to have that much magic at one's fingertips all the time? A few humans had natural magic, though it was usually less strong than in the other races, like elves, dwarves, trolls, and ogres. Magical devices were more prevalent, but they were expensive and still hadn't caught on as much as steam power, since the coal for steam was much cheaper than buying a magical device to do the same thing.

There were only four elves compared to Essie's party of ten. She almost winced at how excessive their pack of seven guards seemed when the elven king only brought two bodyguards.

By the looks of the elven bodyguards, they could more than handle her and her brother's guards. The bodyguard elf on the right carried a quiver across his back and a strung bow in his hand, as if prepared to whip out arrows and shoot all of them in the blink of an eye. His chestnut hair flowed over his shoulders in the light breeze, revealing the points of his ears.

The bodyguard elf on the left was an inch or two shorter than the other, though both were slim and sinewy. His angular face seemed younger than the other elves, but Essie couldn't be sure. This elf had blond hair so pale it was nearly silver, matching the color of his flinty, blue-silver eyes. Something in those eyes was hard. Almost dead. He had a pair of slim swords strapped across his back.

A shiver raced down Essie's back. Was this Laesornysh? That would explain why the elf king was so confident with so few bodyguards.

King Weylind, the elf king, was imposing. Long, nearly black hair flowed over his shoulders and around his long, angled face. An intricate crown of several pieces of silver woven together perched on his brow. A long, purple cape hung from his slim shoulders.

Next to the king stood the least imposing of the four elves. Something about his stance spoke that he was more academic than the other elves. Their professional diplomat, the elven version of Master Wendee.

After all the official greetings—her brother bowing, her curtsying; the elven king pressing his fingertips to his forehead —Averett motioned for their guards to set up the tent they'd brought along.

As soon as the tent was up, the chestnut-haired bodyguard elf produced a table from somewhere. Essie hadn't even seen him carrying a pack or anything resembling a table.

At least negotiating this meeting had gone smoothly enough. They offered to bring the tent, the elves the furniture. They would both bring food and drinks for themselves. Hopefully the negotiation that all that preliminary diplomacy had arranged would go as smoothly.

In short order, she found herself seated on one side of the table next to Averett with the elf king and his diplomat beside him. Master Wendee sat on the other side of Averett.

The two elf bodyguards stood behind their king while two of Averett's guards stood behind Averett and Essie. The rest of the guards remained outside of the tent.

King Weylind stared at Averett with dark brown eyes. Silent. Still.

Averett straightened his shoulders and cleared his throat. "We both know why we are here. The incidents lately have been deplorable, on both sides, and I have made it clear to my people, as I am sure you have to yours, that further action will not be tolerated. I have the bodies of your two young elves to return to you with due honor, as I believe you have the bodies of three of my young men."

"The exchange will occur once our negotiations are complete." King Weylind didn't so much as twitch as he said it, but there was something to the tone of his voice. It was an offering of peace and a warning. If things went badly, the bodies wouldn't be returned. He was prepared to play hard if needed.

"Things have been unsettled between our two kingdoms ever since the end of the war. After a war between two human nations, normally we would seal the new treaty with a marriage alliance to guarantee peace. But that is a solution your kingdom hasn't appeared open to exploring in the past." Averett was staring at King Weylind, as if to gauge his reaction to that.

Essie watched too and didn't notice so much as a flicker.

"Would a marriage alliance stop the raids?"

Essie started and glanced up at the silver-haired body-guard. Who was he to dare interrupt a discussion between kings? And why did he sound like he thought his king should consider a marriage alliance?

King Weylind tipped his head toward the bodyguard and spoke in a low tone in elvish. Essie wasn't good enough at elvish, especially spoken elvish, to understand anything. But the first word he'd spoken…she was pretty sure it was *brother*.

Was that silver-haired elf more than simply a bodyguard? If he was King Weylind's brother, then was or wasn't he also Laesornysh?

The silver-haired elf replied in a similar, low tone.

King Weylind turned back to Averett. "Would a marriage alliance as you propose guarantee peace between our kingdoms?"

Averett's face paled, and he glanced at Essie before facing King Weylind.

King Weylind's mouth thinned. "Unless you were not genuine in your offer. We would take it very unkindly if your gestures of peace turn out to be empty."

Averett appeared to be on the edge of squirming, and Master Wendee on the other side was glancing at both Averett and Essie as if he wasn't sure what to say in this situation. The whole marriage alliance thing was supposed to be a ruse. An opening gambit.

But if the elves were serious about taking them up on the offer, this was an opportunity they couldn't refuse.

Essie let out a long breath. It wasn't exactly the marriage alliance she'd thought she would have, but that wasn't necessarily a bad thing. She found the elves and their culture fascinating. She would go to live in their fabled treetop cities, cities that few humans were allowed to visit and no full human had been allowed to live in for generations.

She would be married to an elf. That would be interesting. No worse than any other marriage alliance to a stranger.

She raised her chin. "Yes, we are genuine in our offer."

Master Wendee cleared his throat. "Generally, a marriage alliance would include our princess marrying one of your princes while one of your princesses would marry a prince from Escarland."

King Weylind's face hardened until his pale skin almost seemed to be made from stone. "No. I will not marry my sister to a human."

There was just a hint of derision in his tone. As if it took extreme effort to say human without spitting it out.

Averett's eyes sparked. "And I'm not going to marry my sister to an elf without a reciprocating offer from you. Unless your offers of peace weren't genuine?"

King Weylind glared back. "Your people trespassed into Tarenhiel first. All of Tarenhiel's raids have been in response to your provocation. I believe Escarland should be the first to bend and offer peace as you were the first to harden."

Averett blew out a long breath as if he was trying to keep hold of his temper. "As I already stated, I have decried the actions of the few who crossed the border. I'm the one who sent messengers to arrange this talk. I'm the one reaching out for peace first. I believe I have already done my share of bending."

"Weylind Daresheni, shashon." The silver-haired elf spoke again, his head bowed toward his king so Essie couldn't see his eyes or much of his face past the curtain of his silver-blond hair.

As he spoke, King Weylind's face hardened, and his reply in elvish was sharp. After a few more moments of conversation, King Weylind's expression smoothed, and something in his posture shifted, though Essie couldn't put her finger on exactly what it was. Almost as if his shoulders slumped, but the movement wasn't as perceptible as that.

King Weylind faced Averett. "He has agreed to marry your princess."

"And who is he?" Averett's back was as stiff as the palace's walls. He looked about ready to grab Essie's hand and drag her out of there.

"He is my youngest brother, Farrendel Laesornysh."

CHAPTER TWO

He was Laesornysh. Essie took several deep breaths trying to keep the room from spinning. The elf king's youngest brother was Laesornysh. The same youngest brother she might end up marrying. Who had *volunteered* to marry her.

If they went through with this marriage, she would end up married to the infamous elf warrior-assassin.

She exhaled slowly. All right. This was all right. Focus on the good parts of this.

It would solve Averett's worries about the elves using Laesornysh against them. If he cared anything for his wife and marriage, he wouldn't attack her people. And, as the whispered conversations seemed to indicate, he had some sway with his older brother.

Averett's eyes had narrowed, his jaw hardening. He opened his mouth.

Essie grabbed his arm. "Avie. We need to talk. In private." She sent what she hoped was a winsome smile at the elves. "Your Majesty, please excuse my brother and me for a moment."

She all but dragged Averett from his chair and pushed him toward the side of the tent farthest away from the elves. With their superior hearing, they most likely could still hear every word, but there wasn't a place on this tiny rock of an island that was far enough to be out of earshot, so she'd settle for a semblance of privacy that would hopefully allow Averett to speak freely.

"This is ridiculous." Averett clenched and unclenched his hands. "This was supposed to be just a throwaway suggestion. They weren't actually supposed to...there is no way I'm just marrying you off to some elf assassin. What if he's cruel? I'm not going to let him hurt you."

Essie wanted to let out another sigh, but she'd done enough sighing already. Her brother loved her and wanted to protect her, but this was a princess's job. It wasn't glamorous, being married and shipped off to some foreign land to buy her homeland a bit of peace and safety, but it was what was expected of her. And she was strong enough to be able to handle it and make it into something good.

She sneaked a glance toward the elves. Laesornysh's head was tipped down, but she got the feeling his eyes were still focused on her and Averett. Probably hearing every word they said.

King Weylind's dark eyes were stormy, for lack of a better word. His jaw hard. Would he consider it a grave insult if they refused a marriage alliance after the elves had deigned to take them up on the offer? After all, it was a huge deal for the elves to bend that much. Marrying one of their royalty to a human just wasn't something they did. Ever.

Why do it now? It was an action that reeked of desperation. As if the elves were just as terrified as Averett that a war could break out between Escarland and Tarenhiel. Unless the elves thought it was a war they couldn't win, even with Laesornysh on their side. Why? Were they scared of Escarland? Or of something else?

She turned back to Averett. "It's gone too far already. I don't think we can refuse. Nor do I want to."

"You *want* to marry that elf?" Averett's face twisted. "Elves killed Father."

"On the battlefield. Honorably. They could've sent in elven assassins against us, but they never did. Only against the trolls. Besides, Laesornysh didn't kill Father. He was captured by trolls at the time. So he's actually one of the few elves I can marry without worrying about marrying Father's killer." Essie gripped Averett's arm. She needed to make him understand. This was best for their country. And, it might even be best for her. "Marriage alliances are always a chance. I would be running the same risk if I married into a human kingdom. Maybe more of a risk. Elves aren't known for their cruelty. Cold and distant, maybe, but not cruel."

"Essie, I…" Averett pulled her into a hug and mumbled over her shoulder. "I can't lose you."

"You won't." Essie patted his shoulder. "This is an opportunity—and adventure—that I'm not about to let slip by. I will be invited places few humans ever see. I will be able to learn their language, their culture, in a way we can't from the outside. And they will learn ours from me. Perhaps I'll be able to foster trade between our nations and an understanding that will prevent future wars even decades after you and I are long dead."

Averett shook his head, but a hint of a smile played across his face. "You're actually excited about this idea."

"You know? I think I might be." Essie twitched her skirts. "I've heard elvish women don't have to wear petticoats or corsets."

Averett snorted and tapped her nose with a finger as he'd done when she was a little tot of five following her older brothers around. "I guess I have no choice but to approve, if for no other reason than to see the utter chaos you're going to bring to the staid and stuffy elves."

Essie tried her best to temper her grin as she and Averett returned to the table and took their seats once again.

Averett pulled himself straight in his chair, returning to his professional, cool demeanor. "We find a match between my sister and your brother acceptable. I believe her presence with your people will reassure my people that they have an advocate to maintain peaceful relations. Peace will still take time, but I believe it is achievable along this path."

King Weylind tipped his head, the equivalent of nodding enthusiastically for an elf. "As do I. If, after a period of six months, your sister's marriage to my brother has sufficiently cooled tensions, I will agree to send one of my sisters for an extended visit to your capital as an ambassador to further peaceful relations."

It wasn't a reciprocating marriage, but it was probably a huge concession for the elves.

Averett opened his mouth, and Essie nudged him under the table. It was the best offer they were going to receive. Maybe the elf princess would fall madly in love with one of Essie's brothers and accidentally bring about a strengthening of the marriage alliance. Even if Avie was already wonderfully married to Paige, Essie's friend, Essie still had two other brothers who were both free.

Averett shot glares at both her and Master Wendee, so Essie probably hadn't been the only one nudging him under the table to prevent him from saying something they'd all regret. He straightened his shoulders and expression. "Very well. Now that we have worked out that part of this treaty, let's get to the particulars."

It turned out the first particular they had to work out was the wedding. The elves insisted they didn't want to leave the treaty signing without her in tow, and Averett seemed reluctant to just hand her over on such short notice.

It took all of Master Wendee's diplomacy and Essie's insistence to keep the wedding meant to keep the peace from turning into the thing that sparked the war.

In the end, they agreed on two weddings. The first, a human-style wedding, would take place on the Escarland side of the border in two days immediately after the treaty was signed. Essie would leave with the elves shortly afterwards and journey to their capital city Estyra where a second, elven wedding would take place to make things official.

After Essie and Averett were rowed from Linder Island to their steamboat, which took them across the Hydalla River toward the Escarlish shore, they were shown to a suite of guest rooms in the army fort guarding this section of river.

Essie made herself comfortable on one end of the settee, kicking off her shoes and curling her legs beneath her. Based on Avie's expression, this was going to be a long discussion.

Sinking onto the other side of the settee, Averett took off his crown and rubbed at the mark it had left across his forehead. His auburn hair stuck up in places, dimpled in others. "I'm sorry. I tried to give you more time. Two days…"

She couldn't let him beat himself up over this. "Will be more than enough time. If we wire Mother tonight, she will be able to arrive here in time."

Avie massaged his forehead. "I know you will want Paige here. But she needs to stay with the boys back home. The elves seem committed to peace, but if this is some trick to lure Escarland's royal family here to be slaughtered..."

Essie hadn't thought of that. She didn't think it was a scheme the elves were likely to pull, but it never hurt to be cautious. It was never wise to have the whole royal family in one place except at the palace where they were well guarded.

Perhaps Paige could come while Essie's nephews stayed behind, but if the worst should happen, they would need at least one of their parents to survive.

Essie shook herself. Nothing was going to happen.

Nothing besides a wedding, anyway.

She pasted her smile into place and forced the laugh back into her voice. She was getting married in two days. She wasn't going to spend the days before her wedding moping. "I'll miss her terribly. I never imagined I'd get married without her to gush with me. But I guess we'll just have to do that later."

Whenever that would be. Once Essie moved to Tarenhiel with her new elf husband, when would she see her family again? Would her family be allowed to visit? Would they dare step foot in Tarenhiel? Her elf husband wasn't likely to want to visit Escarland.

No moping. This was an adventure. The best adventure she was likely to get.

"Edmund and Julien should be able to come, if they can be spared from their duties, so I'll have most of my family here." Essie's smile came less forced now. She leaned forward, thinking through the details. "Mother can bring a few of my personal items and favorite dresses, but I doubt I'll need to pack much. He's an elf prince. He can probably afford to outfit me with a new wardrobe."

Averett grimaced. "I'm not going to send you off to the elves looking like a pauper. What will they think?"

"They will probably think my human dresses are horrid and be offended by how much luggage I have. They seem to travel light." Essie shook her head. "No, the lighter the better. I'll take my two favorite dresses, which will be enough to introduce human culture and fashion to the elves if I deem appropriate. Taking my personal jewelry—the pieces you have given me that aren't a part of Escarland's royal jewels—will be enough to show wealth while still being easy to carry."

And, if she was going to blend human fashion with elven, it would probably go over better if she wore a few human pieces of jewelry with elven clothing. She was, after all, marrying their prince. She would need to adapt to their ways as much as possible or they would never see her as anything other than an outsider at best and an intruder at worst.

"How are you so calm about all this?" Averett rested his elbows on his knees, his shoulders drooping.

"There's no point getting all hysterical. It won't change anything but make me and everyone around me miserable." Would a good shake get that notion through Averett's thick head, or would she have to take more drastic measures? "I told you. I always knew a marriage of alliance would be in my future eventually. I can be thankful it didn't happen until I'm twenty-years-old instead of a sixteen-year-old child paired off with a fifty-year-old somewhere."

Averett's face turned a shade of green in the fading light of dusk. "I never would have done that to you. I don't even want to do this to you." He dropped his head in his hands. "I'm such a horrible brother."

He probably felt like he was sacrificing her and her happiness for the sake of the kingdom's peace. While it warmed her to know her brother would put her happiness above the kingdom's wellbeing, this was her duty as it was his.

Besides, it wasn't as if a true love, story book romance would be in her future if she refused this arranged marriage. A romance between a princess and some guard or regular citizen sounded wonderful in stories.

But those stories didn't take into account the realities such a couple would face. The commoner would either be out for the money he could wheedle from his princess bride, if he was the unsavory sort, or, if he was a better man, he might resent that she would forever have more money, rank, and prestige than he did. If he was truly a good man, maybe he could work through the difficulties of marrying a princess. Maybe he could overcome the differences.

The chances of that were slim. Essie had chased off—or had her brothers chase off—enough gold diggers to know there were a lot more of them than good men out there who would actually approach a princess and spend time with her long enough to fall in love.

No, this was the best Essie could hope for, really. This elf was also a prince, so he had no need of her title or money. He was even a younger prince, meaning they were probably in similar places in their respective lines of succession. It was about as equal a marriage as she was likely to get, and that equality meant she would be able to interact with him without titles getting in the way.

She patted Avie's shoulder. "I told you. I chose this. I'm determined I'll be happy. So that's exactly what I will be."

"I hope that elf learns to appreciate your eternal optimism as much as I do." Averett raised his head from his hands, though he wasn't smiling. "You do realize that those elves probably see you as little more than a child compared to their long lives? For all we know, the elf you're going to be marrying is the human equivalent of a fifty-year-old."

Essie snorted. "That's one of the first things I'll have to ask him. But, I don't think he's that old. I don't know why, but I got the impression that he's young, relatively speaking, for an elf. King Weylind certainly seemed extra protective of him. Not like he would be for a younger brother near his own age, but one that he still sees as his little brother. Much like how you are with me."

Averett gave a small groan and flopped his head back

24

into his hands. "How am I going to explain this to Mother?"

"I'll take care of it. You worry about negotiating the rest of this treaty." Essie patted his shoulder.

That's how she ended up spending the day before her wedding back on the Escarlish shore, sending telegrams back and forth between the capital and the outpost where she and Averett were staying. She would've liked to go with Averett to Linder Island again and at least see her groom-to-be, maybe even talk with him, but organizing her wedding dress with her mother and packing her personal belongings long distance via telegram took precedence.

Oh, well. She'd have time to talk with him on the trip from the border to Estyra. While they would be married in her kingdom's eyes, they would be more like betrothed in the elves' eyes until the elven ceremony so she would have some chance to get to know him.

Not that she was expecting romance. After all, this wasn't a story book where the handsome, brooding elf prince whisked her away to his home and fell passionately in love with her.

But she could dream he would tolerate her. Maybe even be mildly fond of her.

Either way, she was determined he wasn't going to steal her joy or her happiness. She didn't need him to make her happy.

CHAPTER THREE

His fingers were long and slim clasped around hers. And kind of cold. Did elves' fingers go cold when they were nervous? Or did elves have a naturally cooler temperature than humans?

Essie gave herself another mental shake and tried to concentrate as the officiant droned the ceremony. Her groom was too elf to shift uncomfortably. Or even change his expression from stony-faced blankness into boredom. But he had to be bored. She was bored, and this was supposed to be her culturally significant ceremony.

But maybe the elves had a similarly boring wedding ceremony. She would find out once they reached Estyra.

She wore a white dress with voluminous petticoats aiding the crinoline in puffing the skirt to large proportions around her. Lace overlaid the soft silk, flowing into a long train.

How her mother had managed to pull together such a

princessly wedding gown on such short notice, Essie didn't know. Still, there had been plenty of tears and hugs when her mother had unveiled it.

Across from her, her elf groom wore a long, flowing blue-silver tunic that nearly matched his eyes. It was stunning against his silver hair cascading down his back. He wore a circlet made of twining silver branches complete with tiny maple and oak leaves.

Her fingers itched to touch his pointed ears and slide through his hair. Not in a romantic way. But out of curiosity. Did elven ears feel like human ears? Or did they have a waxy texture? Was his hair really as silken as it looked? What sort of shampoo did they have over there in the forests that kept their hair so soft and shiny? Was it magic? Would she be able to use it on her own hair?

Not that it would do anything about the color. For those in the audience, her red hair must be shocking against her white dress and her groom's silver clothing and blonde hair.

Did his mouth just twitch? The change in his expression was so fast she would've missed it if she hadn't been staring at him.

Then again, she was unabashedly staring at him. That twitch could've been a sign of his discomfort.

They were in the middle of one of their weddings. She was supposed to stare, right?

It was hard not to stare when his hair was so perfect, his sharp cheekbones so perfect, his eyes so sharply blue-silver.

Ugh. She gave herself another mental shake, harder this time. She was not going to turn into one of *those* princesses. The ones in books where they went on and on describing the absolute perfection of their handsome lover's face, chest, muscles, and so on.

Yes, this Prince Farrendel Laesornysh was almost too flawlessly handsome. But *all* elves were, at least to human eyes. To an elf, he probably had numerous flaws. That scar running deeply across the hollow of his right cheek, for example. It wasn't like he was unusually handsome for his people. Rather ordinary and plain to them, probably. That might even explain why he was willing—and maybe desperate enough—to marry a human. None of the elf women would have him.

In that case, it was just as well he was marrying a human who would appreciate his looks for what they were and not make him feel bad for not being as handsome as the other elves.

Um, yes. That's exactly what she was doing by swooning over him.

But she was in the process of marrying him. Being attracted to his looks wasn't a bad thing, as long as it didn't become the only thing their relationship was based on.

Admittedly, right now it was all their relationship had since they knew absolutely nothing about each other besides their names.

Finally the officiant reached the vows. She vowed to stick by him in sickness and health and all that, then it was her groom's turn.

He spoke in her language in a nice, rich baritone. She hadn't paid that much attention to it, back in the diplomatic meeting. But it was a nice voice. Not too high, but not intimidatingly low either. The kind of voice Essie would enjoy listening to for the rest of her life.

That was a good sign, right? It would be truly terrible if she hadn't liked the sound of his voice, considering she was going to be stuck with him for a rather long time.

When the elf prince was prompted, he slid a silver ring onto her finger. It was simple, without the diamonds or other gems she might have expected to receive from a human groom. But it was etched with a pattern of maple and oak leaves, much like the circlet he wore. Where had he gotten this ring? There surely hadn't been time to have it custom made for her. Did he just happen to have a ring that matched his crown lying around?

Then they were declared man and wife, and that was that. No kiss. That was one part of the ceremony the elves had nixed. Something about it violated some propriety for them. Essie wasn't sure if she was glad or disappointed.

As they turned to face the gathered crowd of a few Escarlish dignitaries, outpost soldiers, the three other elves including King Weylind, and the members of her family who could make it in time, her new almost-husband dropped her hands, leaving her fingers feeling even colder than when they'd been clasped in his.

He was just so hard to read and there was so much about elven culture she didn't know. Maybe he didn't mean anything by letting go of her hand. Elves might not consider handholding a romantic gesture that couples did even at their wedding.

Of the elves, he had pushed for their marriage the most. Surely that meant he wasn't entirely indifferent to her, right?

As she stepped from the platform to head for the light supper laid out at the other end of the military barracks that had been cleared for the occasion, her mother rushed up and gathered Essie in yet another warm, tight hug.

Essie wrapped her arms around her mother and hugged her back. How many more chances would she have for her mother's hugs? With how long elves lived, they might not understand her need to see her family frequently, if possible. Would it be five years before she saw her mother again? Ten years? Never?

She wouldn't let herself think about it. She would write letters that could be shared across the border. It would be slow. The elves would probably censor them to make sure she wasn't telling information they would rather keep to themselves. But she wasn't going to be cut off completely. At least, that's what she hoped. Avie had specifically made sure there was a clause for sending messages and letters across the border included in the treaty.

"I'm so proud of you, Elspeth." Mother stepped back, though she kept a grip on Essie's arms. "Your father would've been proud."

That soothed something deep inside her. She'd barely had a chance to know her father. But from what she'd heard about him from Averett, Julien, and Edmund, he valued courage. And surely marrying an elf, a former enemy, took courage.

"I'm going to be all right, Mother. I'll write and tell you all about my new home." Essie patted her mother's hands. "No crying. This is my wedding, and I want it to be a happy occasion. Now let's go enjoy the feast the army cook managed to put together on such short notice."

Essie should also probably track down her groom and at least put on a show of a happy, adoring couple. That was the purpose of this marriage, to convince her people to stop raiding into Tarenhiel. They would only do that if they thought she had some power in Tarenhiel to look after their interests.

Where was her almost husband? He wasn't by King Weylind. The elf king stood off to one side with his bodyguard and diplomat talking with Master Wendee. Being distracted?

Yep, that's exactly what Master Wendee was doing. Averett and Julien had cornered Farrendel at the far side of the room. Edmund would've been there, cornering her elf husband as well, but Edmund had been on some mysterious mission for the Intelligence Office and couldn't be spared.

Both Avie and Julien had their arms crossed. Based on their stances, they were giving Farrendel the if-you-hurt-our-sister-we-will-hurt-you lecture. Not that the lecture would do any good for an elf who could probably toss both of them aside as easily as brushing away a pair of feathers, but it was the thought that counted, right? At least her brothers were taking the time to make sure she would be cared for.

The elves seemed to be in a hurry to leave. Maybe they didn't like to be surrounded by so many humans. Or maybe they didn't like crowds. Or they were wary of being alone and barely protected over on the Escarlish side of the border while surrounded by soldiers at the outpost.

While Essie would've liked more time with her family, in some ways it wasn't all bad cutting the goodbyes short. Long goodbyes just turned maudlin.

She hugged her mother one last time. Julien gripped her in a bear hug. Averett embraced her last and whispered in her ear, "If he hurts you, you send me word, all right? Don't try to hide it or push through on your own."

"I love you too, big brother." She patted his shoulder and pulled away. "I'm going to be fine."

At least, that's what she had to hope.

She reached for her one, large sack of belongings, but Julien snatched it from the floor before she could. He marched over and shoved the sack at Farrendel. "You're her husband now. Be a gentleman and carry Essie's things."

Farrendel didn't take the sack right away, but his face was too blank for Essie to tell if he thought carrying her things was beneath him or he was offended by Julien's tone or if he was simply confused because the whole concept of being a gentle-man was part of human culture.

After a long moment, Farrendel took the sack from Julien, spun on his heels, and strode to Essie. He held out his arm to her.

Apparently, elves did have some idea about gentlemanly behavior. That was something. Essie tucked her hand around the crook of his arm.

He stared at her hand as if she'd done something wrong. Though, he had been the one to offer his arm, so she wasn't sure what else he could've expected.

Then, with a lift to his shoulders that might have been a shrug, he headed for the door with her keeping pace. She had to trot to keep up with his long strides, not an easy thing to do with the volumes of skirt puffing around her. She tried not to focus too much on the feel of his biceps through the silken fabric of his tunic, but it was hard not to notice when his muscles were so firm and strong beneath her hand.

King Weylind preceded them out of the building while one of Averett's guards held the door open. Essie had to let go of Farrendel's arm long enough to yank her skirts through the doorway before they continued out the outpost's front gate, down the slope, and to the elven ship docked next to her brother's steamship.

Even as they all climbed the gangway and boarded the elven boat, none of the elves said a word. Did elves not talk among themselves? Ever? Or was it simply that her presence was just as awkward for them as it was for her?

She would just have to make herself at home and start the conversations. It was the only way they were going to get anywhere. After all, her somewhat, half-way legal husband had yet to say one word directed solely to her. The marriage vows hadn't really counted.

"Unless you're fine with me stumbling around in this fancy dress all night, is there any place I can change aboard this vessel? There should be time enough before we reach the other side." Essie took the sack of her belongings from Farrendel.

Farrendel glanced back at the other elves. The diplomat and the bodyguard elf scurried past, heads down, as if they really didn't want to be consulted. As far as Essie could tell, they were the only crew members on this boat, so they probably had things to do before they could shove off.

King Weylind stared back at Farrendel, then flicked his hand in her direction, as if to tell his brother, *Well, go on then. She's your human. You take care of her*.

Farrendel turned to her, his expression blank. But there was something in his eyes. Almost like he was wishing someone would show up with a book on *How to Care for Your Human*.

She suppressed a sigh. That made her sound more like a new puppy than a new wife. But, for all she knew, that's how these elves saw her. A pet Farrendel was going to have to keep happy and fed for a couple of decades.

She would make the best of it. If she had to, she would be an affectionate, loveable puppy.

Forcing on a wide smile, she turned toward the hatch that looked like it led below decks. She'd been on enough boats that she should be able to navigate her way around long enough to find an unused room to change clothes in.

"Never mind. I'll just explore and find something."

Next thing she knew, Farrendel was beside her, then striding ahead of her. "This way."

He'd said something to her. Finally. A curt command, but it could've been worse.

She trailed behind him as he led the way across the deck to the far end of the boat and down a different hatch than the one she would've entered.

It took some maneuvering to squish the fabric of her skirt and petticoats and crinoline enough to fit through the hatch. Farrendel probably got a whole eyeful of ankles and petticoats and bloomers underneath, but at this point, Essie didn't care. He probably didn't even know what all the layers of fabric were or that it was considered scandalous that he saw them.

Well, not all that scandalous. They were married according to Escarland, after all.

Once she had her feet firmly on the floor in the passageway, he led her past the first door and opened the second one on the right. By his hand motion, he wanted her to enter.

She worked her voluminous dress through the doorway and popped out on the other side. The room inside was surprisingly spacious, considering this was on a steamboat.

Not a steamboat. Essie swayed in time with the boat's

movements as it pulled into the current, yet she couldn't hear the sounds of churning paddlewheels or the whistle of pressure being released from the boilers.

"What is powering the ship? Is it magic?" She turned back to Farrendel.

He hadn't moved from the doorway. "Yes."

She waited, but he didn't provide more information. Guess that was too much to expect.

She took a good, long look at the room. A bed in an odd, curved shape was woven into the wall with long branches, as if it had been grown that way. A shelf across the room from the bed held a few folded items of clothing. All of the woodwork was etched with leaves and branches. Green wisps of fabric formed gauzy curtains at the edges of the windows.

"This is a beautiful cabin. It looks like someone is staying here." Essie glanced back to Farrendel.

There was the barest shift to his stance, his gaze swerving away from her. "It is mine."

His? She glanced around again, trying to figure out something about his personality from it. It was too empty for that, but it was only a cabin to stay in for a few days. Not his home.

"Thank—" She turned back to the doorway, but Farrendel was gone, the door shut behind him.

At least he was giving her privacy.

She opened her sack and fished out the simplest dress she'd brought. It was the same one she'd worn to Linder Island for that first diplomatic meeting with the elves.

It was wrinkled. Rather sad-looking.

And, for some reason, she didn't want to dress in one of her human dresses. She was married to an elf—well, halfway married to him. It was time to embrace her new life. If only she had elven clothes to wear.

She didn't have any but...she walked over to the shelves. Would it be too presumptive to wear his clothes? How shocking would the elves find that?

A slow smile crept along her face. She was going to do it. He might get mad she touched his things, but better to find out now than later. And maybe she could get some reaction out of those pointy-eared elves besides flickers and twitches.

As carefully as she could, she took the tunics, shirts, and flowing pants from the shelf. One of the tunics was the somewhat fancier, dark blue one he'd worn to the diplomatic meetings. The other was a simple green color with some fancy stitching around the collar and sleeves in a darker green. It was shorter than the other one, perhaps for ease of movement for an everyday tunic.

Would he be annoyed since this was most likely the tunic he wanted to change into when she was done using his room? He probably didn't want to remain in his wedding finery any more than she did, even if his looked silky and comfortable compared to her dress.

He'd have to put up with it. If he was annoyed, he would have to talk to tell her.

She worked her way out of her wedding dress. The ties were placed so she could reach them—one request she'd made of the seamstress. She dumped her petticoats in a pile on top of her dress, forming a white, poufy mound on the floor, with the crinoline perched like a massive birdcage on top. What was she supposed do to with the dress? It wouldn't fit in her sack.

She'd let Farrendel figure it out. Surely he'd tell her where he wanted it or he'd quietly have servants take care of it.

Her undergarments would have to remain. As far as she knew, there wasn't any other option available here. But she did loosen her corset ties as much as possible to make it more comfortable.

The pants and shirt were far too big, but the silk was soft and smooth against her skin. She could get used to wearing fabric like this all the time. After adjusting the pants and shirt as much as she could, she pulled the tunic over top and tied it all in place with a dark green sash she'd had for one of her dresses.

The tunic fell past her knees and the pants sagged onto the floor. She rolled up the ends of the sleeves and the pants. She had a pair of low boots in her bag that worked well enough. Better than the fancy, heeled shoes she'd worn for the wedding.

She glanced over her shoulder one last time at the pile of her wedding dress and petticoats with her sack of belongings next to it. No reason to haul all of that around this boat.

Strolling to the door, she yanked it open and stepped into the passageway.

Voices died. She glanced to the left, then the right.

King Weylind and Farrendel stood near the hatchway to outside. Both turned toward her.

Farrendel started. Full on started. And did his eyes widen? "Those are mine."

His tone wasn't accusatory. It was more...bewildered. At least, that's how she was going to interpret it. There wasn't a whole lot of inflection to work with.

"I hope you don't mind if I borrow them. I don't have any elven clothes yet, and these are much more practical for scrambling around boats and whatever else we are going to do for the next part of the journey to Estyra." Essie ran her palms down the front of the tunic. "You don't mind if I borrow it, do you?"

King Weylind was giving his brother that *she's your human, you deal with her* look again.

Farrendel shook his head, making his silver hair slide

across his shoulders.

Essie clenched her hands. It was becoming increasingly hard to resist running her fingers through his hair. But she kept the smile on her face. "I will take that as a no, you don't have a problem with me borrowing your clothes. I'm sorry I left your room in a mess. I didn't know what to do with my wedding dress. I like it. It made me feel like the princess I am. But it will hardly be in style in Estyra."

Both elves were staring at her. Probably inwardly gaping. She'd just spouted more words than they ever heard in one paragraph. Avie had been right about her bringing chaos.

Neither of them said anything. What had they been talking about? Her, probably.

"Anyway, your room is available. If you want to change into your other tunic. I'm sorry I took this one." Essie shifted from foot to foot. Where was she supposed to go? Up on deck? Stay right here? "What am I supposed to call you? Farrendel? Or do you prefer Laesornysh? Do elves have nicknames? Can I call you Farren?"

"Farrendel is fine."

Good, considering that's what she'd taken to calling him in her head. Thinking about him as Farrendel was a lot less intimidating than Laesornysh.

CHAPTER FOUR

A hand was on her shoulder. A slight, gentle shake. And a baritone voice was saying something she couldn't understand. A pause, then the voice spoke again. "Wake up."

Essie blinked and pushed herself onto an elbow. They were still in the elven version of a train car they'd boarded after disembarking from the boat on the Tarenhieli side the river. The train glided nearly silently on a set of rails that hadn't looked like the iron Essie had been expecting, though she hadn't gotten a good look in the dark as she'd been swaying on her feet in exhaustion.

As soon as she'd been shown inside the train car with its two long rows of plush benches facing each other, she'd curled up, told Farrendel to wake her when they neared Estyra, not fully expecting he would, and dropped off to sleep.

But he had. That was something to think about. Was he

being nice to her or was there something more to the gesture? Or maybe something less? He might not have thought anything of it since she'd need to be awake to get off the train regardless.

Essie sat up and peered through the large windows of this passenger car.

The train was gliding through a deep, dense forest. Most of the trees and the undergrowth were nothing but a blur passing close to the train with a few of the farther tree trunks seemingly lingering longer before they too were swept from sight.

Sight. She could see the trees outside the window. It was still gray and hazy, but morning had come even if she couldn't see the sky or the sunrise.

Ahead, lights glittered amongst the trees, still too indistinct for her to make out details. A few shafts of sunlight streamed long and slanting from in front of them and to the left. The sun must be peeking above the horizon somewhere.

Essie nearly pressed her face to the window to see better but stopped herself just in time. She couldn't act like a child here, not among these seemingly ageless elves. She didn't need to give them any more reason to dismiss her. Or turn away in disgust.

Still, she couldn't help a few bounces in her seat as they neared the fabled elven city.

The undergrowth cleared and the tree trunks widened, soaring higher and higher into the sky. She craned her neck as she peered through the window. How had these trees grown so tall? They were taller than any building in Escarland. Taller even than some of the rolling hills they called mountains back in her homeland.

The train began a gentle curve, skirting the edge of what appeared to be truly gigantic trees. To the left side of the train behind the bench where King Weylind and Farrendel sat with inscrutable expressions, there was only forest.

But on her side of the train, a bustle of activity appeared. Gauzy awnings and leafy canopies designated what appeared to be shops on the ground floor of this forest while winding staircases that appeared to be made from the trees' own living branches wound upward into the spreading branches overhead. Did the elves live above their shops much as her people did back in Escarland? Or were there more shops up there?

She caught glimpses of swinging bridges connecting some of the trees together while on the forest floor, the suggestion of streets wound between the trees. Not the straight, grid-like streets of her home city of Aldon, but meandering streets that followed the pattern of the forest.

Here, the land dictated the city, not the other way around.

The train slowed and glided to a halt by what must be a train platform. Here in Estyra, it was more a moss-covered rise with a ring of trees keeping sentinel.

A squad of six elves waited in the center of the flat stones. Four of them were obviously guards in the way they stood tall, carrying swords and bows on their backs. The other two were just as expressionless, but they didn't carry any weapons. Perhaps they were servants to carry any luggage the king had brought on this diplomatic mission.

Had word been sent ahead about the addition to their number? Surely King Weylind would've at least wanted to warn his staff to expect Essie, as well as let his family know their youngest brother was bringing home a bride.

How big a family did Farrendel have? Essie seemed to remember King Weylind was married. Did he have children? What about other siblings? She had heard there were elven princesses, but she wasn't sure how many or if they had more brothers. Between the elves' tendency to keep to themselves and the tensions breaking down diplomacy, there hadn't been a lot of information about the elven royal family making its way to Escarland.

When was the elven wedding going to take place? Tomorrow? The day after? After the rush of her first wedding to Farrendel, Essie didn't know if the elves planned to also rush the second wedding or if their customs dictated they needed more time. Where would she stay before the wedding?

Where would she stay *after* the wedding? Was Farrendel expecting for them to be husband and wife and all that came with it right away? Or would he marry her and shove her off into a corner of the elven palace and ignore her as if she wasn't his wife?

What did living as husband and wife even look like for an elf couple under normal circumstances?

Unless she found someone willing to answer her questions, she would just have to bumble along and hope Farrendel found her missteps endearing rather than annoying.

Would it even matter if he found her annoying? The whole point of this marriage was peace between their kingdoms. That was it. Not romance. Not love. Not even kindness was truly required. In the end, it didn't matter if Farrendel liked her or ignored her or whatever as long as peace was achieved.

Essie would make the best of it. With or without her new husband's love or kindness or even consideration. Even if he never said a word to her at all.

Which, was entirely possible. He'd said a total of seven maybe eight words to her so far. Quite the eloquent elf she'd married, that's for sure.

An elf that was standing by the doorway to the train

car, staring at her.

How long had she kept him waiting? Had she awkwardly been staring off into space?

She hopped to her feet. "You're lucky I only say a fraction of the questions I have in my head."

That got a tilt of his head in reaction. Great. He was probably already regretting being stuck with her, and they hadn't even gone through with the second wedding yet.

He held out his arm, and she tucked her hand in the crook of his elbow as she'd done before. This time, however, he took her wrist with his free hand and adjusted her grip so that her hand rested lightly on his forearm.

"So that's why you gave me that look." It was gratifying to know what she'd done wrong back in Escarland. Apparently, elves did the whole escort-on-the-arm-thing like this. Essie glanced up to find Farrendel looking down at her with some stormy look in his silver-blue eyes. "Yes, that look. I still haven't figured out if it means you're angry with me, annoyed, bored, disgusted you're stuck married to a human, or just plain confused. Or maybe you're inwardly laughing at me. I really can't tell."

Essie forced herself to bite off her words before she kept talking. All this silence was driving her to talk far more than she normally would at home. Back home, there were so many people to listen to that she didn't need to fill the silence with chatter.

That could be the thing she missed most from home. Conversations. Interaction. If all elves were as silent as Farren-del and his brother, then living with the elves would be lonely.

Farrendel was still looking down at her. Studying her, maybe.

She couldn't keep the words in any longer. "Are all elves as silent as you? Or maybe you can't speak a lot of Escarlish and this whole time most of what I've been saying has been gibberish to you and that's why you keep looking at me in confusion." She waved toward the platform. "In that case, we'd better get going. Looks like everyone else is waiting for us."

Essie took a step in that direction, but Farrendel still didn't move.

He swung his gaze away from her. "I am not angry."

With that succinct pronouncement, he set off from the train and onto the platform with ground-eating strides. Essie trotted to keep pace at his side. At least she wouldn't have to worry about exercising to keep in shape with all the fast walking and trotting she had to do to match Farrendel's longer stride.

They joined King Weylind, and the four bodyguard elves who had been waiting on the platform closed around them.

As they strolled along what served as a broad, probably main street in Estyra, elves stepped from the shops and nodded to their king. A few waved and smiled. It felt oddly relaxed. No one was bowing or completely halting what they were doing as the king walked by, like they did in Escarland when Averett traveled into town.

The smiles faltered, though, when the elves' gaze focused on her. With her hair mussed from sleep and wearing Farrendel's clothes, she probably looked like some human waif he'd taken in out of the goodness of his heart.

Ahead, the tallest and broadest tree she'd seen yet loomed over them. Lights twinkled among the leaves and branches, playing off touches of gold that seemed to be a part of the living tree.

"*Ellonahshinel.*" Farrendel spoke in a low tone, not looking at her as he said it. "In your language, it means *Heart of the Forest.*"

If she'd been less in awe of the tree before her, she may have taken more time to celebrate the fact that he'd just spoken a whole sentence to her.

But this tree *Ellonahshinel* was like nothing she'd ever seen before. Leaves as broad as she was tall shaded the forest far overhead. Many of the branches were as broad as a road, and elves were walking back and forth on them as easily as if they were on the ground instead of hundreds of feet in the air.

Built in the center where all the branches met to form the massive trunk was a palace of wood and gold and green. Living branches formed walls and spiraling towers. Windows glittered in the light of what sunlight managed to penetrate the foliage overhead.

It had to be the elven palace. A place few humans had ever been allowed to see from the outside, yet she was going to see the inside. Perhaps even live there, depending on if Farrendel had a room there or lived somewhere else. She wasn't sure what sort of accommodations the elven king had for his siblings.

A set of broad stairs appeared to be grown into one of the massive tree's roots. Essie couldn't stop herself from gaping as they ascended the stairs up the root and circling the trunk until they entered through a curving archway of branches into what had to be the entry hall for the elven palace.

There, a whole group of elves waited for them. Three tall, dark-haired women waited with two younger elves, a male and a female. Their postures were relaxed, the hints of smiles gracing their faces, until their gazes swiveled in Essie's direction. Then eyes hardened. Smiles disappeared.

Essie kept her own, serene smile in place. No need to get offended just yet. This was, after all, just as sudden to all of them as it had been to her family.

An elf woman with brown hair stepped forward, the

younger two elves behind her. A crown matching King Weylind's rested against her hair. With the warmest smile Essie had yet seen among the elves, the elf woman gripped King Weylind's upper arms and said something in elvish.

King Weylind held her upper arms in return, his own warm smile in place.

Was this King Weylind's wife? What was the elf queen's name? Essie tried to remember. Surely, she'd heard it once or twice over the years.

King Weylind moved to grip the shoulders first of the younger male elf, then the teenage female elf. Both of them looked not that much younger than Farrendel. That had to be strange, for elf families. With how long they lived and the decades or even centuries that could occur between siblings, the generations had to get rather muddled.

Essie glanced up at Farrendel. Was he going to introduce his family to her?

Had she introduced her family to him back in Escarland? With the whirlwind of planning the wedding, then the wedding itself, she couldn't remember.

The two other elf women in the room also greeted King Weylind. The first had long, flowing black hair while the other's hair verged more on brown than black.

Were these sisters? Cousins? Was this all the family, or were some attending to duties as Essie's family had been and unable to come?

The whole pack of them turned to stare at Farrendel and Essie. Well, mostly Essie.

She tried not to shift under their scrutiny. Compared to them, she must look a frightful sight. Flaming red hair frizzing around her head. Farrendel's much too large clothes sagging from her. While all of the elves were stunningly beautiful with their long, straight hair and flawless pale skin. Even the male teenage elf was a beautiful kind of handsome.

She studied them, seeing some resemblance in the shape of their eyes and the line of their mouths to King Weylind and Farrendel.

But...she flicked a glance at Farrendel's silver-blond hair and back to their dark hair. Why did all of Farrendel's relatives have such dark hair while his was blond?

It was a question she didn't dare ask. Not yet, anyway. She'd ponder it for a while first. Maybe she could find a book on elven genealogies in this palace's library. Surely, it had a library. Elves had invented books way back when humans were still using scrolls.

King Weylind said something and gestured toward Farrendel and Essie. Essie drew herself as tall as she could and smiled what she hoped was a friendly-looking smile to elves.

No one smiled back. Instead, the elf woman with the black hair, one Essie guessed was a sister, turned to King

Weylind and said something in a sharp tone.

Angry. Essie gritted her teeth and forced her smile to remain in place. It had been too much to hope for that she would be greeted as a sister, but why would they be angry already? It wasn't like Essie had even had a chance to do anything to offend them besides simply exist.

King Weylind replied, but whatever he said didn't calm the black-haired sister down. She snapped something back, pointing at Farrendel, then Essie, and back to King Weylind.

Farrendel took a half step forward, putting his shoulder in front of Essie as if to shield her. His tone was nearly as sharp as the sister's had been, but firm somehow. Essie couldn't pick out a word of what he was saying, but it did seem like he went on for several paragraphs.

Good to know he could string together several sentences when he wished. Just not when he was talking to her.

The black-haired sister crossed her arms and glared. The brown-haired sister's shoulders sank a fraction. She nodded and said something in elvish to Farrendel.

Whatever she said made the other sister huff. The elf queen said something in a smooth, diplomatic tone that relaxed some of the tension Essie sensed in the room.

Farrendel turned back to Essie, stepping to one side so he could face her and his family. He gestured to the elf queen and the two younger elves. "Queen Rheva and my niece and nephew Brina and Ryfon."

All three of the elves made a hand motion, touching their fingertips first to their mouth, then to their foreheads. It must be some greeting gesture. At least, it didn't seem to be an insult.

Essie bobbed as much of a curtsy as she could while wearing Farrendel's tunic and trousers. "It is nice to meet you."

Farrendel waved first to the sister with the black hair, then to the one with the dark brown hair. "These are my sisters Melantha and Jalissa."

Melantha made a sniffing sound, but Jalissa's mouth twitched in what could have been a tentative smile. Essie smiled in return.

Farrendel then gestured to Essie and said something in elvish. Essie managed to catch her own name Elspeth and the word *amirah*, meaning princess.

She widened her smile. "But you can call me Essie."

A slight wrinkle formed on Melantha's nose. She looked like she wanted to say something sharp once again, but Farrendel held up a hand and said something to her in elvish, his tone almost pleading.

All at once, her stance softened. She spoke in a low, earnest tone, whirled, and strode from the room with her long, silken dress flowing in dark green waves behind her.

First chance she got, Essie was going to learn to speak elvish and hone her ability to read it. Not being able to understand what was going on was terrible. At least Farrendel seemed to understand her language and appeared to be fluent, when he did speak. It would've been so much worse if they couldn't understand each other in any language.

King Weylind also said something to Farrendel before he and his family exited the room in the direction Melantha had gone, leaving just Essie, Farrendel, and Jalissa in the entry hall.

Farrendel turned to Essie. "The wedding will be tonight."

Essie barely tamped down her start of surprise. Tonight? So soon?

"Rheva and Melantha have agreed to arrange it while Jalissa will help you prepare." Farrendel gave Essie's back a gentle nudge, as if he thought she needed prodding to go with Jalissa.

Maybe she did. She didn't know Farrendel at all, but he was at least more familiar than this place or Jalissa or anything around her.

Essie drew in a deep breath. She'd agreed to this. It was a little late to start panicking or have second thoughts.

Farrendel started for the door, but he paused next to Jalissa. "Look after her."

He'd spoken in Escarlish. So that she'd know he was looking out for her?

"I will, shashon." Jalissa patted his arm, then turned to Essie. "Come. We will talk. Do you know anything about our wedding ceremonies?"

Essie shook her head. "No. They aren't something my people are invited to often."

The small twitch of a smile was back on Jalissa's face. "No. Not in many years. I see I have much to teach you before tonight." She glanced at Farrendel's retreating back. "But, for my brother, I will."

There was something to those words. A deeper meaning. But Essie couldn't even begin to guess what it was. Whatever dynamic existed in this family, she would have to figure it out sooner rather than later. It seemed like that information could become very important to know.

CHAPTER FIVE

E ssie tried to hold still as Jalissa and her maid put the final touches on Essie's hair. The different texture and slight curl to Essie's hair had given the two elf women fits until they'd finally settled on an intricate braid down her back, laced with silver strands. Silver strands had been plaited together to form something almost like a circlet, complete with silver maple and oak leaves tucked into her hair.

Another elf maid bustled into the room, carrying a pile of white fabric. She puffed out something between panting breaths.

Jalissa let out a sigh. "The dress is finally ready."

Good. Even Essie had been able to sense the tension as Jalissa and her maid worried the dress wouldn't be ready in time. Essie probably would've been worried too, but she had been too busy practicing the elvish words she needed to know and pronounce correctly for the ceremony.

Unlike her rushed wedding in Escarland, the whole elven court was going to be there, and this would be their first impression of her. She couldn't mess this up. Not if she wanted a chance at finding a place here.

And, strangely, she wanted to make a good impression for Farrendel's sake as well. She didn't know all the reasons why he'd agreed to this marriage, but he was doing just what she was. Marrying someone he barely knew for the sake of peace for his people. He'd made an effort to learn the vows and say them correctly for their Escarlish wedding. It was the least she could do for him to do the same for their elven wedding.

The maid let go of the dress's skirt and held it up.

Essie froze, her breath catching in her throat. Not just because the dress was the most exquisite piece of clothing she'd ever seen—and it was stunning with its flowing white-silver fabric and overlay of lace—but because she recognized that lace overlay. It was from her first wedding dress.

She eased to her feet and walked over to the dress. Much of the bodice was the same beadwork and embroidery as before, though it had been reshaped so that it was flowing instead of tight. The upper part of the bodice and the sleeves had been removed to leave her upper chest, shoulders, and arms bare while a strip of fabric had been added at the neckline, a band of fabric that would hold the bodice in place now that the sleeves and shoulders were gone.

Instead of puffing out with the help of yards of fabric and several underlayers of petticoats, this skirt draped straight down, falling like a waterfall to the floor and flowing in a graceful train behind.

Essie had loved the dress before, but now it was the type of dress it was an honor to be able to wear. She reached out to touch it but halted just shy of the fabric. "How did you know to remake this dress?"

"Farrendel requested it." Jalissa was glancing from Essie to the dress, as if trying to figure out what was so special about it.

He had? She'd only made that one, brief comment to him about her wedding dress, and it had been buried in a bunch of other chatter. Yet he'd remembered. Had brought the dress along from the boat. And asked that it was altered for this second wedding.

It was all so thoughtful of him. She hadn't known he'd been paying enough attention to her to be thoughtful.

Everything was so new. So foreign. So sudden. But perhaps this marriage would work out. Somehow. He was making an effort, not simply ignoring her. And that would make all the difference in the world.

The maid draped the dress over a chair that looked like it had been grown into its shape. Then she held out two more items to Essie that Jalissa explained were under-garments. They were almost scandalous, compared to her layers of chemise, corset, bloomers, and petticoats.

But they weren't scandalous to an elf.

Essie grinned. She'd always wanted to shed a few of the confining layers. And here in Estyra, she didn't have to worry about being proper by Escarlish standards. Only by elf standards.

Quickly, Essie changed into the new undergarments and dumped her old things on the floor. When the maid knelt to pick them up, Essie nudged the corset with her toe. "You can dispose of those things however you wish. I don't plan on ever wearing them again."

The maid glanced to Jalissa, and Jalissa nodded. "Do as she says."

With Jalissa's help, Essie eased into the remade wedding dress. It slid against her skin in a way it hadn't in its previous, flouncy state. With a few final touches, Jalissa turned Essie to the smooth surface of the mirror set in a frame that appeared to be a tangle of branches.

Essie caught her breath at the vision her reflection portrayed in the mirror. Yes, she was shorter and curvier than most of the elves. She had more color to her cheeks and a pink tint to her skin instead of silver. But in that dress with her hair styled as it was, she almost looked like she had been born with elven blood in her veins.

Jalissa stood beside her. "Tonight, you will become a princess of the elves. Hold your head high with pride. Do not let anyone make you feel ashamed because you are human. If you do, they will never let you forget it."

"Thank you." Essie turned, barely resisting the urge to hug Jalissa. "I know you aren't happy about your brother marrying me, but I promise I will do my best to make him happy."

Jalissa didn't meet her gaze but instead turned to their twin reflections in the mirror. "I was upset that circumstances were forcing him to marry a human. If he finds happiness with you, it will be a happiness that will be fleeting and short, even if you have a long life for a human."

Essie tried to think like an elf. What must it be like to live so long that a human's lifespan of eighty or ninety years seemed short? "I will do my best not to be a burden to him."

"I think you will try." Jalissa patted her arm. "We elves do not give our hearts easily, but when we do, it is a weighty thing. We do not give and take back the way you humans do, calling every passing fancy love. You live short, passionate lives, and any mistakes you make will only be regretted for a few decades before you die. But we elves live too long to live so recklessly. What we regret, we regret for centuries."

"What you're saying is that I shouldn't expect Farrendel to ever love me." Essie tried not to let that sting. It was all right if her husband never loved her. She hadn't expected anything like love or romance going into this.

Who was she fooling? That deep down, foolish part of her wanted romance. Wanted Farrendel to eventually love her.

Jalissa finally met Essie's eyes. "No, I am asking that you do not let him love you. My mother died young for one of my people. I watched my father die that day, even though it was another hundred years before a troll ended his life. My brother is too young and has already suffered too much for me to wish such grief on him. Please. If you come to care for him at all, do not do that to him."

Essie tore her gaze away from Jalissa's. What could she say to that?

A lump formed in her throat, and she swallowed it down. That was the worst part of facing the cold, hard truth. No, she hadn't expected love. Or romance. Or even fondness.

But she'd wanted them. She could easily find herself falling in love with Farrendel.

Could she manage to love him knowing he wouldn't —couldn't—love her in return? Would it be better or worse than spending her whole life keeping herself from ever loving him?

She didn't want him to spend centuries miserable. But she also didn't want them to spend the decades of this marriage miserable either.

Hold her head with pride. Don't let anyone make her feel ashamed to be human. That was Jalissa's advice, and Essie drew every scrap of courage together to face Jalissa with her chin up. "No, I don't want to hurt Farrendel. Now or after I'm gone. But I'm not going to make both of us miserable now either. I will do my best to keep our relationship to a friendship filled with caring and kindness, even if we can't have love."

Even if Essie's love would be always one-sided.

"That is all I can ask, as a sister who cares for her brother very much." Jalissa tilted her head in what Essie was beginning to recognize as a nod. She glanced toward the door-way. "It is time."

Essie turned. Melantha stood in the doorway, her face a beautiful mask. Without a glance in Essie's direction, Melantha clapped her hands together and gave something—most likely an order based on the tone—in elvish.

The two maids picked up the ends of Essie's train while Jalissa joined Melantha. Together, the two sisters began singing, a song with high, ringing notes that few of even the best human singers could hope to match.

Essie couldn't understand the words, but Jalissa had told her it was a song about love and wishing happiness on the bride and groom. It was a traditional song to be sung as the bride walked to the hall for the wedding and wouldn't be changed even in the unusual circumstances.

As she'd been told, Essie fell into place behind them with the two maids carrying her dress's train behind her.

It was a short walk down a spiraling staircase and along a broad branch to the hall. Essie didn't look to either side of the branch to the long drop to the ground below.

Two male elves opened the double doors into the hall. Essie kept her head up as they entered the elves' grand hall.

Branches the size of trees grew upright to form the walls. Windows lined each side while a tangle of branches formed the roof far above. Lights twinkled among the roof branches. Gold filigree glinted on the arches above the windows and above the doors.

Elves lined each side of the room, much as humans would have if this was a wedding in Escarland. At the far end of the room, Farrendel's silver hair was a shining beacon against the dark hair of his brother standing next to him.

Melantha and Jalissa led the way down the aisle between the elves, still singing their lilting melody. At the front, they stepped to either side, leaving Essie to walk the last few feet alone.

She halted in front of Farrendel. He was dressed in a

silver tunic and trousers only a few shades darker than the tunic. He didn't wear a shirt beneath the tunic, leaving a V of skin exposed on his chest.

His chest was well muscled. Slim and sinewy.

She shook herself. Focus.

No, she was already focused. Too focused. On the wrong place at the moment.

She gave herself another good shake and forced her gaze to lift to his face.

His expression was annoyingly blank, his eyes hard and cold as ice. Not even a twinkle to tell he'd noticed her ogling his chest.

King Weylind began the ceremony. Essie couldn't understand any of it beyond a word or two. At least she had a vague idea of what he might be saying, thanks to Jalissa's explanation. It would be a short message about the binding of two hearts into one. Something similar to the message the officiant had given over in Escarland.

At the end of the message, King Weylind picked up a shallow bowl filled with a liquid that looked like light green paint. He held it out to Essie.

She let out a long breath and took the bowl. This was the part she'd been memorizing all morning and afternoon to make sure she got right.

Facing Farrendel, she held the bowl out in both hands.

Farrendel dipped his finger into the paint, then lifted

his hand to her face.

Essie braced herself as Farrendel traced an elven symbol on her forehead and spoke in elvish. It was a wish for their minds to sharpen each other. Though wish was a small word for it. Jalissa had explained it was more like a blessing.

Farrendel touched the paint again before he traced a symbol on her right cheek while speaking another elven blessing. This one for kindness to fill their speech with each other.

After dipping his finger in the paint a third time, Farrendel reached for her again, but this time he drew the symbol on her chest just above the neckline of her dress above her heart. She tried not to shiver. His touch was gentle, the paint cold against her skin. The elven blessing this time was for their hearts to be bound as one.

Something zinged deep in her chest. It didn't hurt, exactly, but it was powerful enough to make her catch her breath.

Farrendel's expression didn't change, exactly, but his eyes searched her face.

No time to ponder what just happened. She held the bowl out. Farrendel took it from her and cradled it in his hands.

Her turn. She dipped her finger into the paint then reached up and traced the symbol on Farrendel's forehead, repeating the elven blessing and hoping she got the pronunciation right. She did the same thing with the symbol on his cheek.

Then it was her turn to draw the symbol on his chest. With a deep breath, she refreshed the paint on her finger, then, tentatively, touched his chest over his heart.

His skin was warmer than she'd expected. Or maybe her hands had gone cold from nerves. She traced the symbol over his heart, and as she nudged aside the tunic to complete the symbol, she caught sight of a scar running from his collarbone, down his shoulder, and onto his upper chest. She looked closer, paying more attention to his skin than the muscles beneath as she had earlier.

More scars cut across his skin, only their ends visible before they disappeared beneath his tunic.

He was Laesornysh. Death on the wind. And he was marked because of it.

Was it her imagination, or did his muscles stiffen beneath her finger?

She needed to finish the ceremony and worry about everything else later. She repeated the blessing for binding their hearts into one. This time, she didn't feel the zing of power, but Farrendel started almost imperceptively. She might not have noticed if her finger hadn't still been on his chest and felt the twitch of his muscles.

Farrendel set the bowl aside, King Weylind said the

closing words, and just like that, Essie was officially, for-real-on-both-sides-of-the-border married to an elf prince.

Farrendel held out his arm, and this time Essie laid her hand on top of his forearm as she was supposed to. Instead of leading her anywhere, Farrendel stayed in place, as if waiting for something.

Melantha and Jalissa approached them first, each gripping Farrendel's shoulders and saying something in elvish in turn. Melantha walked past Essie without so much as a gesture or word, but Jalissa gripped her upper arms and said in Escarlish, "Make my brother happy."

Essie nodded, not daring to even glance at Farrendel beside her.

More elves walked up to them and gave Farrendel what Essie could only guess what some sort of congratulations. For most of them, the tone of their voice didn't sound all that happy or congratulatory. More like they were giving Farrendel their condolences.

An elf woman approached them. Her dark black hair had a single streak of gray running one side while the hint of lines cut around her eyes and mouth. She must be very old for an elf. When she spoke to Farrendel, her voice held a warmth Essie hadn't heard from many of the other elves.

The elf woman turned to Essie. "I am his father's mother, Leyleira."

His grandmother. Essie smiled and bobbed a curtsey.

"It is a pleasure to meet you."

Leyleira's dark eyes studied Essie for a long moment before she reached out and gripped Essie's arms. "May your love be as Daesyn and Inara."

Essie didn't recognize the names, but they meant something. She could feel it in the stiffening of Farrendel's muscles beneath her hand and the way, behind Leyleira, several elves shot glances toward King Weylind.

Essie wouldn't ask about them now, but she would note those names. Maybe, if she could find a library around here and if she could brush up on her elvish enough to read whatever she found, she could figure out who Daesyn and Inara were and why Leyleira thought their love would be important.

Maybe Leyleira's statement was meant to be ironic? Maybe that was a story of tragedy and not one of true love? Maybe Daesyn abandoned Inara for someone else?

No, Essie was not going to assume the worst. Not until she knew the story.

While the elves gave their congratulations—or condolences—to Farrendel, tables and food were set up in the hall. Essie was relieved when it was finally time to sit and feast.

The elven food was delicious, even if it was short on spices to her taste. They didn't have much for vegetables, only a few roots and greens that probably grew in the forest. But the venison was juicy and tender even if it lacked pepper.

She glanced around as she ate, making sure she wasn't making a fool of herself by eating too much. The elves were all so thin, it seemed they must eat sparingly.

But, as far as she could tell, the elves feasted as much as humans would have, though much more quietly and with less raucous jokes shouted across tables. It was almost like a sedate tea party, yet with lots more food.

After the feasting was dancing. A slow, twirling, graceful sort of dance far removed from the fast-moving, dizzying dances that were a part of Escarlish weddings. Farrendel didn't lead Essie into a dance, and Essie wasn't sure if that was because he was ashamed of his new human bride or he wanted to spare her embarrassment.

Finally, Farrendel eased to his feet and held his arm out to her. With his sisters, brother, and sister-in-law dancing, it seemed he had timed their exit to cause as little stir as possible.

That was fine by Essie. She took his arm and slipped with him from the hall.

Outside, the cool night air wrapped around them as they climbed one of the outdoor staircases that wound higher into the tree. Essie drew in several deep breaths, the crisp air filling her like they were her first decent breaths all day. Maybe they were.

They left the staircase and traversed a broad branch as wide as the street far below before they reached another winding staircase. Essie tried not to think about how high in the air they were.

At the top of the staircase, they reached a spot where a branch split into many, smaller branches about three or four feet wide.

Farrendel started across one as if it was nothing to stroll across a four-foot-wide branch hundreds of feet in the air with not even a single handrail for balance. Darkness had fallen over the treetop palace, making the space below the branch nothing but black highlighted with a few bubbles of light.

Essie dug her feet in. She couldn't walk out there. What if she tripped on her dress or her foot slipped or...she shuddered and wrapped both arms over her stomach.

Farrendel turned back to her. Silent. Not even a twitch to his eyebrows to let her know what he was thinking.

She tried to calm her breathing. "I take it there aren't any clumsy elves? Not that I'm terribly clumsy for a human, but humans do tend to have accidents happen to us, and that branch is awfully small to walk across. My balance isn't quite like yours."

He was probably ruing the day he got himself stuck with such a helpless human female. Essie didn't want to be helpless or go all shuddery over crossing a branch, but she also didn't want to fall hundreds of feet to her death on her first night in Estyra.

Farrendel strode back to her and bent like he planned to pick her up.

"No, wait!" Essie took a step back. She closed her eyes and let out a trembling breath. She probably should've let him carry her. That would've been more romantic, right? Being held in his strong, sinewy arms.

But another part of her need to prove she was strong enough to survive in Estyra. He couldn't go around carrying her over every little branch and bridge in this treetop city. Besides, there was nothing romantic in having to be carried because she was helpless. It was only romantic if he wanted to carry her and she wanted to be carried in return.

She opened her eyes and faced him. He was still crouched, eying her with that look again. The look he'd said wasn't an angry look. Confusion, perhaps? She wasn't making a whole lot of sense to herself at the moment.

"Sorry. I just...I can do this. I have to do this. I'm going to be living here, and I have to get used to walking across these branches." Essie clenched her fists and forced herself to walk forward.

He stood and held out his arm again. She latched onto his upper arm with both her hands.

He didn't adjust her grip or shake her off but set out

across the branch once again, this time at a much slower pace.

He probably felt like he was inching across, but it was still too fast. Essie's heart pumped harder in her chest. She hung back, forcing her feet to move inch by inch.

She wobbled, and her heart lurched into her throat. For a moment, the whole world spun, and all she could do was stare down into the darkness below their feet, imagining herself falling, falling, falling…

His arms were around her, steadying her. One of her hands still gripped his arm, but the other was fisted in his tunic, her knuckles brushing the warmth of his chest. Her nose was level with the symbol she'd painted over his heart.

For a moment, all she wanted to do was rest her head against his chest and soak in his strength. Pretend that he would someday return the attraction that beat in her chest, an attraction that could turn into love if given the right chance.

She wanted to know the stories behind his scars. Know why his hair was a different color than his siblings. Have him trust her enough to tell her how and why he got the title Laesornysh. If he would give her the chance, she would come to love him as he was because love was something she could choose, and she would rather choose to love this elven husband of hers than stay loveless and lonely among the people she'd married into.

Instead, she forced herself to look up. Farrendel was looking down at her. Was there a hint of softening around his mouth and in his eyes?

He eased back, putting a few inches of space between them. She forced her fingers, one by one, to release his tunic and return to her death grip on his arm.

"Relax." Farrendel gently gripped her elbows. "If you are tense, you will fall."

Her tension was causing her wobbles. She tried to take in a deep breath. She could do this. She had to do this.

One step forward. Another.

She glanced down. Her stomach lurched, the world a breath from spinning again.

Farrendel squeezed her elbows. "Do not look down."

Don't look down. She dragged her gaze back up to him. His silver-blue eyes were fixed on her, as if asking her to trust him.

He took a step back, walking backwards along the branch with the sure-footed grace of a cat.

Did she trust him? She couldn't be sure. He'd been gentle—kind even—with her so far. But he'd barely spoken with her. She didn't really know him. After all, he'd gotten the name Laesornysh, and it hadn't been for being kind and gentle with his enemies.

Was she his enemy? His friend? Or just some scared

puppy he would take home and award with few gestures of affection now and then.

Until he proved her wrong, she had to trust him. She held his gaze and took another step forward.

She didn't look down. She didn't look away. Instead, she focused on his eyes as he led her across the branch.

He halted. "We are here."

Essie blinked and glanced around. They were no longer standing on the branch but on a porch-like platform in front of an arching doorway to a wooden structure nestled onto a split in the branches. Twigs and branches arched into the beams and roof for the house.

Farrendel pushed the door open and spoke a word in elvish. Light flared inside, filling the space with a warm, white-yellow glow.

Essie stepped inside. Unlike the grand hall and the room she'd been taken to in the main part of the palace with grand, soaring branch ceilings above and gold gilding in the woodwork, this space was cozy. Cupboards filled one wall while large, plush cushions filled one corner, inviting even if they were on the floor. Three doors were cut into the wall across from the door they'd come in. It was as if a palace kitchen and sitting room had been smashed together into one room.

How self-sufficient were the elvish royalty? She wouldn't be expected to cook and clean and those sort of things, would she? Not that it terrified her necessarily, but she'd been raised a princess. She hadn't been taught how to fend for herself in that way.

Farrendel's boots barely whispered over the wood floor as he strode across the room. He tapped a finger against the door in the middle. "This is your room." Without turning to her, he opened the door on the right. "This one is mine."

Without another word, he stepped through the doorway and shut the door behind him, leaving her alone.

Essie let out a long, slow breath. A human marriage alliance would usually have to be consummated to be considered official. But that was probably one of those mistakes Jalissa had been talking about. The ones elves didn't make.

Did Farrendel see Essie as a mistake or a potential mistake? Maybe he never intended for this to be more than a platonic friendship since she was a short-lived, going-to-die-in-a-few-decades-anyway human.

Maybe she truly was just a pet to him that he planned to keep fed and somewhat happy for a few decades before she died, leaving him free to move on with a real, elf wife.

Essie straightened her shoulders. She would make the best of it. That's what she'd decided back when she'd agreed to this arranged marriage, and that wasn't going to change now.

After crossing the room, she opened the center door. A staircase led up a branch to another, smaller structure perched even higher in the tree. A staircase without handrails led toward it.

She swallowed and glanced back at the room behind her. She didn't know how to turn the lights off. As they were magic, they wouldn't catch anything on fire like a candle would. If the light bothered Farrendel, he could come back and turn them off himself.

Besides, she needed the light to navigate the staircase. No way would she go up it in the dark.

She forced herself up the staircase, holding her breath the whole time until she reached the platform at the top. Stepping inside the room, she glanced around. The light from the building down below cast a glow through the windows, enough for Essie to make out the vague shapes of the furniture.

She could try to speak the word Farrendel had used to turn on the lights, but she didn't know how to turn them off. Nor did she see any curtains to draw across the windows to prevent anyone who might be looking in this direction from seeing inside. As she didn't know how close other rooms might be in this palace in the trees, she didn't dare risk it.

It felt odd to sleep in nothing but her undergarments, especially the scandalous elven ones, but Essie wasn't sure if there were any other clothes in this room and her wedding dress wasn't comfortable enough to sleep in.

Shrugging, she slid out of her wedding dress, stumbled to the hammock-shaped bed along one wall, and crawled into it. She pulled the blankets around her, curling on her side.

Hopefully this wasn't a day she would end up regretting for the rest of her life.

CHAPTER SIX

Birds sang obnoxiously loud outside her windows. Louder than Essie could ever remember them being. There weren't many places for birds to land near her windows.

Essie opened her eyes, blinked, and brought the room into focus.

This wasn't her bedroom in Winstead Palace. The memories of the wedding, Estyra, and Farrendel jolted through her.

This was her new home, as foreign and unhomelike as it felt.

Wrapping a blanket around her shoulders, Essie slid from the bed. The floorboards were cool beneath her feet with a few patches warmed by the thin shafts of sun penetrating the foliage above to cascade through the wide, open windows.

Across from the bed, a mirror framed with twining

sticks seemed to be embedded in the wall. Below it, a few shelves held folded pieces of clothing. A mound of clothing on the bottom shelf caught her eye, and she recognized the two dresses she'd brought from home. Apparently some elf maid had attempted to fold them and stuffed them on the shelf, not realizing that humans hung their clothes in wardrobes.

No matter. Essie didn't plan to wear either of those dresses any time soon.

The shelf above Essie's dresses held two folded elven dresses while the shelf above that held pants, shirts, and a few long, flowing tunics. Yesterday while watching Estyra flash past, she'd seen many of the elven women wearing tunics similar to the men's. It was more practical for wandering around in treetops than dresses.

Next to the shelves, a door led into a water closet complete with all the facilities, including a spigot that spouted warm water from above her head. She didn't see a tub, only a basin. Did elves wash in the water pouring down on them instead of soaking in a tub?

Essie changed into the pants, a shirt, and one of the tunics, belting it with a leather belt hung on a peg nearby. A pair of boots made of a soft buckskin sat under the peg. Essie put them on. The boots reached nearly to her knees and only squished her toes a little bit. Not enough to be bothered by it. Not bad for a pair of boots that had been scrounged for her last minute.

As she brushed and braided her hair, Essie's stomach rumbled, sending gurgles twirling around her insides. Where would she find breakfast here? Would there be food in the main room below or would she have to walk all the way back to the main palace?

Only way to find out was to start exploring and hope she found Farrendel while she was at it. Maybe he would be in a talkative mood this morning.

She checked her appearance one last time in the mirror. The green symbols were still visible on her cheek and forehead. Was she allowed to wash them off? Or did they have to stay painted on her until they naturally wore off?

She'd leave them until she had a chance to see Farrendel and know for sure what she was supposed to do.

The staircase outside was less scary in the daylight. She couldn't see the ground as she'd feared. Instead, a network of branches, leaves, and even the roofs of a few rooms far below blocked her view of the ground, and she could almost convince herself that if she fell, she'd be bruised, but some-thing would stop her fall before she was killed.

When she stepped inside, she found the main room empty, though a wooden plate with a thick slice of bread and a piece of cheese waited for her on the wooden countertop. Had a servant left it for her? Or had Farrendel? How early did elves normally rise in the mornings?

As she ate, she poked around the main room, opening all the cupboards and exploring their contents. While many of them contained dishes and one cupboard was chilled, acting as an ice box even if she didn't see any ice, there weren't any pots, pans, or a stove for cooking. All of the food seemed to be bread, cheese, cold meat, and other items that could be eaten without cooking.

Did elves only have hot meals for special occasions? Or did they eat cold meals in their rooms for most of their meals while one meal was hot in the main part of the palace? And how was this different from non-royal elves?

She peered out all the windows and explored the stairway outside of the third doorway. It led to a third bedroom, this one empty of clothing like it was a guest bedroom.

Last night, she hadn't noticed that the main room and her bedroom had porch-like walkways circling them on the outside, thankfully with railings. She walked the perimeter of both her bedroom and the main living and dining room.

While she could see the roofs of structures far below and one structure almost buried in the leaves and branches in the distance, it was almost as if this set of rooms was a secluded wing of the elven palace. No other elves were wandering in this direction. Not even servants.

Though, if this were the morning after a wedding in Escarland, the servants would be shy about disturbing the bride and groom.

Still, there was a sense that this quiet part of the treetop palace was normally this quiet. Farrendel seemed the sort who would choose to live in the most out of the way part of the palace as possible.

Where was he? Surely he hadn't wandered back to the main part of the palace and left her here by herself?

Unless he got bored with waiting for her to get up and left, figuring she'd stay sleeping for hours. Or maybe he never planned to wait for her and had just gone on about his day as normal.

This constant uncertainty about her status and his motives was going to eat her from the inside out if she let it.

She would check his room. She wouldn't go inside—she didn't intend to be that nosy on her first day here—but she could knock on the door and walk the porch perimeter. If he wasn't there, then she'd decide if she should try to find her way back to the grand hall or if she'd camp out in the main room and hope he deigned to return sometime that day.

She climbed the stairway to his room and halted on the

platform, listening. She couldn't hear any noises from inside, though she wasn't sure what she'd expected. It was silent. Almost too silent.

The birds were quiet. She cocked her head. The birds were still singing nearer to her bedroom structure a branch over, but near Farrendel's bedroom, the birds had gone silent, as if scared off.

A faint thumping sound came from the far side. Not inside the room, but in the tree branches.

Essie crept around the walkway. As she reached the far side, she halted, frozen in place.

Wearing only a pair of pants and his boots, Farrendel was running along a tree branch only about four inches wide, his silver-blond hair floating behind him. With a leap, he somersaulted in the air, spun, and landed on his feet in a crouch, his hands held out like he was wielding weapons, though he wasn't carrying his swords.

After only a second's pause, he leapt to his feet, dashed along the branch, and launched himself across a several feet wide gap to land on another branch, turning the move immediately into a spinning kick.

Essie tiptoed closer and sank onto the edge of the walkway where he'd left his swords and his shirt.

The sunlight glinted on the sweat covering his torso, highlighting the scars tracing across his back, down his shoulders, and across his stomach. But the scars hardly detracted from the sinewy play of the muscles beneath.

Essie couldn't swallow, much less breathe. She didn't even want to think about the adjectives going through her head at the moment for him. They would all sound too swoony.

She was ogling him. Full on, unabashedly ogling.

But he was her husband. It was perfectly fine for her to ogle him. That was the gist of the marriage vows after all, that she'd ogle only him and all that.

And she was perfectly content to sit right here and stare. All morning, if he kept this up. Based on how sweaty he was, he must have been at this for quite some time.

Tomorrow, she was going to get up much earlier if this was the view she could look forward to.

He continued racing across the branches, flipping in the air, always landing on his feet, his silver hair whipping through the air in a shining arc as he moved.

Was this what made him Laesornysh? From the stories, she'd always thought most elves were naturally athletic, graceful, and balanced. She'd certainly seen the evidence of that in the way their palace was built.

While Farrendel's athletic display was magnificent, was it more so than any other elf's? Since Essie had never watched any other elves while they performed feats of balance and agility, she didn't know, but something told her that Farrendel's muscles and balance weren't the only things that had made him Laesornysh.

Farrendel spun and raced toward his bedroom and Essie's hiding place. Should she move? Had he seen her?

With a leap and a flip in the air, he somersaulted over the railing and landed in a crouch within arm's reach of Essie. All at once, he went rigid, staring at her.

Coming from him, that was the equivalent of him falling backwards and gaping in surprise.

"I, um…" What could she say? She shouldn't be embarrassed to be caught spying on him, but it was rather awkward anyway. "I didn't know where you were and then…you have…" She stopped herself just short of saying he had a lot of muscles. "A lot of scars."

It was the wrong thing to say. She didn't know how she knew, but something in his eyes dimmed as he ducked his head. He reached for his shirt. "I will cover them."

Did he think she found his scars disgusting? Horrifying? She put a hand on his shirt, stopping him from picking it up. "Sorry, that didn't come out like I meant it to. Your scars don't bother me."

No, that still wasn't enough. He still had his head down, his hand clenched in the fabric of his shirt like he wanted to tear it from her grip. Like he needed the fabric to hide behind like a shield.

Why would scars bother him so much? Why would he just assume she would be disgusted by them?

Unless...would an elf woman have been disgusted? Essie thought of all the flawlessly handsome and beautiful elves she'd seen since arriving in Estyra. Perhaps elves didn't live recklessly and make foolish mistakes, but did they also so highly prize beauty that a scar—something that could hardly even be considered a flaw—was despised by them?

She wanted to reach out and touch him. Lift his chin so she could see the expression in his eyes. But she focused on the cascade of his hair hiding his face, the rise and fall of his back with his panting breaths. "Where I come from, a scarred warrior is honored. It means he has faced battle and death and survived. Scars are something about which the men boast and the women admire."

His head raised slowly, and his silver-blue eyes searched her face.

Just as slowly, Essie reached out and traced the length of the scar across his cheek, feeling the tightness in him, as if he was torn between staying still and pulling away. "I don't know how scars are viewed by your people, but the only thing I mind about your scars is the suffering you must have gone through to get them. But you survived, and for that, I admire you, scars and all."

His fingers uncurled from his shirt, and he eased away from her hand, sinking into a cross-legged position on the floor of the walkway. He was still eyeing her, as if searching for a look of disgust to cross her face.

If she was the all-too-happy puppy, then he was a tentative forest creature whose trust could be too easily shattered if she said or did the wrong thing.

Too bad she couldn't be sure what the wrong thing was.

Perhaps she hadn't been too far off, when she'd wondered if the only reason he was desperate enough to marry her was because he was too flawed for an elf woman to want. She'd thought it funny then. Now she ached for how true it might be.

Did his family know how bad the scars were or how much they bothered him? Was that the hurt Jalissa said Farrendel had already experienced?

If his scars were disgusting to his fellow elves, what would that mean for him once Essie was gone and he was free to marry again? Would it be better if he never married again rather than face a marriage to an elf woman who might find him disgusting?

Essie shook those thoughts away. She was here now, and, at least while she was his wife, Farrendel wasn't going to have to feel ashamed of his scars around her.

She forced a smile onto her face. "It's a good thing you married me, then. Since I find all of this," she gestured to his shirtless, sweaty torso, "rather attractive."

He didn't move. Or speak. Maybe he stiffened. Had

she offended him? Was talk of being attracted to him offensive to the elf culture? Or was it too soon for such talk? They were married after all, so in some ways, it was a little late rather than too soon. But they were still mostly strangers, and elves had an odd sense of decorum as far as Essie could tell.

Maybe it was time to have a frank discussion—if he could manage enough words for it to count as a discussion. There was no way to say this except be blunt. "We need to talk."

Farrendel remained where he was silent and still. At least he hadn't bolted the moment she said those words. That was something, right?

Essie tried to gather her thoughts. "I need to know what you expect from this marriage and from me. I don't want to embarrass you or make you regret marrying me any more than you already do, but I don't know elven culture well. If I'm doing something wrong or there's something I should know, then please tell me. I won't always know the right questions to ask."

He wasn't piping up with anything to add, and now that the words were pouring from her, she couldn't seem to make them stop.

"I know I'm probably not the wife you expected to marry someday, and you didn't have any more time to prepare for this wedding than I did." Essie clenched her fingers in the end of her tunic. "I know love probably isn't an option, but I'm willing to put an effort into at least making this a really good friendship. I'm willing to be the person you can trust and confide in and smile with you. But I need to know you're going to put an effort in too and aren't just going to go about your day ignoring me. It's hard to know what you're thinking when you don't even talk to me and I don't know if you find me annoying or you don't understand half of what I'm saying. I just…"

She blew out a breath, all wrung out and talked out for a moment.

Farrendel was still staring, but something in his gaze seemed like he was waiting for her to start spouting words again.

This time, she would wait him out. She could hold off talking for five minutes if it meant he would say something.

After another heartbeat passed, he finally looked away. "I do not want to say anything to offend you."

Really? That was his concern? It was sweet, that he was worried about offending her. It meant he cared what she thought about him.

She put on her widest grin. "You won't offend me. I've been saying the first things that come to my mind this whole time, and I haven't offended you. Or I don't think I have. Would you even tell me if I offended you? Will you at least tell me if something I say is considered horribly offensive to elven culture so I know not to say it in the future?"

He tilted his head in something of a nod. After a pause, he added. "I like when you talk."

He did? She nearly started talking again but bit her lip to keep the words inside.

His gaze flicked toward her, then away. "When I wait, you keep on talking. It is humorous."

Great. He'd been inwardly laughing at her.

But, she'd told him she wouldn't get offended. And, she wasn't. Not really. His tone and gaze seemed to say he found her chatter the endearing sort. "Thanks for telling me. Now I can laugh inwardly along with you. I'm glad you find me entertaining."

He tilted his head, a pause coming between his intake of breath and speaking as if he weighed his words. "There has not been much that is humorous in my life."

Her heart ached at that. Both for the pain of his words and at how much that small bit of honesty cost him.

She wanted to ask about that past and pain. About his scars and the name Laesornysh. But he was only beginning to be this raw with her, and he needed to know he could trust her before she dug deeper into this wound.

She reached out and gently rested a hand on his knee. She wanted to touch his face, run her fingers through his hair, but he probably wasn't ready for that yet. Maybe he never would be if this remained nothing more than a platonic friendship.

When he met her gaze, she hoped he could see the depth of her sincerity. "Then I am especially glad you find me humorous. I will endeavor to be plenty ridiculous. I may even see you smile some day."

Instead of the small tilt in an almost smile she'd been expecting, he turned his face away, the glimpse she'd caught in his eyes even more pained.

Time to change the subject and let it drop.

She withdrew her hand from his knee. "So what do we do now? I would love to see more of the palace and the city."

His expression faded back into his blank mask. "It would be...unusual for us to venture anywhere this week, but especially today."

A long sentence from him. Their talk must be making some progress. "I see. It would be unusual for a couple in my kingdom to go out and about the day after the wedding too. Though, considering our circumstances, it might not be totally unexpected."

Yet, Essie wasn't sure she wanted to give the appearance of anything other than a happy couple. She was determined for this to work.

"Why don't we stay here and talk today?" Essie waved

over her shoulder toward the main room. "Well, maybe not here specifically. Maybe down there where we can sit on those comfy cushions. At least I think they are comfy. I haven't tested them out yet. Is that all right with you? I don't even know how old you are or your favorite color or anything like that. And you can ask me questions. As you've probably learned, I would be happy to answer anything you want to ask. Then tomorrow maybe we can see some of Estyra. Touring the palace can wait."

Farrendel tilted his head in his version of a nod. "There is a back way to leave to visit Estyra. I would...like to avoid my family. They are protective."

Essie let her relief gust out in a sigh. "That sounds fine by me. It would be nice to be more sure of myself here before facing your protective siblings. I am even kind of glad my siblings are a kingdom away. They are just as protective of me and suspicious of you as your family is of me."

"I know."

She winced. "Yes, sorry about my brothers cornering you at the wedding. They probably would have been threatening even if I'd married a human, but they were more so because you're an elf. Sorry."

"They value you."

"As your family does you."

He turned away, something in his eyes pained again.

Did he doubt how much his family loved him? Or did he doubt his own worth to his family?

Essie couldn't see how that could be. He was Laesornysh, the elves' most feared warrior. Not to mention their little brother.

Essie pushed to her feet. "I'll meet you in the main room, if you want to wash up after your morning routine."

He would probably show up in the main room with his shirt on, and she couldn't help but feel a twinge of disappoint-ment at that. So she made sure she especially appreciated the play of his muscles as he rose to his feet.

She swallowed and forced herself to turn away before her staring turned awkward.

"Elspeth?"

Essie froze. He'd said her name. Even if it was her whole name and sounded odd coming from him. It was the first time, and it sent something skittering through her stomach. A pleasant sort of skittering, the kind she would be happy to feel every day. Every minute of every day.

She turned. "Yes?"

Farrendel's silver-blue eyes were focused on her, but as soon as she met his gaze, he looked away. "I do not regret marrying you."

He didn't? Essie clasped her hands, so filled with... something that it was all she could do to stay where she was. She wasn't sure if she wanted to hug him or grin or swoon in a puddle of gooey warmth right there.

Instead, she forced herself to put on a soft smile. "I don't regret marrying you either."

She spun and headed for the staircase to the main room before she could see his expression. She would know his reaction if he showed up in the main room after cleaning up.

CHAPTER SEVEN

E ssie made herself comfortable on a stack of the cushions in the corner of the main room. All this really needed was a nice fireplace to make it the perfect place to curl up with a good book. Though, elves seemed to have a thing against fire. What did they do for heat in the winter? They must have a way to spell their houses to stay warm. What about snow? Those branch pathways would get awfully, dangerously slippery with ice and snow.

How long would it take Farrendel to wash up? Essie tapped her fingers on one of the cushions. Too bad she didn't have a book to read while she waited. As she had already snooped through all the cupboards that morning, there wasn't much point in snooping through them again except to give herself something to do.

She was just about to push herself to her feet when the door to Farrendel's room opened, and he crept inside, moving with the wariness of a mouse that knew the cat was on the prowl.

Farrendel lowered himself to a cushion a couple of feet away from her. He went perfectly still, staring at her as if expecting her to start talking.

Well, that was she normally did. She probably should just start firing away with her questions. He wasn't likely to start on his own.

"Um, well, do you have any questions? Because I have a lot of questions. Don't let me ask all the questions, all right?" Essie paused long enough for him to give her something that could almost count as a nod. She'd better come up with an actual question if she wanted to hear his voice instead of her own. Probably best to start with something easy and not too personal. "My favorite color is dark green. Mostly because of this." She picked up her long braid and waggled it. "Green always looks good with my hair. Blue too. But the other colors can be iffy, depending on the shade. It makes it difficult when picking out fabric for dresses. But green is my dependable color. What's your favorite color?"

He stared back at her, head cocked, for several moments, as if still processing all the words she'd just spouted. "Blue."

One word. It was a start, right?

Essie settled more comfortably on her cushions,

leaning against the wall. What she wouldn't give for a mug of hot chocolate or tea right about now. But this room didn't seem to have anything for heating water, and Essie wasn't going to ask a servant to cart a mug all the way from wherever this treetop palace's kitchen was located. She tried to remain relaxed as she asked her next question. "How old are you?"

He studied her, as if unsure of how she would react. "One hundred and five."

One hundred and five years old. Essie ran the calculations in her head. The baby stage for elves was about the same length as a human, but the growing stages kept getting longer from there. The teenage years lasted from about fifty to a hundred. "That makes you something like nineteen or so years old in human years."

Making her slightly *older* than him.

Essie had to smother a snort. Instead of marrying someone far older than her, as Avie had feared, she'd actually married someone younger. Sort of. If someone a hundred and five years old could be considered young.

Farrendel shifted, ducking his head. His hair fell across his face, hiding his expression and revealing the tips of his ears. "One hundred and five is scandalously young for an elf to marry."

"Nineteen is somewhat young for humans as well. Not scandalously young, though." Essie shrugged. "I'm twenty. Does that make me a hundred and ten or twenty or something like that to you elves?"

Farrendel gave her a tiny nod. "Still young. Elves consider it best to wait to marry until full maturity at one hundred fifty to two hundred."

"I guess when you have the luxury of nearly a thousand years of life, waiting doesn't hurt. We humans tend to marry young. Not everyone does. Avie didn't get married until he was twenty-three, and both Julien and Edmund will probably be at least that if not older before either of them even thinks about marriage. When you only live eighty to ninety years or so, every year counts." Essie swallowed back an unexpected ache inside her chest. She'd only left Escarland a day ago. Surely, she couldn't miss her family that quickly.

But she had so much she already ached to tell them. This treetop palace. Her elven wedding. Farrendel. If Paige was here, they would've sat cross-legged on Essie's bed and giggled about it all.

Essie's sister-in-law and best friend was far away in Escarland. Here, all Essie had was the far-too-silent elf sitting across from her, studying her with an inscrutable expression.

She eased the smile back onto her face. "Do you have a question you would like to ask? I've asked two."

Farrendel glanced at her before looking away. "Why

do your people shorten your names?"

"Like a nickname?" Essie shrugged. "Usually because it is shorter and quicker to say than a person's full name. But nicknames are also endearments. Usually only close family and friends will use a nickname. Don't you use nicknames?"

Farrendel shook his head, his gaze flicking to her before looking away. "No. Our names have meaning. To shorten them would take away the meaning."

That made sense. The meaning must be something deeper, more personal than the meanings human names had. "What does Farrendel mean?"

He touched the strand of his hair falling over his shoulder. "Fair one."

Interesting that his hair was the feature pointed out in his name. Was there a deeper reason behind it? Something that answered why his hair color was so different than his siblings'. She tugged her braid over her shoulder. "I would've been named after my hair color too. It's rather bright."

"It is pretty."

When she glanced up at him, he wasn't looking at her. But the tips of his pointed ears poking through his hair looked a touch pink. Was he blushing?

"I'm glad you think so. Back in Escarland, a lot of people dismiss it as a vulgar color. And they expect me to get angry easily because, of course, I must have a terrible temper." She rolled her eyes.

"Why would they think you have a temper?" Farrendel cocked his head, facing her once again.

"For some reason, people associate red hair with getting angry easily. As if red hair has anything to do with it." She shoved away all thoughts of the whispered insults she'd heard over the years. "Ask me another question."

He paused for a moment before he asked, "What is it like in your kingdom?"

Not exactly a personal question. But he had to be curious. He'd fought the trolls, not her people. He likely didn't know much about Escarland.

Once Essie started talking, she found it all pouring out. About the city and palace where she'd grown up. About her family and growing up with three older brothers. About her friendship with Paige and how her friend had fallen in love with her brother.

Farrendel turned out to be good at listening. He was quiet, but his gaze didn't waver. A few times, he even asked questions to show he'd been listening. He cared enough to listen to her, even if he said little about himself or his own childhood. She had the impression there was something there. A hurt he wasn't ready to tell her yet.

"And then there was the time Julien and Edmund decided to steal Avie's crown and see how long it would take him to notice it was missing." Essie paused to draw in a breath, but her stomach grumbled and gurgled. Had Farrendel heard?

He pushed to his feet. When she moved to stand as well, he shook his head. "Stay."

Essie settled back on her cushion. It wasn't a command, necessarily. More a *please, you don't have to get up* request.

She continued telling the story while Farrendel took food from the chilled cupboard. He returned a few moments later and held out a wooden cup and a plate piled with bread and what looked like some kind of cold meat and vegetable mash.

There was something to that gentle kindness in seeing to her needs before his. Perhaps he was being extra nice since this was the day after their wedding. Maybe she was reading more into his gesture than there really was.

But she wanted to believe he was the gentle, thoughtful sort of man—well, elf—that she was seeing now. Kind. Quiet. She could work with that easily enough.

Even though her stomach rumbled, she didn't dig into the food and instead set to work using the fork to move some of the meat and vegetables onto a corner of the bread while she waited for Farrendel to spoon his own food onto a plate. He moved with a graceful efficiency, telling her he was used to taking care of his own meals. Did the royal elves not have servants see to their personal quarters the way royalty in the human nations, including Escarland, did?

Perhaps, with their lower population, the elves didn't have a large enough workforce to employ an excess of servants to do every menial task. Or maybe the elves were simply so independent that they wouldn't want servants to do that for them, even if the option were available.

From what Essie had seen as they'd strolled through Estyra, the elven royalty didn't stand with as much ceremony as royalty in Escarland did. For as much as the elves had a reputation toward traditionalism and stuffiness, they had, at times, less rigidity.

Farrendel returned to his seat across from her, eyed her plate, then glanced at her. "Is it not to your liking?"

Maybe she was reading too much into the tone of his voice, but he almost sounded worried. She smiled. "I don't know. I haven't tried it yet. I was waiting for you."

"Why?"

"It's considered polite to wait until everyone has their food before you start eating. Is that not how it works here?" Essie speared the bite of bread and meat with her fork and popped it in her mouth. Maybe if he saw her mouth was full, he'd give her a longer answer.

"No, we wait for formal meals." Farrendel paused, as if he was trying to figure out what he wanted to say. "You were hungry. You did not have to wait."

She finished chewing, trying to figure out what he was trying to tell her. Was he saying this was informal so she didn't have to wait? Or that he would've understood if she'd gone ahead and started eating since her stomach was raucously growling? Or possibly that he didn't want her to feel like she needed to be stiff and formal around him?

In the end, she settled for a simple, "I know."

That seemed to satisfy him. Their conversation died away as they ate, her piling the meat and vegetables on her bread and Farrendel carefully keeping the meat and vegetables from so much as touching his bread. Essie wasn't sure if all elves didn't like their food touching or if it was just Farrendel's quirk.

Once she had finished, she set her plate aside. So far, she'd kept the conversation light. But there was one question she'd been itching to ask. He might not give her an answer. She wouldn't know if it was the truth even if he did.

But she needed to ask.

Something in her posture must have given away the seriousness of her question because Farrendel stiffened, the look in his eyes back to that wary, about-to-run look he'd had that morning.

"Why did you agree to this marriage alliance?" Essie studied his face, trying to read his reaction. "You didn't have any warning it was coming. I, at least, knew earlier that ending up married to an elf was a possibility, but a marriage alliance to a human wasn't in your plans, I don't think. So why agree to it? More than that, why talk your brother into it?"

Farrendel didn't meet her gaze. "My people need peace with your people."

"Yes, I know." There was probably something deeper that Essie didn't know about yet that was fueling that desperation. But that wasn't what she wanted to know. Not right now, anyway. "But why would you agree to a marriage alliance so quickly? You could have tried to talk your brother into marrying one of your sisters to one of my brothers instead. You didn't have to marry me if you hadn't wanted to."

"Better me than my sisters." Farrendel's shoulders slumped a fraction, his head ducked so she couldn't see his expression.

Well, she had pushed. So she really didn't have an excuse if that came off as mildly insulting. Better if she focused on the fact that Farrendel was self-sacrificial and not that it was considered a sacrifice for him to have to marry her.

"I see." She tried to keep the disappointment from her voice. She didn't even know why she felt hurt. She'd known they'd only married for political reasons. Why had she even been hoping there had been something more to Farrendel's quick agreement to the marriage alliance?

Perhaps some of her hurt came through in her voice. Farrendel met her gaze. His expression held something she couldn't name. Vulnerable. More open. "But not only that."

She waited, holding her breath as Farrendel's gaze searched her face.

He gestured to her. "Your smile. No one else was smiling. They were looking at each other as enemies. But you smiled, as if we were people you were happy to meet."

She'd smiled? She honestly couldn't remember doing it. But, she was always smiling. She purposely tried to go through life smiling and happy. If she could brighten someone's day with a smile, she might as well do it.

Farrendel ducked his head. "I thought that marriage to someone like that would not be miserable."

Not miserable was a good start. But she sensed he meant more than that. She reached out and rested a hand on one of his. "I hope for much more than not miserable."

"Yes." Farrendel didn't take her hand, but at least he didn't pull away. He glanced back to her. "Why did you agree to this arranged marriage?"

It was only fair if she was just as vulnerable as he had been a few moments earlier. "Actually, I kind of suggested it. It started off as a joke, sort of. I was somewhat serious when I said it. Avie decided to use it as an opening gambit, but then you agreed, and I found I was glad you did. Marrying you and coming here has been the best opportunity for an adventure I've ever had. And, I've always been fascinated by your people and your culture. I read every book our library had on elves. I studied your language as best I could. I read some elvish, but I can only understand a few spoken words. I'll have to work on that."

"I will help."

"Thanks." It would be nice to be able to understand the elvish conversations around her. "What was your plan going into that diplomatic meeting?"

He gave her something that was almost a smile. "We planned to agree to almost anything your people suggested. We expected a ceasefire treaty and perhaps an exclusive trade deal. Maybe even exchanging hostages. Marriage was a surprise."

The elves were desperate. Why? What would drive them to be willing to walk into a diplomatic meeting ready to agree to nearly anything Avie suggested?

Essie shook the darker thoughts away. She would figure out the reason eventually. Today was about her and Farrendel. She grinned and leaned forward. "Well, let's not tell my brother that. He will be disappointed that he could've gotten peace with a whole lot less than marrying me off. But, I'm glad this is the end result."

Farrendel gave her his hint of a smile in return.

CHAPTER EIGHT

The next morning, after Essie figured out the elven water spigot for washing and used some of what she hoped was the magical elven shampoo on her hair, she dressed in a dark blue tunic over a white shirt and dark gray pants.

She studied herself in the flawless mirror. Since she and Farrendel were going into Estyra today, she needed to look her best. Like a princess worthy of the younger elven prince.

Would she disappoint the other elves no matter what she looked like? More importantly, would she disappoint Farrendel? That's what really mattered. More than it should, considering she'd only known him for a few days.

But she was married to him. He should mean something to her, and that meaning would, hopefully, only deepen in time. It already had, after spending yesterday talking.

Essie ran her hand through her hair one more time. Was it softer and shinier than it had been before? At least it seemed less frizzy, even if the elven shampoo smelled like grass. A decent scent, but not something she was thrilled about smelling on her hair all day. For nicer hair, it was worth it. She turned away from the mirror and headed for the door.

After navigating down the staircase, through the main room, and up the stairs to Farrendel's room, she raised her hand to knock, but the door opened. Her hand was already in motion, swinging to knock on the door that was no longer there, headed right for Farrendel's nose.

Farrendel was a blur of movement as he ducked and grabbed her hand, stopping her fist. There was an undefinable crackle in the air.

"I'm sorry." Essie yanked her hand back. Was that magic she was sensing? "I was about to knock, then you opened the door, and..."

Farrendel let out a breath and lowered his hand. The crackle dissipated so quickly, Essie couldn't be entirely sure it had been there in the first place. But the look in his eyes...Essie wasn't sure what memories she'd triggered, but she didn't want to do it again.

"I'm so sorry. I didn't mean..." Essie shook her head. The way he was pulling himself together, he didn't want to talk about it. She put on a smile. "I'm ready to visit

Estyra if you are."

"Yes." Farrendel stepped from his room and led the way around the perimeter walkway. He wore a dark green tunic, a light green shirt, and dark gray pants the same color as Essie's. His long, silver-blond hair flowed down his back past his shoulders.

Essie had to curl her fingers to keep from touching his hair. Hopefully continued use of the elven shampoo would do wonders for her hair. She would put up with smelling like grass if her hair would flow and shimmer like that.

At the back of Farrendel's room, a short, swinging rope bridge—thankfully including handropes—led to a platform ringing a branch. As they approached, Essie spotted what looked like a small gazebo with a thick rope attached at the top. The rope looped over a pulley system on a higher branch while the long, trailing end coiled inside the lift.

"It's a lift." Essie hurried over to it, though she didn't get in. "We have a few similar lifts in Escarland, but ours are usually operated by a hand crank. There was some talk that an inventor was trying to figure out a way to power it with steam."

Farrendel stepped into the lift, untied it, and gripped the rope to lower them down. Essie hopped inside and leaned against the lift's railing as Farrendel lowered them hand over hand. Safe inside the lift, she could appreciate the beauty of the verdant green surrounding her, from the broad leaves to the patches of the thick grass she could occasionally glimpse far below. The branches spread far into the distance, twining in and out of each other.

"We don't have trees like this." Essie gazed first up as far as she could see, then back down toward the ground, still a couple hundred feet below. "How do they grow this big? Even the trees that aren't cut down usually die before they grow like this."

"Magic." Farrendel wasn't even out of breath as he worked the rope to lower the lift.

"I heard elves worked magic on plants, but I didn't realize it was to this level." Essie tore her gaze from the trees to look at Farrendel. "Do all elves have plant magic?"

"No, but it is the most common." Farrendel wasn't looking at her.

There was something about it. Essie studied him. He'd said just magic earlier. Not our magic as might have been expected. Almost as if he didn't have magic, but she was nearly positive that crackle she'd felt earlier had been magic. Perhaps he didn't have plant magic. He had a different kind of magic. A kind that was uncommon for the elves, perhaps?

It wasn't time to ask yet. This seemed to be another thing Farrendel kept close, and Essie wasn't going to pry.

Today she just wanted to enjoy the city and hope that the day would continue to deepen Farrendel's budding trust in her. At least, she hoped he was beginning to trust her.

About thirty feet above the ground, the lift settled onto another platform. Farrendel tied off the rope, walked to the edge of the platform, and tossed a rope ladder to the ground. A thin rope connected to the bottom of the ladder.

Essie grimaced. "I knew it was too good to be true that we'd be taking this nice, safe lift all the way to the ground."

"I will go first." Farrendel swung over the edge of the platform and descended the rope ladder.

Essie drew in a deep breath. At least this was better than facing Farrendel's family and walking across those handrail-less branches. And she was wearing one of the elven style trousers, shirt, and tunic. This would have been impossible—not to mention scandalous—if she'd been wearing one of her old dresses.

On her hands and knees, she crawled to the edge, turned around, and eased her foot down, feeling for the ladder. There was nothing to grip with her hands. There was nothing for it but to reach down and grab the ladder with one hand, nearly folding herself in half with her feet on the first rung. Gritting her teeth, she dropped from the platform.

Her body weight yanked on her arm and she scrambled for the rope with her other hand. The rope ladder swung wildly, and she struggled to keep her feet in contact with the rungs.

After a few seconds, the rope steadied. Essie forced herself to move one foot and one hand at a time. A glimpse below showed her that Farrendel was already on the ground. Probably tapping his foot impatiently at how slowly his unathletic, human wife was navigating the ladder.

If this was one of the romance novels she'd read from the palace library, then she would've caught her foot in the ladder, given a small, adorable shriek, and fallen backwards, only to be caught by Farrendel's strong arms.

Instead, she made it to the ground without mishap. She might not be athletic, but she didn't manage to be charmingly clumsy either. Just average. Nothing stunning to attract a handsome elf besides the fact that he was stuck with her and didn't have much of a choice but to tolerate her.

No, she wasn't going to let that train of thought continue. She shook herself just in time to notice that Farrendel had taken down the end of a thin rope and was pulling on it. The rope ran over a pulley and lifted the rope ladder off the ground until it hung twenty feet off the ground. Farrendel tied the end of the rope high in a tree branch where the leaves obscured it from sight.

He turned to her. "Security."

"I guess you wouldn't want to leave a back door open, even for a small trip into Estyra." Essie fell into step next to him. Did she dare ask her next question? "How is this going to go once we reach Estyra? Are we going to pretend to be a blissfully happy couple? Or walk around like we're still awkward with each other?"

"Elves do not lie." Farrendel didn't glance at her. At least, not a glance she managed to catch.

"It's not a lie. At least, I don't think it is." Essie focused on the ground as she thought of how to phrase it. "But there's the truth that you show to other people and the deeper truth that only you know. It's true that, for a marriage of alliance arranged on such short notice, we're doing really well. And, I'm optimistic that we will be blissfully happy eventually, considering you find me humorous, and I adore your battle scars. Yes, it's also true that we're still awkward and getting to know each other, and I don't know what you're thinking most of the time, but I'm not sure that is a truth everyone else needs to know. Does that make sense?"

"Yes." This time, Essie for sure saw a flick of Farrendel's eyes in her direction. "My family will hear about our trip to Estyra."

"Rumors travel fast around here, I take it. It would be best if they believed we are happy. You are happy, right? Or, at least, you said you don't regret marrying me." Essie grimaced. She should've swallowed back those words before they popped out. She sounded so shallow, always harping on him trying to get him to admit he was all right with this arranged marriage. She kept going before he felt the need to answer. "In Escarland, a newlywed couple often holds hands in public. It shows everyone they are disgustingly happy together. Do elves hold hands?"

"Yes." Farrendel halted and half turned in her direction. He reached for her hand but halted a few inches short, as if he didn't dare touch her, not even her hand.

Essie sent him a small smile and clasped his hand, threading her fingers through his. He didn't close his fingers over hers, his fingers staying limp as if he wasn't sure what to do. "This is how we humans hold hands."

Farrendel slipped his hand free from hers.

Essie forced her smile to stay in place, even as her stomach twisted. For a moment, she'd thought they were making progress. She couldn't say why, but it was important to hold his hand. Take a step toward trusting him and him trusting her.

Then he twined his first two fingers with hers so that the backs of their hands were pressed together. "This is how we elves hold hands."

Essie couldn't help the grin that bloomed on her face. Clasping Farrendel's fingers, she fell into step with him as they strolled through the forest.

Within a few minutes, the outskirts of Estyra came into sight and hearing. Even though it was the elves' largest city, the bustle wasn't as loud or crowded as even a back street in Aldon. Estyra had a calm, leisurely pace and air to it. Essie shrugged. Probably had to do with the elves' long lives. Taking a few extra minutes to get from one place to another seemed like less of a waste compared to a life of several hundred years instead of a few decades.

The grass and moss covering what served as a street was still green, without patches of dirt as Essie would've expected from a place highly trafficked. Only magic could keep grass that green while it was being trampled.

Though, the elves didn't trample it as much as would be expected. The grass bent around their feet, their steps so light and soft they almost seemed to float above the ground.

As she and Farrendel joined the sedate, ambling elves on the street, a few of the elves gave them sidelong glances. Not that Essie would have expected anything less. The elves' youngest prince was married to—and holding hands with—a human princess. Of course that would get a few looks.

Most of the looks were too blank for her to read. Some of the elves narrowed their eyes and their mouths tightened in what Essie guessed was an elven grimace.

But others watched her and Farrendel pass with

something almost like curiosity. They didn't smile, but at least they seemed to see possibilities.

After winding off the main street onto a side road, Farrendel pulled her toward the base of a tree where tables—spindly tables that looked like they had grown there—were placed underneath a spreading canopy of either leaves or fabric, Essie couldn't tell.

"Hungry?" Farrendel steered her into the short line that waited before the counter at the rear of the shop.

"Yes." Essie rubbed a hand over her stomach. She hadn't taken the time to eat breakfast before leaving, though Farrendel had probably eaten when he'd gotten up insanely early in the morning. Her stomach had rumbled the entire walk here. With his elven hearing, had Farrendel been able to hear it?

When it was their turn, the elf woman behind the counter smiled at Farrendel, though her smile turned tight as she glanced at Essie. Essie wasn't sure how old the woman was, but something about her seemed mature.

The woman spoke to Farrendel in elvish. Farrendel glanced at Essie, smiled, then replied in Escarlish. "Yes, she is. Essie, what would you like?"

Essie couldn't read the menu board on a stand next to the elf woman nor did she have any idea what sort of breakfast foods a place like this would serve here in Estyra. She smiled back at Farrendel. At least he was politely keeping his side of the conversation in Escarlish so she could understand. "I'm sure all of it is wonderful. Surprise me."

Farrendel gave the order in elvish. Possibly because the elven dishes didn't have a good translation into Escarlish. Farrendel handed over a few coins from a pouch at his waist, then turned away, probably headed for a table.

As they turned, Essie caught a glimpse of the hard stare the elf woman was giving her, the look more antagonistic now that Farrendel's back was turned. This elf didn't like Essie. Was it because she was human? Or because she'd married Farrendel? Both? Essie wasn't sure.

Farrendel led her to a table on the far side of the café. The table nestled against the base of the tree and was sheltered from the street and most of the café by one of the tall, spreading tree roots.

Essie took a seat in one of the chairs. It gave a little beneath her, as if the wooden legs still held some of the bend of a living tree. She glanced back the way they'd come, then lowered her voice. "She didn't like me very much, did she?"

Farrendel slipped into the seat across from her and shook his head, making his long hair slide across his shoulders. "No."

"We'll probably get a lot of that today. I expected as

much. If I were to walk hand in hand with you down the streets of Aldon, we would probably get more than a few angry stares. We'd probably have to endure shouted insults and maybe even a few rotten vegetables thrown at us. At least elves don't seem prone to such outright, impolite displays of anger." Essie resisted the urge to reach across the table to hold his hand again. Funny how she missed it, even if they'd only held hands with two fingers. It had felt surprisingly right, even walking in a foreign place like Estyra, to be walking beside him.

Farrendel's gaze was focused on the tabletop rather than at her. "Humans are disliked here. But you are not the enemy to us the way we are to you. In the last war, you were but a nuisance that had to be repelled so we could fight the real danger."

"The trolls." Essie said it softly. He was Laesornysh, and it had been the trolls he'd fought in that war. Trolls who had given him the scars he was so ashamed of. Trolls who had captured him and…had they tortured him? Her stomach churned, and she pushed the thought away. Now wasn't the time to ask nor was she sure she wanted more of an answer to that question than Farrendel's scars already told.

Farrendel nodded. "We lost far more to the trolls than we did to your people. While humans are resented, they are not hated."

119

"That still doesn't make anyone here particularly happy about me marrying you, not even to ensure peace between our peoples." Essie glanced around, but no one sat close enough to hear their conversation.

"The resentment has more to do with the fact that humans are not elves than that we were once at war with you." Farrendel flicked a glance at her before focusing on the tabletop again.

"Ah, I see." He'd told her elves valued perfection highly. So highly they would find the battle scars of their greatest warrior disgusting. "Humans are rather annoyingly flawed, after all. Not exactly perfect."

"No, humans are not perfect. But I have seen that my people are not without their flaws, even if they do not acknowledge them. It can be just as much of a flaw to idolize surface perfection."

Essie bit her tongue to keep from agreeing out loud. She didn't want to sound like she was complaining about his people.

Farrendel finally raised his head and met her gaze. "But you will have an easier time being married to me than if you had married a different elf. I am already known for my flaws."

"Because of your scars."

"Yes, among other things." Farrendel looked away once again.

At that moment, a younger elf woman approached their table carrying a tray with food balanced on one hand. She spoke in elvish to Farrendel, smiling and…did she just bat her eyes? Or the elven, equivalent, anyway. She cocked her hips as she set the plates on the table, Farrendel's set gently in front of him while Essie's was bobbled and probably would have fallen into her lap if Essie hadn't caught it.

Knowing the elves' propensity for gracefulness, the bobble wasn't an accident.

Farrendel didn't smile at the young elf woman. He barely glanced at her as he said something in elvish. Something so impassive and cold it sounded more like the Farrendel Essie had met that first day than the one she'd gotten to know in the days since.

The young elf woman shot a glare at Essie, whirled, and sashayed off. Essie snorted a laugh. It had been a while since she had seen such purposeful sashaying. That elf woman had her cap set for an elven prince, that much was certain, and wasn't too happy having the prince snatched out of her grasp by a human.

When Essie faced Farrendel again, his head was cocked and one eyebrow tipped up. "You do not look offended."

"Oh, her actions were offensive, but I can hardly stay offended when her attempts to flirt with you failed so miserably." Essie picked up the fork¬-like utensil. There were only three prongs, but they were long and slim.

"I am sorry. She is the daughter of this café's owner." Farrendel picked up his own fork. "We were friends. Years ago. That gave her ideas that we could be more than friends."

"Relationships can get complicated as they change. It must get more so when you live so long." Essie was too hungry to keep talking. She filled her fork with a bite of the food. It looked like a fancy omelet layered over some vegetable on the base, but she wasn't sure what all was in it. It didn't matter. She stuffed it in her mouth. She gave a groan, swallowed, and wolfed down another bite. "What is this? It's amazing."

"Srilysh. It is partridge eggs with various vegetables over one of our carili peppers."

Essie dug into the breakfast. She had her plate polished off even before Farrendel finished his. She was tempted to steal a few bites from his plate, but they weren't up to that level of sharing in their relationship yet. Two days of marriage was probably a little too soon to start stealing his food.

As soon as Farrendel finished, he stood and reached for Essie's hand. She smiled and twined her fingers with his. She didn't even care that the café owner and her daughter glared at them as they left.

As they set off down the street, Farrendel glanced over his shoulder at the café. "I am sorry for how they treated you."

"I am a human married to their prince. I didn't expect to be welcomed with open arms." Essie kept her voice light and cheery. She refused to let the attitude of one miffed café owner bring her down.

"But I expected different. From them, at least."

"They are friends of yours?" Essie wasn't sure she liked that thought. The young elf woman was stunningly beautiful, even if Farrendel seemed immune to her flirting.

"Yes." Farrendel turned down an even smaller, winding street farther away from the main bustle of Estyra. "Lislela's husband was killed in the war."

"On the front with my kingdom or against the trolls?" Essie wasn't sure she wanted to know the answer. It made the elf woman's anger all too real.

"Your kingdom. But I thought my patronage would be enough to overcome the sting."

Essie squeezed his fingers. "It's all right. I understand. Truly I do. It's no easy thing to overcome the war and bloodshed that happened between our people. My people haven't been able to forgive and forget, and twenty years is a long time for us. For your people, twenty years is nothing. Not nearly enough time for anyone to begin to heal."

"Perhaps not." He tugged her closer as they meandered between small shops tucked into the trees. Above them, rope bridges swung, connecting a second level of shops in the trees. "But I know your reception at this next shop will be better."

With their fingers still linked, Farrendel led Essie between two shops to a set of small stairs winding their way up the side of one of the massive trees. About twenty-five feet in the air, they reached a platform that connected to several swinging rope and wood bridges. Farrendel led her across one, and they entered a small shop built around one of the trees, balanced on its spreading lower branches.

As soon as they stepped inside, a barrage of sweet scents filled Essie's nose. She closed her eyes and took a deep breath. It smelled like a garden with all the flowers blooming at once.

But it wasn't a garden. When she glanced around, she spotted rows of shelves curving around the tree's trunk on the inside of the shop. Jars lined neatly on the shelves, filled with a similar, viscous substance to what she had been guessing was elven shampoo that morning.

"Is this...does this shop sell elven shampoo? Like for my hair? Or your hair, I guess. Is this where you get it? Because whatever you use on your hair must be amazing because it's always so perfect." Essie winced and bit her lip. She hadn't meant to say all of that out loud. "It's probably more elven magic, isn't it?"

An elf woman bustled from around the far side of the shop, her long, blond hair hanging to her waist in the most shimmering, sleek perfection Essie had ever seen. While Essie couldn't be sure on her exact age, the elf woman seemed slightly older than Farrendel. More mature, but not as old as the elf woman who ran the café.

This shopkeeper swept a glance over them and a smile crossed her face. She spoke in elvish to Farrendel and reached out to grip his upper arm with only one hand.

That's when Essie caught sight of the stump of the elf woman's right arm below her elbow. Essie dragged her gaze to the elf woman's face and didn't let her smile slip.

Farrendel glanced from Essie to the elf woman, saying something in elvish. Essie caught her name and the elvish word for either *bride* or *wife*, she wasn't entirely sure. Then Farrendel turned to Essie with a nod in the elf woman's direction. "This is Illyna."

"It is a pleasure to meet you." Illyna inclined her head in what seemed a formal, stiff bow compared to the warmth she'd greeted Farrendel with a moment ago. But it wasn't an angry sort of stiffness. She was wary. Tense. "The rumors have been swirling in Estyra about the human princess our Laesornysh brought home."

Our Laesornysh. There was something about the way Illyna said it. Not with the hushed tones of someone worshipping their hero or with disdain over what the name implied. More like she had fought alongside him. Had gained her scars where he had gained his.

"You fought against the trolls, didn't you?" Essie kept her voice soft and didn't let her eyes so much as flicker down to Illyna's missing hand.

If anything, Illyna stiffened further. Her gaze darted from Essie to Farrendel.

Farrendel's fingers tightened around Essie's. "She was with the unit who rescued me."

And had lost a hand in Farrendel's rescue? Or had the loss of the hand come later, in the final battles of that war? Essie wasn't going to ask. All that mattered was this woman had helped rescue Farrendel. Had seen him bloody and battered from torture and didn't turn away in disgust like many of the elves. Perhaps because she too carried her own scars and what the other elves deemed a disfigurement. An unsightly blemish.

Essie stepped forward. "Can I give you a hug? A real, human hug? Because you deserve a hug for helping rescue Farrendel from the trolls."

"A human hug?" Some of the wariness drained from Illyna shoulders.

"Yes. Like this." Essie pulled her hand free from Farrendel's and eased her arms around Illyna in a gentle hug. Not like the leaping, enthusiastic bear hug she would've given one of her brothers, but she didn't want to scare Illyna more with such a boisterous invasion of personal space.

Essie stepped back after only a moment. Hopefully Illyna wasn't too offended. Or at least tolerated the human interaction.

But a small smile crept across Illyna's face. "I see the rumors have been wrong. But I should have known. Our Laesornysh does not let people into his life without good reason."

Essie glanced at Farrendel, but he was half-turned away from her, the tip of his pointed ear pink beneath his silver-tinted skin. The elven version of a blush.

Illyna's smile widened, as if she enjoyed making Farrendel uncomfortable. It struck Essie then that, even now with Illyna's teasing, Farrendel was more comfortable here than he'd been with his own family. This Illyna seemed more a sister to him even than Jalissa, though Jalissa cared enough for him to threaten Essie about his happiness. Why did Farrendel feel so out of place with his family? Was it because they didn't understand him and his scars the way someone who had fought in the war would?

Except his brother King Weylind had also fought. He'd led the elven armies. Yet the tension remained there as well.

There was some secret Essie had yet to figure out. One it was unlikely anyone would tell her, nor did she dare ask. Making it rather difficult to figure out until something clicked into place.

Essie couldn't spend time contemplating it now. She shrugged. "I'm beginning to be really curious about these rumors."

"I am sure you are." Illyna waved to her shop. "But you are not here to trade gossip. You are here for some of my products."

Hair products. Essie would gladly let herself be distracted by that. "What do you have for shampoo? Not that I need anything. The shampoo I was given will work fine."

Illyna reached out, lifted a lock of Essie's hair, and sniffed it. "No, it will not. Basic grass is a perfectly reasonable scent to keep on hand for guests when you want a generic smell, but it is not suitable for a princess."

Essie wasn't sure what to make of that. It was a good thing she'd already crossed personal space boundaries or she might have been more shocked. At least she didn't have to feel bad about not liking that grass smell since it was meant to be just a basic smell, the way unperfumed soap was used back in Escarland.

"Farrendel, unless you need anything, you might wish to step out and come back in an hour or so." Illyna pressed her right forearm to Essie's back to steer her further into the shop.

Essie glanced over her shoulder. Farrendel was shifting, glancing between her and the door as if he wasn't sure if he should abandon her. Essie sent him a grin and waved before she turned back to Illyna. She was more than happy to explore the wonders that elven shampoo had to offer.

CHAPTER NINE

B y the time Farrendel returned, Essie had learned far more about elven shampoo than she'd realized there was to know. Apparently it was magic. Doubly magical, since the plants used to make the shampoo were infused with magic, then Illyna added more magic as she made the shampoo.

Illyna also custom tailored each shampoo for each elf's—or human's—hair. She spent a lot of time rubbing, smelling, and touching Essie's hair. Turned out personal space only existed for certain parts of elf life. When Illyna was done assessing Essie's hair, she had Essie sniff several of the scents to pick out her favorite—or mix together if she desired—and gave her several samples to take home to figure out which worked best for her hair. Illyna would create a shampoo specifically for Essie and have it delivered to the palace in a few days.

Essie also discovered that the elves had far more hair

products than just shampoos. They also had something called conditioner that was apparently responsible for most of the gleaming, shimmering silkiness of their hair along with several other oils. Not to mention lotions for face and hands. No wonder the elf women were so beautiful with all the magical beauty products they had on hand.

As Farrendel reached Essie's side, Essie put back the lotion she had been considering. She didn't need it, and it wouldn't do to tread too heavily on Farrendel's generosity on her second full day of marriage to him.

She struggled to stand with her arms filled with several small jars of shampoo and conditioner. "Sorry this took so long. I'm ready to go when you are. Is this too much? I really don't need all of it."

"I am a prince, and I spend very little on myself. I have more than enough." Farrendel picked up the jar of lotion she had been considering, added it to the pile in her arms, and turned to Illyna and began talking in elvish.

Essie stared down at the jar of lotion. He was being so generous. Yesterday, she'd wondered how much he was going to make an effort. He'd told her elves didn't take things like marriage lightly, and they'd agreed to work on being friends. But today, he was acting almost like he was courting her, downright spoiling her with gifts.

Did his gestures mean anything deeper? Or was this

just what he considered part of his duty to take care of her properly since she was his wife?

It was so hard to know. She'd never had a long-term relationship ever, much less with an elf with a different culture and cultural expectations.

If only she had something to give him. Everything she had—her status as a princess, her allowance from the crown, her inheritance—only mattered in Escarland. Here, she had nothing of her own to buy him a gift, even if she knew of something he would like. All she had was kindness and her smile. They seemed to be more than enough for Farrendel.

But was it enough? Should she be doing more? After all, she was a princess of the elves now. What was she expected to do besides sit around and be Farrendel's wife?

Farrendel was digging in his pouch again and pulling out more coins. Larger coins, and more of them than he'd paid for their breakfast that morning.

Essie shouldn't feel guilty he was spending so much on her. She was his wife. But she didn't want to seem demanding. Or like she expected to be spoiled and given everything she could possibly desire.

If only her mother was here. Essie would dearly love a healthy dose of marriage advice right about now.

She drew in another deep breath of the competing, floral scents of the shop. Mother and Paige would love this shop. If Essie closed her eyes, she could imagine bringing Paige here on a visit.

Essie froze, her mind whirling. Did she dare ask for him to spend more on her today? Was her idea even possible?

But the more she thought about it, the more both the economics and politics of it formed in her mind…

Farrendel touched her elbow. "I have a bag you can put that in if you would like."

"Oh, right. Of course." Essie eased the jars into the canvas bag he held open for her. As she took it from him, she searched for a way to ask her question. "Do you think…can I order a shampoo and conditioner for my mother and my sister-in-law? If it's possible to get it across the border. I can write to let them know it is coming, and they can let the border guards know not to dispose of it as a suspicious substance. I can write letters, and they will get through, won't they? That was part of the treaty my brother and your brother signed, wasn't it?"

"Yes." Farrendel was eyeing her almost warily, though she wasn't sure if the wariness was because of her request or because she was still tense with the words building up inside her.

Had he been saying yes to buying shampoo for her family? Or yes that Essie could write letters? "I know it must be expensive, but I think it will benefit both our kingdoms—well, actually, yours will benefit the most financially probably. Once the ladies of the court see the results of the elven shampoo and conditioner on my mother's and Paige's hair—assuming it works as well on humans as it does on elves—they will all clamor for their own. The trade potential for elven hair products—even generic, non-personalized ones—would be huge. And, once the ladies of Escarland depend on elves for their hair products, it would take a great deal before Escarland would go to war against Tarenhiel. The women would never let their men go to war against the source of their haircare products."

Both Farrendel and Illyna were staring at her. Farrendel slowly gestured at the shop around them. "You think we can secure lasting peace through shampoo?"

"Yes, though I'm sure shampoo and conditioner will only be the beginning. Though I'd think you'd want to keep the trade limited to specialty items. It doesn't seem in your nature to want to turn something like this into mass-produced, large-scale business like we have in Escarland. Nor would I want the charm of Estyra taken away with that." Essie clamped her mouth shut. Perhaps this was a horrible idea and Farrendel was only waiting to get a word in edgewise to tell her so.

"You could get trade with Escarland started? They would want something as simple as this?" Illyna held up a jar of shampoo.

"Believe me. The ladies in Escarland will be scrambling for it. It just has to be brought to them in the right manner. And that is by having my mother and Paige start a trend. None of the ladies of the court want to be left out of the latest fashion trend."

It sounded so superficial, but apparently the elven court had similar dynamics since Illyna nodded with a knowing glint in her eyes.

Farrendel nodded, and his eyes too got a gleam to them. He glanced from Essie to Illyna. "Send along a few smaller, sample jars as well."

He liked the idea. Essie grinned. "Yes, good idea. Mother and Paige can gift them to a few ladies. Once they see the results on their own hair, they will clamor for more. I'll pick a scent for my mother and Paige and a few scents I think will do well in Escarland. My mother's hair is similar to mine while Paige's is thinner and finer. The samples can either be a generic batch or make it like the ones for me and my mother, whichever is easiest."

Illyna smiled. "It will be my best work."

By the time they returned up the lift to Farrendel's room in the elven palace, orange rays from the setting sun were slanting through the broad foliage overhead. Essie's face hurt from smiling, yet she couldn't stop.

After Illyna's shop, they'd gone to a shop where Farrendel told her to pick out fabric for new dresses and three everyday tunics, shirts, and trousers. Then he'd shown her more of Estyra. She'd met more elves who had fought with Farrendel against the trolls or fought to rescue him. A few of the elves she met hadn't been as welcoming, but most had. Perhaps the elves who had fought and been scarred had less against a human than the rest of the elves.

Essie stepped from the lift and turned to Farrendel as he tied it in place. "Thank you so much for today and everything you bought for me. And for breakfast and lunch and…" She tried to put everything into words, but for once, the gush of words was failing her. Finally, she just said, "Thank you. It was amazing. I had a good time."

The words hardly seemed enough for the glow she was feeling inside. Was it possible to begin to fall in love with someone in a single day?

Maybe it was. After all, if love was a choice as she'd been told, then how long did it take to make a choice? Only a moment, really. A series of moments as a person kept living out and making the choice again and again.

Was Farrendel feeling a similar happiness? Hopefully he was, but she couldn't be sure. After all, their handholding in town had been for show. She already missed the back of his hand pressed against hers, their fingers twined together.

Farrendel joined her on the platform and held out his hand. He wasn't smiling, and the look in his eyes was more wary than happy as he said, "I did too."

Essie smiled and held his hand again in the elven style that was becoming more comfortable after spending the whole day holding his hand like that. Maybe he was feeling some happiness or romance or something. Holding her hand now wasn't for show for anyone.

She tried to think of something to say. Was this the moment she was supposed to lean in, tip her face up, and hope he got the message and kissed her? What would it be like to be kissed by him?

She was swaying closer to him, her breath catching in her throat. Was it too soon to be feeling such warmth and tenderness for him? She'd been married to him for a total of two days. Well, two days since her elven marriage. Three days since she'd been married in a human ceremony.

But she was married to him. It would be foolish to hold back and not let herself feel for him when she was already married to him.

"Farrendel, I…" Her voice was a whisper as she gazed up at him. They were standing closer than they had been a moment ago, their breaths mingling in the scant space between them.

A loud gurgling, rumble shattered the stillness of the evening air. Essie grimaced and eased back as her stomach let loose with another peal of roars and growls. "I must be hungry."

The noise Farrendel made was like a suppressed snort. She wouldn't have even realized it was his stumbling, out-of-practice laughter except that he was also smiling. "I did not feed you enough today."

And now she was back to being the puppy he had to make sure he gave enough food and water. Essie suppressed her own snort.

With their fingers still twined, Farrendel led her around the walkway surrounding his room and down the staircase to the main room.

At the bottom of the stairs, Farrendel halted so quickly Essie stumbled against his back. She steadied herself with her grip on his hand. "What is it?"

"Someone is inside." Farrendel went so hard and stiff he was more stone than a living person. After a moment, he relaxed a fraction. "My brother."

Essie hadn't even realized how much she had tensed until her stomach tightened further. For some reason, she was less terrified of some random attacker waiting for them than she was of his brother. Farrendel was Laesornysh. He presumably could handle an attacker or two.

What was his brother doing here? It had to be important if he was waiting for them. How long had he been waiting? All day? Or had he come after being tipped off that they were wandering the town and something about that made him angry?

Farrendel started forward again. Stalked would be a better word for it. He didn't let go of her hand, and Essie took that as a good sign. Hopefully it meant they would be presenting a united front when facing his brother.

After shoving the door open, Farrendel barked the word to turn the lights on, then said something in elvish that ended with King Weylind's name.

King Weylind unfolded himself from one of the cushions on the far side of the room. His face was blank, though as his eyes flicked down to their linked hands, his jaw tightened.

Farrendel tugged her closer to his side. "What is it?"

King Weylind glanced between them, then let out a breath that might have been a sigh for anyone less dignified. He said something in elvish, his tone low and somehow weighty.

Farrendel stiffened again, but only for a moment, before everything in him seemed to sag. He drew in a breath and replied in elvish in a flat, emotionless voice.

King Weylind said something, then headed for the door.

As soon as he was gone, Farrendel took a step away from Essie, his hand sliding free from hers.

Cold wrapped around those fingers and started up her arm, into her chest. What was going on? Moments ago she and Farrendel were smiling, and now it was as if the last two days hadn't happened and he had returned to his silence and distance.

She wasn't going to let him retreat, especially when she didn't even know what was going on. She gripped his arm. "What happened? What did he say?"

When Farrendel turned toward her, his expression was the same blank one that had seemed so impenetrable. "Trolls have raided the border. The border guards have asked for my help to end the raids."

They'd called for their warrior. For Laesornysh to bring death swift and terrible to the raiding trolls.

And he would have to go. It was his duty.

Essie forced her breathing to remain calm, even as everything in her churned and tightened and twisted. Part of it was fear for herself. Nerves at being left alone in this foreign place.

But most of the fear was for him. He could be hurt again. Gain another scar. Die inside a little more.

She didn't even know all his secrets or his past to know why this seemed to weigh on him. But it would. It did.

She swallowed down the churn in her stomach. "When do you leave?"

"Tonight."

In other words, immediately. She drew that reality in, then pushed it down into her core. The best thing she could do for him now was be strong. Show him that she wasn't afraid to navigate her new life on her own and that she would be waiting here when he returned, however much or little that would mean to him.

Essie lifted her chin as she faced him. "Don't worry about me. I'll be fine here. Just stay safe and come back to me, all right?"

His silver-blue eyes studied her face, as if looking for any insincerity in those words. He wouldn't find any. After a moment, he nodded and turned toward the stairs to his room.

Essie let out a breath. That was it? No touching goodbye? Not even an unemotional, impassive farewell?

At the door to his room, Farrendel paused, then half-turned around to face her. "If you want to write a quick note for your family, I will make sure it is sent before I leave."

He did care. Maybe they weren't up to grand declarations yet, but for two days of marriage, they were doing fairly well, all things considered.

With barely a sound, Farrendel headed for his room, the door giving only the faintest click as it closed behind him.

How long would it take him to pack? Essie rushed for

the cupboard where she'd seen paper and ink on her first day here. She would have to seriously limit her words to the essentials if she was going to get everything written that needed to be written by the time he returned.

In the end, she settled for a quick note explaining that she was fine and Farrendel was treating her well and to expect a longer letter and a package of elven shampoo and conditioner soon.

She was just sealing the letter with wax when Farrendel strode into the room. He was dressed in a dark green tunic over a black shirt, black pants, and knee-high, matte black boots. His swords were buckled across his back while vambraces were laced on his forearms. While he always moved with an easy, light grace, his steps had an extra menace to them. His face was hard as the stones of Winstead Palace.

Essie eased to her feet, her chest tight. Her breathing was coming hard.

She couldn't be afraid of Farrendel, could she?

No, maybe she wasn't afraid of Farrendel. But he wasn't Farrendel at the moment. He was Laesornysh.

She drew her shoulders back, lifted her chin, and held out her letter. "I kept it short."

Farrendel took the letter, nodded without so much as a flicker of expression in his eyes, and strode past her.

That was it? Yes, he had changed into Laesornysh

from his clothes to his expression. But surely he could spare something for her.

"Farrendel?" Essie held her breath. Would he turn around for her? Or was he so focused he wouldn't so much as turn around?

He paused, then glanced over his shoulder at her. His silver-blond hair was stark against his dark clothes.

What did she want to say to him? She probably should have thought of what she wanted to say before she'd stopped him.

"Stay safe." Essie clasped her hands behind her back. "I thought you should know. I'll miss you."

He met her gaze for only a heartbeat—but what a breathless heartbeat it was—before he turned and disappeared out the door.

CHAPTER TEN

E ssie woke to sunlight streaming through the eastern window of her room. She groaned and rolled over.

It was so tempting to lie there for the whole morning and hide in these rooms all day. She didn't want to face anyone here without Farrendel at her side.

But she couldn't be a coward. What had Jalissa told her on her first day here? Hold her chin high and never let them make her feel ashamed for being human.

She would not be ashamed. She would face them. Today.

In some ways, it might be easier without Farrendel. With him at her side, they would hide their true thoughts behind fake smiles and false kindness. By herself, she would know the truth of the elven court.

After rolling out of bed, Essie picked out the nicest of her tunics, shirts, and pants. If only she had one of the outfits from the fabrics she'd picked out the day before with Farrendel, but it would be a few days at least before the first of those arrived.

Essie left her hair long, though she braided the sides in small braids to keep the hair from her face. It felt a little softer and sleeker than it had before. It should become even more so if the shampoo and conditioner Illyna was custom making for her did everything she said it would.

Once she navigated the stairs to the main floor, she stood for a moment in the center of the main room. No food waited for her on the countertop like the first day. Farrendel wasn't in his room where she could sneak up and gawk at him going through his morning workout.

It was…lonely. Essie grimaced and headed for the ice chest that held the food. She wasn't the type to enjoy alone time. Or loneliness. People, even slightly unfriendly elves who would probably spend all day gossiping behind her back, were better than staying here all by herself.

Essie grabbed some cold meat and cheese and headed out the door. She would be finished with her breakfast by the time she found her way from Farrendel's out of the way room to somewhere inhabited. Considering Essie had no idea how to even access the main hall.

When she reached the narrow branch, Essie kept her eyes up and inched her way across. When she successfully arrived on the other side, her hands were shaking. But she made it.

If she kept following the branches until they grew larger and larger, that should take her close to the heart of the tree and the palace's hall.

The closer she came to the main palace, the more the branches bustled with servants and those she assumed were courtiers of some kind. She tried to stay out of their way, and most either ignored her as if she didn't exist or gave her a disgusted look complete with a slight curl to the lip.

Essie expected someone to stop her. Maybe direct her to the royal apartments. Instead, everyone just ignored her.

No matter. Essie explored the elven palace with no one bothering to stop her. She found the hall where she'd married Farrendel and from there she discovered the fancy dining room decorated with gilt maple and oak leaves and a sitting room nearby. The lower levels of—what was the elvish word Farrendel had called it?—the Heart of the Forest contained the kitchens.

Higher in the branches above the dining room and sitting room, Essie discovered some fancy guest rooms with far more gilt and silk and furniture than Farrendel's rooms. Which begged the question: why was the elven prince living in such out-of-the-way, simple rooms? Especially since he was also the honored warrior Laesornysh?

The way his siblings doted on Farrendel they would've let him have his pick of the rooms at the palace. It was almost as if Farrendel didn't want to claim one of the fancier rooms. Why?

After more wandering, Essie stumbled across the library. It tucked into the crook of several twisting branches with no other rooms around it. Spires of shelves curved in multiple levels on the inside of the library. They enfolded Essie inside as she wandered, always revealing another curve and another layer of books.

This was her new favorite place in the whole palace, except for the coziness of her and Farrendel's set of rooms. She could see herself spending hours here, curled on one of the padded benches grown into the walls under the arching windows formed with living branches arching around panes of glass.

Too bad all the books were in elvish. Essie could read elvish better than she could understand it spoken out loud, but she was far from fluent.

Maybe she could come back with Farrendel sometime, and he could point out the children's section or the elf equivalent.

"Elspeth Amirah?"

Essie jumped and turned. An elf woman dressed in a simple green tunic, white shirt, and gray trousers with soft, knee-high boots stood a few yards behind her and lower down on one of the staircases. A servant?

"Yes?" Essie leaned against the arching handrail-bookcase formed of a curving, living branch.

"Leyleira Ellendirah requests your presence." The elf woman spoke slowly, as if speaking Essie's language was difficult for her.

"All right." Essie guessed the stilted sound to the words meant Essie was requested to come now. Not that it bothered her. It was closing in on lunch time, and Essie had no wish to eat alone nor was she ready to attempt to find her way back to her and Farrendel's rooms. Besides, it wasn't like Essie had anything better to do, and Leyleira had been the most welcoming of Farrendel's family.

Essie strolled down the stairs. "Lead the way."

The elf spun on her heels and strode from the library. Essie hurried to keep up.

Outside, the servant led Essie across a series of branches—thankfully all wide branches—to a series of rooms not far from the main section of the palace.

At the door to what was probably the sitting room-kitchen like in Farrendel's suite of rooms, the servant knocked, open the door, and spoke in elvish. Another voice answered from inside. Essie thought it was Leyleira, but she'd only heard her speak the one time at the wedding.

Essie stepped inside the room. It was draped in silk curtains with plush cushions and chairs clustered on one side and an ornate table carved with maple, oak, and beech leaves on the other side.

Leyleira perched on one of the chairs on the far side of the table as if it was a throne, her long, dark hair flowing over her shoulders and an emerald green silk dress draping around her body.

If Essie had known her wanderings would turn into a formal occasion, she would've dressed for it.

Or, perhaps not. It would have been more difficult exploring if she'd been wearing one of the flowing dresses.

Essie took a step forward and curtsied. What was the correct title for Leyleira? She would've been the Queen Mother and deserving of the title Your Majesty still in Escarland, but Essie wasn't sure of the protocol here. Still, it couldn't hurt to go with the title. "Your Majesty."

Leyleira tilted her head and gestured at the seat across from her. "Please. Have a seat. I heard that my Farrendel's bride was wandering Ellonahshinel and decided it was time we shared the midday meal."

Essie tried to figure out the edge to Leyleira's voice. It didn't seem to be the suspicion or even contempt she'd heard in those who didn't like that Farrendel had married a human. It was more like Leyleira was assessing her. Studying whether she was worthy of Leyleira's grandson.

Essie slid into the seat across from Leyleira and forced an easy smile onto her face. She had nothing to hide, and her best choice at this point was to be genuine and honest. She truly wanted to make Farrendel happy and be happy herself here in Estyra. "I was hoping to have a chance to get to know Farrendel's family better. Especially you. You were…" Calling her the nicest wasn't the right word for it, "the most accepting of Farrendel marrying me, a human."

The elf servant woman bustled around their table for a moment, pouring a deep pink liquid into china cups that looked like teacups yet without the handles, before she left the room. To fetch the food, perhaps?

"Ah." Leyleira picked up her china cup with both hands, holding it by her fingertips in a regal and delicate manner that must be the proper etiquette for holding this type of cup, and sipped at the drink. "I have lived long enough to remember a time when friendship rather than fear existed between my people and yours. When elf children and human children often crossed the border to play together and elf and human couples, while not common, were not the rare and frowned upon thing that they are today."

Essie picked up her own china cup and sipped at her drink to buy herself more time to come up with a reply. The liquid was sweet and cool, some sort of juice if she were to guess. It didn't have the burn or tingle to indicate that it was alcoholic.

What was Leyleira expecting her to say? Leyleira's

probing eyes were focused on Essie above the rim of her china cup.

Essie took a moment to study Leyleira in return. Her posture was guarded. Not exactly friendly, but not antagonistic either. It was almost as if she was waiting for something from Essie. As if this was a test of some sort.

If this was a test, then Leyleira might be willing to give Essie a few of the answers she sought. But only if Essie asked the right questions.

Essie set down her china cup. "At the wedding, you mentioned Daesyn and Inara. Who were they?"

Leyleira's mouth tilted upward at the corners. The barest hint of a smile that said Essie had asked a good question. "When I was a child, theirs was our greatest love story. It is not told as often now, and I fear your people have forgotten it entirely."

"My people. Why would my people know an elven love story?" Essie tried to sort through the riddle Leyleira was giving her. It seemed Essie would get answers, but those answers would hide more questions.

"Because Daesyn was a human who married our princess Inara." Leyleira sipped from her china cup again.

Essie tried to wrap her head around that information. "Your greatest love story is about a human and an elf princess?"

It hardly seemed possible that a people who scorned

humans as weak, flawed, and fleeting would also venerate a love story between an elf and a human.

"Yes." The corners of Leyleira's mouth curved in what was almost a smirk, her dark blue eyes glittering with the hint of more secrets behind that word.

What else was there to the story? What was Essie missing?

But she couldn't figure out what question she was supposed to ask so she decided to change the angle of the conversation. "That would explain why Farrendel's siblings weren't pleased with your mention of Daesyn and Inara. They…" Essie paused to choose her words carefully. She didn't want to sound like she was disparaging Farrendel's siblings, especially not King Weylind. "They don't want to see Farrendel hurt by loving a human."

"No, they do not." Leyleira set down her china cup. "But I have lived a long life. I know love, especially true love, has its costs. But I also know that the truest of love is always worth that cost. It is a cost I gladly paid, even though I lost my Ellarin too young. It is a cost I know my son gladly paid, even though he also lost."

Essie held her breath, trying to pick apart those words. It felt like each one was weighted with hidden meanings that Leyleira was waiting for Essie to find.

The door opened, and the servant returned carrying a tray.

Essie set her china cup aside, breathing out slowly. Good. The servant's presence gave Essie a chance to think before she had to come up with an answer or a question for Leyleira.

While the servant set plates with meat, cheese, and greens in front of them and laid out utensils and refilled glasses, Essie let Leyleira's words churn inside her.

Cost of love. Love lost far too soon. Something about that niggled at her, and she remembered being told that Farrendel's father had mourned for his wife for a hundred years before he was killed in the war by the trolls.

King Weylind's and Farrendel's father was killed almost fifteen years ago now. And if he had mourned for his wife for a hundred years before he died…

The numbers gnawed at her. Because certain things weren't adding up. How approximate was that hundred years? How much was it rounded up or down?

Essie felt herself grow tense. Did she dare ask the question? Because if her spinning thoughts were anywhere close to the truth, then she was treading close to secrets the elven court might prefer to remain hidden. How dangerous would it be to gain the answers to this particular question?

She waited until the servant left the room, closing the door firmly, before she met Leyleira's eyes. "How long ago did…" she nearly said *Farrendel's mother* but that didn't seem correct anymore, "the late elf queen die?"

Leyleira was still but not tense as if Essie was poking into a place she didn't belong. If anything, Leyleira's gaze turned sad beneath its layer of calculation. "My son's wife died a hundred and thirteen years ago."

Farrendel was only a hundred and five years old.

The late elf queen couldn't possibly be Farrendel's mother.

Essie struggled to keep her breathing even. Her thoughts jumbled until it was a struggle to organize all the answers tumbling through her.

King Weylind, Melantha, Jalissa…they were Farrendel's *half* siblings.

Unless the elf king wasn't Farrendel's father? Was he adopted? Was that why he didn't look like his siblings and felt so distant from them?

How did she even go about asking these questions? This seemed like something that it might not be her business to pry into.

Yet she was married to Farrendel. Whatever the answers here, they weighed on him. They formed the very core of who he was…or, at least, who he thought he was. She would never be able to understand him if she didn't understand this.

Essie swallowed and asked in a quiet voice, "Is the late elf king Farrendel's father?"

The sadness was deeper in Leyleira's eyes, along with

a searching look. Seeking Essie's reaction? What reaction was Leyleira hoping to see? "Yes."

Then not adopted. And Essie knew enough about the elven court to know the late elf king had never married again.

Not adopted. Illegitimate.

We elves live too long to live so recklessly. What we regret, we regret for centuries.

That's what Jalissa had told Essie, and back then, Essie hadn't realized the deeper meaning behind those words. Elves tried not to make mistakes, mistakes that would haunt them for centuries.

Mistakes like an illegitimate child.

And, in this case, a mistake that haunted not just the late elf king, but Farrendel and his entire family. Is that what Farrendel saw when he looked at himself in the mirror? Did he see himself as the reminder of his father's mistake?

So many, many questions. Would Leyleira tell Essie the answers? This couldn't be easy, discussing what was probably her son's greatest failing. This couldn't be something the elven court would want Essie reporting back to her brother or airing about widely for the world to scorn.

But Essie wasn't going to do that. Because doing so would hurt Farrendel.

"Farrendel doesn't bear the guilt for his parents'

mistakes. He can't help how he was born." Essie forced her fingers to uncurl, trying to relax her muscles. Why was she so tense? Almost like she was ready to start a fight to defend Farrendel, though she didn't know who she thought she'd be fighting against.

"No, he does not." Leyleira's face and posture relaxed just enough to let Essie know she'd said the right thing. Not that her words had been anything other than sincere. "His family sees that. But Farrendel often does not. He sees only the dishonor that he takes as his own."

He must feel like his very existence was a constant dishonor to his father's memory. As if anyone who saw him would be reminded of his father's mistake and remember the former king only in that light.

How did Farrendel feel about his father? His mother? Did he resent them? Love them?

Perhaps those were questions Leyleira couldn't answer. But Essie ached to understand.

Essie stared down at the plates of food both she and Leyleira had yet to touch. Perhaps, before Leyleira would say more, Essie needed to offer a reassurance. "I know this can't be easy for you to talk about. It isn't something to be ruthlessly bandied about. What I ask and want to know is only because I want to understand Farrendel better and this seems to be something that forms much of how he sees himself. I won't share this with my family. It would serve no purpose for creating peace between our peoples, and I see no point in promoting a scandal that would only hurt everyone involved."

Leyleira tipped her head in a small nod. "If I did not think you were sincere, I would not reveal what I am about to tell you. But, I do believe for my grandson's happiness, you need to know. Eat. The story is long."

Essie picked up one of the pieces of cheese almost by reflex. She'd been hungry when she'd followed the servant from the library, but now her stomach was churning so much she wasn't sure she'd be able to swallow.

"After my—what is your word for her?—daughter-in-law was killed, it rocked our family, but especially my son. Her death was sudden. A troll attack at the border. A common occurrence now, but back then the trolls had been peaceful for a hundred years. But their new king had recently taken the throne and decided to expand their empire down from the north and sparked the war that has yet to truly end." Leyleira held her china cup in her hands, but she didn't sip from it. "A year after her death, Lorsan placed the rule of the kingdom temporarily into Weylind's hands and disappeared into one of our remote manor houses near one of the small border villages with the kingdom of Mongalia. He would disguise himself and stroll through the local villages, driven from the manor out of loneliness but not really knowing what he was searching for. Simply an end to the ache inside him."

Leyleira's gaze dipped, as if she knew that ache all too well herself.

Essie choked down her bite of cheese. "That's when he met Farrendel's mother, isn't it?"

"Yes." Leyleira's gaze lifted briefly to Essie before dropping back to the china cup in her hands. "We elves pride ourselves on not making mistakes. Pride ourselves too much, a mistake in itself. But like any society, there are those who wish to live more recklessly and outside of society's norms. And, yes, even outside of morals in many cases. Those of my people who crave such a life tend to live in the border villages where they find more in common with your society, and even the fringes of your society, than they do with their own. Farrendel's mother was such a one."

Now Essie was definitely having trouble swallowing another bite. She gulped more than sipped at her juice. But the lump in her throat didn't fully leave.

"The pain of loss made Lorsan desperate, and for that, he did things he normally would not have done. It woke him up to how low he had fallen, and shortly afterwards he returned to Estyra and took up his duties as king once again, though a sadder, still lonely and hurting version of himself. As we elves do not have the ability to become pregnant as often or as easily as you humans do, he did not think more would come of a single night."

But there had been Farrendel. Essie set down the piece of cheese she'd been worrying in her fingers. She wasn't going to force another bite into her twisting stomach.

"As we learned later, as soon as Farrendel's mother realized she was pregnant, she began a search for the father. She did not know Lorsan was the king, but she had known he was from an upper-class family."

"She wanted money to support her child." Essie barely whispered the words, not really intending to say them out loud. It wasn't too uncommon. Her kingdom even had laws mandating that fathers provide for illegitimate children and their mothers.

"In a way, yes." Leyleira's gaze turned liquid and deep with the sadness there. "It is the duty of the elven queen to sit in the hall when the king meets with women asking for aid or judgment on a matter so that our women know they have a sympathetic ear who will help the king hear them. As my son's queen was dead, I had stepped back into the role I had held when my husband was the king. Thus, I was there in the hall when she came before Lorsan, a barely two-week-old babe in her arms. A baby she had not yet bothered to name."

A sick feeling twisted deeper inside Essie's gut. She wasn't sure she wanted to hear the end of this story.

"She announced that her son was Lorsan's, and she

demanded payment for his care, threatening to expose Lorsan's mistake to the kingdom if he did not pay her. After some questioning, it became clear she planned to abandon the child to the first person who would take him while she took as much of Lorsan's money as possible to live her reckless kind of life."

Now Essie was in danger of losing what little she'd eaten. "She blackmailed your son."

"That is what she attempted to do, yes, and I feared that she would continue to do so any time she needed more money. I counseled Lorsan against paying her, but he instead offered her three times the amount she had been asking for."

"He offered to pay her more? After she'd shown up to blackmail him?"

For the first time since she'd begun telling this story, the curve returned to Leyleira's mouth. "Yes. Even though he was not fully certain the child was his, Lorsan knew he could not leave the child in her care. Not when she intended to abandon him. So, instead, he offered her an even larger sum if she would give the child into his care and sign a statement that she would never demand more money or have contact with the child ever again."

"And she signed?" What mother would give her child away like that?

"Without a moment's hesitation. Then, once she was

paid, she walked away without so much as a farewell to the babe she left behind."

"What happened to her?" Essie fisted her hands in her lap.

"About twenty years after that, she was killed in a back alley of the same village where she met Lorsan. It seems she attempted to blackmail a human lord from across the border, and this lord was a less honorable sort who decided permanently silencing her was better than either paying or facing the truth when it came out, which it did anyway." Leyleira shook her head, letting a moment of silence fall between them.

What could Essie say to all of this? Poor Farrendel. How old had he been when he realized the date of the late queen's death and the date of his birth didn't line up as they should?

"He was such a tiny babe, much too young to be away from his mother. There were times those first few days and weeks when we were not sure he would survive." Leyleira's expression was such a mixture of sadness and joy it was hard to figure out what emotion to call it. Perhaps bittersweet was the closest. "For all the guilt he takes upon himself for his birth, I do not think Farrendel realizes how much he saved his father. Having Farrendel did not take away Lorsan's grief for Vianola, but Farrendel eased the grief and gave Lorsan much joy after those first difficult weeks. He loved his youngest son deeply, just as much as his other children, and did his best to never treat Farrendel differently or make him feel unworthy because of the circumstances surrounding his birth. If Farrendel feels that way, it is not because Lorsan made him feel that way. That came from others."

That eased some of the ache Essie felt on Farrendel's behalf. At least his father had been good to him. Loved him. But even in that, there was hurt. When King Lorsan was killed by the trolls, Farrendel lost the only parent who'd loved him at a time when, in elf years, Farrendel was still a teenager.

"How did King Weylind, Melantha, and Jalissa feel about him? I can tell they are protective of him now, but it couldn't have been easy on them." If Essie had the ages figured out correctly, they all would've been a couple hundred years old by then. Adults in elf years.

"They were understandably hurt and bewildered at first by what was a betrayal of their mother's memory. But they all eventually grew to love their youngest half-brother, and by the time he was one, they had become the fiercely protective older siblings they are now. In some ways, because of the circumstances, they are more protective of him than they are even of each other. They spent years protecting him from the snide remarks and scorn of the court while he was growing up." Leyleira picked up one of the pieces of meat, but only nibbled at it before setting it down again, as if she too couldn't bring herself to force food into a churning stomach.

"A scandal like that would be difficult to face in my kingdom's court. I imagine the scandal here must have been terrible." Essie shook her head, staring at her plate of uneaten food.

"It was. Lorsan wanted to raise Farrendel with all the love he had for his older three children, and that meant he could not quietly hide him away even if he had wanted to. Instead, he had to confess to me, his children, the court, and the entire kingdom what he had done and officially make Farrendel a part of the royal family. The court even demanded Farrendel be officially and magically tested to verify for certain that he was Lorsan's son. The dishonor was something Lorsan struggled with for the rest of his reign and life, though he did his best to shield Farrendel. And that is perhaps the cruel irony of it all. Even though he is the innocent one in the scandal, Farrendel will forever be the most marked by it."

If Tarenhiel was anything like Escarland, then Farrendel wasn't in line to inherit the throne because he was illegitimate, even though he had been acknowledged and raised as part of the family.

Would Averett have agreed to let her marry Farrendel if her brother had known the truth of Farrendel's standing in the elven court? Most likely not. He probably would've seen it as an insult that the elves would marry off their illegitimate prince to Escarland's princess.

Well, Averett was never going to find out. Essie had been truthful when she'd said she wouldn't tell him, and now she was even more determined. There was no reason Averett had to know.

Besides, even if he was illegitimate, Farrendel was still a part of the elven royal family. A dearly loved younger brother. And he had earned respect as Laesornysh.

Essie stilled, letting that thought seep into her. Was that why Farrendel had become Laesornysh? Because he felt he had to earn the place that should've been automatically his as an elf prince? Did he feel he had to prove himself worthy of the love his family had given him?

That ached in her chest. Because a family's love wasn't earned. It was given no matter how worthy or unworthy the family member was.

What would this mean for her marriage to Farrendel and their future together? If he saw himself unworthy, did that mean he saw himself unworthy of being loved by a fellow elf? Had he chosen to marry her, a human, as sort of a penance? Marrying a less worthy bride to match his own unworthiness?

She didn't want him to see her as less worthy. Less than

an elf bride he might have married. Nor did she want him to see himself as unworthy of love—any love, even that of a human—because she would never be able to build a relationship with him like that. Even a friendship would be difficult.

Leyleira was still looking at Essie, waiting for an answer.

This answer had to be right.

Essie let out a long, slow breath and met Leyleira's gaze. "I won't hold any of this against Farrendel."

Another hint of a smile crossed Leyleira's face. "And that is why I believe it is a good thing Farrendel married you, a human. Humans can be fierce, and some elves need a human's fierceness. Farrendel, I believe, is one of those elves. You and he will find your way to a love like Daesyn and Inara's."

Were her cheeks heating up? Essie ducked her head and focused on her plate. It wasn't only her cheeks that warmed. Her chest had a warmth too, the part of herself that was already falling for Farrendel.

She'd thought she'd be content with mere tolerance. Maybe even a mild friendship.

But she wasn't going to be content with that. She wanted to love Farrendel and wanted—desperately wanted—him to love her in return.

Was it possible?

CHAPTER ELEVEN

After they had gotten the serious topic out of the way, Essie spent a delightful afternoon with Leyleira, listening to stories about Farrendel's childhood.

Two hours before dinner, Leyleira insisted that it was time Essie joined the family for the evening meal. Essie couldn't help but agree. It was time she faced Farrendel's family, and it should be less intimidating with King Weylind gone.

Still, Leyleira informed her that it was etiquette to dress for dinner. Thankfully, she sent along her maid to show Essie to her room and back so she didn't become lost.

Essie dressed in the one elven dress she had that wasn't her wedding dress. It was a light green and silky smooth against her, though it was a touch too long. Not exactly a comfortable situation when Essie had to walk across branches without tripping and falling to her death.

Once she was dressed, she followed the servant across the branches back to the main part of the palace. Essie forced herself to keep her eyes up as she crossed the four foot wide branch.

The branches grew wider and wider until they reached the gilt dining room Essie had explored earlier that day. At the door, Essie paused and drew in a deep breath. She would hold her head high and wouldn't let them shame her for being human. She was married to the elf prince, and that made her a princess of both Escarland and Tarenhiel.

She pushed open the door and glided inside.

Leyleira and Jalissa were already there, standing along the wall on the far side and holding glasses with a dark red liquid. They glanced toward her but didn't halt their conversation. Leyleira's mouth remained in her hint of a smile, but Jalissa's smile wavered.

Essie strode farther in the room. Should she join their conversation? Or try to figure out what seat would be hers for dinner?

Behind her, the door to the dining room opened again. When Essie turned, she spotted Melantha and following her was Queen Rheva with Prince Ryfon and Princess Brina.

The whole family was here. Essie swallowed and forced her chin to remain high as the weight of Melantha's icy glare fell on her. If Jalissa was wary, Melantha was hostile.

And, having learned what she had about Farrendel that day, Essie didn't blame her. Melantha had been an adult when Farrendel was born. She would've been more a mother than a sister to him, especially those early years.

As if their arrival was a signal, everyone headed for the elegantly spindly chairs around the ornate table. Essie waited a moment to see where everyone else was headed.

The chair at the head of the table was left empty. It was probably King Weylind's when he was here. Queen Rheva claimed the chair to the right while her son and daughter sat in the seats next to her. Leyleira sat to the left of the head of the table with Melantha, then Jalissa in the seats next to her.

That meant Farrendel's seat would be either next to Jalissa or next to Princess Brina. Would Essie, as Farrendel's wife, be expected to sit next to him or across from him? Was she supposed to leave his place empty or could she sit next to either Jalissa or Princess Brina so she didn't have to sit awkwardly alone one space removed from everyone else?

If she hesitated too much longer, her hesitation would go from noticeable to awkwardly noticeable.

With her chin held high, she headed for the left side of the table and claimed the chair next to Jalissa. At least

Jalissa somewhat tolerated her and would make the meal less unpleasant than it could be. Hopefully.

Melantha glared while Jalissa sent Essie a sideways glance. Essie couldn't be sure if the glares were for picking the wrong seat or picking the right seat. Somehow, she didn't think this family would like her much no matter which chair she had chosen.

But she needed to show them she was strong enough to face them on her own without Farrendel at her side guiding her. She couldn't let herself be intimidated nor could she let them think she would run off to hide behind Farrendel every time they sent her an icy glare. They would walk all over her if she did that. She was a princess of the elves just as much as Jalissa, Melantha, or Brina, and she would carry herself as one.

Servants glided in carrying trays of food, their footsteps not even a whisper of sound on the wooden floor.

Melantha faced Queen Rheva and began a conversation in elvish, and the others soon followed, filling the room with a hushed murmur of voices speaking the lilting tones of the elvish tongue.

Essie pasted on a smile. She really needed to learn elvish. It wasn't fair to make everyone in this room speak her language just for her, and Essie truly didn't want to be that kind of a bother to everyone forever.

But she could sense the underlying tension in the

room. They were speaking in elvish to purposefully exclude her. Even Jalissa had her shoulder tilted away from Essie, as if to make sure Essie didn't seek to draw her into a conversation.

Instead, Essie kept her smile plastered to her face and dug into the meal. The first course was some sort of thick, vegetable soup that needed a touch more salt. That was followed by plate of cooked vegetables and venison. All delicious, though a hint bland. Did the elves not use spices the way her people did?

After barely eating that afternoon while talking with Leyleira, Essie didn't mind staying silent to polish off the food. While she ate, she tried to pick out the elvish words she could understand. There weren't many, though she caught Farrendel's name a couple of times and a couple of mentions of bride or wife with a glance in Essie's direction.

As the servants cleared away the main course and began setting out dishes with a chilled dessert, Leyleira glanced at Essie. "I had a lovely chat with Elspetha this afternoon."

The switch to Escarlish was so abrupt it cut through the rest of the conversations like a knife, slicing the room into silence in heartbeats, especially since Leyleira had added the a to the end of Essie's name to make it more elven. It made her sound more like one of them. Not the stranger, but Farrendel's wife.

Essie took in the narrowing eyes and pursed mouths around the table, as if no one there was happy their grandmother had been alone with the disgusting human all after-noon. It was as if she was a stray dog with fleas that they didn't want infecting their furniture.

Essie forced her smile to become a tad more brilliant. She would show them she was a nice puppy, if that's what it took.

"It was enlightening and delightful." Essie dipped her spoon into the dessert set in front of her, trying to think of something—anything—to add to the conversation now that Leyleira had so deliberately brought her into it. Honestly, she wanted to say something cutting, but such pettiness was beneath her and would probably come off as childish in this room where the teenagers were ninety years old. Instead, she went for something sincere. "It helped distract me from missing Farrendel."

It scared her how true those words were. How could she miss him when she'd only known him a couple of days?

Maybe it was the companionship he gave her that she missed more than him specifically. Those days she'd spent with him, she hadn't felt as alone here in Estyra as she had today. Today, even while spending time with Leyleira, Essie's *aloneness* here in the elven capital ached inside her. Except for the political ramifications it would cause with her brother, no one sitting around that table would care if

Essie tripped and died on her way back to her room after dinner. Jalissa or Leyleira might care if it hurt Farrendel, but they wouldn't care on Essie's behalf.

But that was it. No one here would give her a hug as warm and loving as her mother's. No one here would look her in the eyes to ask if she was truly all right the way Paige would. No one would rush out and take on anyone who had hurt her the way Averett, Julien, or Edmund would.

Would Farrendel? Essie didn't know, and it was all she could do to keep her smile from wobbling.

At that moment, all she wanted was her family. Their hugs. Their love. Their familiarity. It ached so deeply inside her she set down her spoon and pushed away from the table.

She couldn't do this another moment. With a forced smile, she stood. "It has been a long day. I think I will retire."

She didn't wait for any replies. Didn't care if they all knew she was on the verge of tears. She simply needed to get away and hide in the one small corner of this place that felt safe.

The next day, she let herself take the coward's way out and hide in her rooms. If anyone asked, she would claim she was writing lengthy letters to her family. That was true, but she'd decided to write the letters after spending a chunk of the morning staring at the wall trying to figure out something to do to give herself some excuse for hiding and keep her mind off loneliness.

Writing the letters didn't exactly help with the loneliness part. She wrote between dabbing at tears and aching for her family all the more.

It had sounded all so easy and brave when she'd agreed to marry Farrendel and packed up her life on a moment's notice to secure peace with the elves. But the reality was harder than she'd realized it would be.

As she finished a letter to Paige, a knock sounded on the door to the main room.

Essie jumped. She hadn't even heard someone step onto the porch. But then again, the elves were so silent they didn't go tromping around. She grimaced at the spot of ink that had dripped from the pen onto the tabletop. She blotted at it and thankfully it came out, mostly, without leaving much of a stain. She didn't want to go about ruining Farrendel's furniture while he was gone.

The knock came again, and Essie set aside her pen and stood. Hopefully it wasn't a servant summoning her to dinner or afternoon tea or whatever. She wasn't in the mood to be sociable today. She'd reached the end of pretending to be fine and happy and blithely unaware of the cutting remarks.

Essie yanked the door open. Yes, an elf servant was standing there. A male elf this time. Probably the equivalent of a footman. Essie nearly slammed the door back in his face, but a shred of politeness stayed her hand. It was no fault of this servant that she was in a foul mood today.

"Amirah," The footman said something in elvish and gestured.

Essie caught sight of the elf standing behind him. "Illyna! Please! Come in!"

Her voice must have sounded downright desperate for the footman elf hurriedly stepped aside, his eyes wide, and Illyna glided past him, carrying a canvas bag slung over one shoulder.

As soon as Illyna was inside, Essie slammed the door, not caring if it was impolite to the footman. "You have no idea how happy I am to see you."

Illyna gripped the canvas bag tighter with her left hand and eyed Essie. "You want to hug me again."

"Um, yes. Kind of. But I'll resist." Essie clasped her hands behind her back to fight the urge. "Sorry to sound so desperate. It…" Essie caught herself before rambling on. She'd enjoyed her time at Illyna's shop a few days ago, but was Illyna a friend? Could she trust her? Or was she tolerating Essie merely for Farrendel's sake?

One day mingling with a few members of the elven court, and Essie was already turning paranoid.

"I see." Illyna's mouth curved into a full—and what Essie hoped—was a genuine smile. "I heard Farrendel was called away and thought I should stop by. It seems it is a good thing I did."

"Yes. Thank you." Essie waved to the plush chairs behind them. "How long can you stay?"

"All afternoon, if you would like. I closed shop early." Illyna took her bag from her shoulder and held it out in her hand. "I finished a small batch for you and for your family."

"Thank you." Essie took the bag and set it on the table. She had a feeling she was going to be thanking Illyna a lot that afternoon. She pulled out one of the jars with her name on it, popped off the lid, and sniffed. "It smells even better than it did in the shop."

She sniffed again and closed her eyes to savor the smell. Floral with hints of a sugary sweet scent and a depth of vanilla underneath. This was the type of smell that would have her grabbing locks of her hair just to smell at random times during the day.

"My pleasure, especially for Farrendel's wife." Illyna sank onto one of the cushions. There was something to the way she said it. Not jealousy, like she had wanted Farrendel for herself. More the depth of appreciation of a good friend indebted to another, almost as if Illyna felt indebted to Farrendel.

Which was odd. If Essie had pieced the story together correctly the other day, Illyna had lost her hand rescuing

Farrendel from the trolls. If anything, Farrendel was the one indebted to her, right?

Essie remembered the small shop in a small, nearly deserted alley. In the entire time she had spent in Illyna's shop, no one else had entered.

As she mulled that over, Essie busied herself pulling china cups from one of the cupboards similar to the ones Leyleira had used when serving her. In the cold cupboard, she pulled out an orange colored juice and poured it into the china cups. Hopefully Illyna liked that particular flavor. It was the only one Farrendel had stocked at the moment, and Essie wasn't sure how to go about getting more. Was she supposed to order food for herself and Farrendel directly from the market or was there a palace steward or butler that she was supposed to go to for requests like that?

Essie crossed the room carrying the two china cups and handed one to Illyna before she claimed a cushion facing Illyna. As much as Essie had enjoyed her time with Leyleira, that had been a test. A minor form of interrogation. This felt much more relaxed. Natural.

Perhaps that was why she felt bold enough to say, "Farrendel is one of your best customers, isn't he?"

Illyna held up her right arm, waving it about as if to highlight the empty space where her hand should have been. "My missing hand sometimes makes others uncomfortable. It is harder to hide than most scars from the war. Farrendel helped me get the shop started, and word has gotten around to others who have been scarred by the war, and they are steady customers."

Illyna's shop must feel like a safe place for those who suffered disgusted looks wherever else they went.

"Then I am especially hoping your products take off in Escarland as I think they will. You'll soon have to hire assistants if my estimation is correct." Essie took a sip of her drink before setting it aside on an end table.

"I appreciate the attempt, even if it does not come to anything."

If Essie knew anything of the ladies of the court in Escarland, it would, but she didn't say that out loud. She didn't want to build Illyna's hopes up too high in case the ladies inexplicably didn't clamor for the magical elven shampoo and conditioner.

Instead, she let herself fall into the easy rhythm of talking with Illyna. A faint glimmer of an idea was sparking in Essie's head, but she didn't voice it out loud. Not yet. She needed to talk with Farrendel to see if it was even possible or something that was needed.

By the time Illyna left with plans for them to meet in a week for another chat, Essie could confidently say she had one friend here in Estyra. And that helped curb the loneliness at least for that night.

CHAPTER TWELVE

Five days after Farrendel left, Essie ate a plate of some sort of thinly sliced venison over vegetables as yet another conversation in elvish flowed around her. She kept her smile in place and practiced picking out words she recognized.

She'd met with Leyleira on two more afternoons and spent another day with Illyna. Both times she worked on learning more elvish, though Illyna was the more patient teacher and Leyleira was...Essie wasn't quite sure what she was. She still wasn't entirely sure if Leyleira liked her or was constantly testing her.

Jalissa was another puzzle. At times she seemed to be warming to Essie and would even join with Leyleira in talking with Essie during these dinners. But other times she would glare along with Melantha as if to remind Essie that she was to be as invisible as possible until she quietly died off in a few decades.

The door to the dining room opened, but instead of servants with dessert, King Weylind strode inside. It was a weary sort of stride that apparently both human men and elf males got when gone too long from home and family.

And he was alone. Essie craned her neck and held her breath, but Farrendel didn't follow him inside.

Was Farrendel hurt? Dead? Why wasn't he with King Weylind? Had he remained behind at the border? Was the trolls' incursion more than a mere raid?

Her heart hammered for answers but her body was frozen, her thoughts too jumbled to force herself to move.

Queen Rheva glided to her feet and gripped King Weylind's upper arms. The largest show of expression an elf couple would do in public, as Essie was learning. King Weylind greeted his children, then the others around the table.

Jalissa asked a question that ended with Farrendel's name, and King Weylind replied, also in elvish, without so much as a glance in Essie's direction.

As if Farrendel's wellbeing wasn't her concern. As if she wasn't his wife.

That surged strength into Essie's legs and arms, and she was on her feet before she'd even consciously thought about moving. "Where is Farrendel? Is he all right?"

King Weylind finally looked in her direction, and the

searching look in his eyes was something inherited from his grandmother. "He returned directly to his rooms."

His rooms. Not their rooms. Farrendel's wording or King Weylind's?

King Weylind's, Essie decided. There was too much undertone to them, as if Farrendel returning to his room was a foregone conclusion Essie ought to know and King Weylind was disgusted she didn't.

Well, it wasn't her fault she didn't know all the secrets of this family yet. She'd been married to Farrendel for all of three days before he'd been called away. How was she supposed to anticipate everything about Farrendel after such a short time?

Why hadn't Farrendel gone to the dining room with King Weylind? Didn't he want to see Essie?

Unless he assumed she hadn't gathered the courage to venture from their rooms yet. Maybe he had gone directly there because he was eager to see her?

Essie gathered her skirt and headed around the table for the door. She had to return there as quickly as possible.

Before she reached the door, her path was blocked by King Weylind. She tried to step around him, but he shifted into her way. A tall elf king with his arms crossed was a formidable block.

King Weylind's dark gray eyes stabbed into her. "Give Farrendel space."

The words might have been a friendly suggestion for a wife still figuring out her new husband except for the intensity. There was nothing friendly about King Weylind's tone. It was a warning. A threat.

Essie would've been angry, except for the depth of love for his brother it showed. She lifted her chin and didn't flinch away from King Weylind's glare. "I know you care about Farrendel, and I do too. I will give him space if he wants space."

King Weylind's expression eased a fraction. Not that he looked friendly. But at least he didn't look like he wanted to wipe his boots off on her dress. "After a battle, Farrendel prefers space. Give him space."

It wasn't a warning this time. More an order.

Essie nodded, and this time when she took a step, King Weylind let her pass.

By this time, she was familiar enough with the way back to her and Farrendel's rooms that she didn't need a guide. She didn't even flinch crossing the last four-foot-wide branch to get to the main room.

All three rooms were dark when she arrived. The main room didn't even look disturbed, yet there was something about it. That indefinable sense that a place had when it was lived in instead of when it was empty and hollow.

What she really wanted to do was track Farrendel down, give him a hug, and tell him exactly how much she'd missed him.

Farrendel's room was dark, and after King Weylind's warning, Essie didn't dare knock on his door tonight, much as she wanted to. Instead, with one last glance in that direction, she retreated to her own room, dressed in her sleeping shirt and pants, and crawled into bed.

For a moment, she lay in bed, blinking at the twisting vines and leaves carved into the ceiling and barely visible in the hint of moonlight penetrating the broad leaves of Ellonahshinel. What woke her? She normally slept deep. Too deep to wake for anything minor.

Then a noise rose above the stillness of the night. Not quite a scream. A cry. Muffled, but distinct. Not an animal noise. It was far too human—or elven. After a moment, it faded into silence.

Essie sat up. Had that been Farrendel? If that had been a nightmare, it must be some nightmare for her to hear him crying out in his sleep all the way in her room a whole branch away.

What was she supposed to do? She waited, her breaths held tight in her chest as she listened, her head cocked toward his room. But after several long minutes, no more sounds drifted on the still night.

Did that mean Farrendel was awake? King Weylind had warned her to give Farrendel space, but did that also mean during nightmares? She didn't think King Weylind's warning had been for her safety though she could see that waking Farrendel—Laesornysh—could be dangerous.

But if he was awake? Would he appreciate company?

She was his wife, and he shouldn't suffer through nightmares alone. Easing out of bed, she padded across her room, down the stairs, through the main room, and back up the stairs to Farrendel's room.

At the door, she drew in a deep breath. She could do this. Raising her hand, she knocked firmly on the door.

She waited for a long moment but didn't hear anything from inside. Should she knock again? Was Farrendel lying in bed hoping she'd just go away if he ignored her?

Perhaps she should leave. King Weylind knew Farrendel better than she did, and he'd said to leave Farrendel alone tonight.

But that aching cry was still echoing in her ears, and she couldn't leave Farrendel to face a night of terrors like that by himself. It wasn't right. She had to at least tell him she was here for him even if he turned her away.

She knocked on the door again. "Farrendel?"

The room behind the door remained silent. Was he even in there? Or had he gone off to some hidden spot among the tree branches? She didn't know him well enough to know where he'd retreat, what he was hiding from, or if he'd want her company. Were nightmares like this usual after a battle? What had happened?

Without so much as a footstep or a creak of floor-boards to give warning, the door whisked open, and Farrendel stood there, barefoot, wearing a rumpled pants and shirt, the collar open to show a V of skin. His hair, even after rolling out of bed after a nightmare, was perfect, flowing in silvery cascades across his shoulders and back, not a hair out of place or frizzing above his head.

Even magical elven conditioner probably couldn't pull off such a feat with Essie's hair.

"Your brother said to give you space, and I was going to, but you cried out in your sleep loud enough I could hear it in my room, and I wanted to make sure you were all right and if I could do anything to help, even if it's just sit with you for a while if you don't want to go to sleep again right away. But if you want space, that's fine too. I'll go back to my room and let you have space if that's what you need right now. I under-stand." Essie snapped her mouth shut against more babbling.

Before her, Farrendel was as still as stone, one hand braced against the door frame. Was he wishing she would just be quiet and leave? Or did he want her there?

Her heart pinched with missing him and ached for the light moments they'd had in Estyra before he'd left.

She glanced up and caught a glimpse of something in

his eyes before he looked away. The hardness there was brittle, a thin veneer to hide the shaking underneath. His hand on the doorframe wasn't casual but a prop to hold himself upright. His body was too rigid, as if only his willpower was keeping him from breaking.

If he'd been a human, he would've been in desperate need of a hug.

Essie eased a couple of inches closer, moving slowly as if he was a wild animal she didn't want to spook. She wasn't sure what would happen if she moved too fast, too boldly. "Would it be all right if I hugged you?"

If she'd thought him still before, now he was still as a breathless morning. For one heartbeat, then two, he didn't move. Didn't so much as breathe. Then his head tipped in his shallow nod, the movement shifting his hair to reveal the points of his ears.

At least it was a nod. Essie closed the last few inches between them and brought her arms around him slowly, carefully, as if he'd bolt if she moved with the giddy sureness she had in her hugs with her family.

As she wrapped her arms around him and pressed her palms against his back, it struck her just how small he felt. He wasn't much bigger around than she was, though he was all hard muscles where she was softer and curvier.

The ends of his hair brushed her hands, and it took all her self-control to refrain from running her fingers through the strands. Somehow, she got a feeling that might be something that would spook him.

He held perfectly still. Not pulling away, but not leaning into the hug or putting his arms around her. Maybe he didn't know how to respond to a hug. Maybe he was doing his best to tolerate this very un-elf-like close physical contact between two barely-not-strangers, for all they were married.

She rested her head against his chest. As he'd been gone fighting trolls, she'd almost expected him to smell of sweat and blood and death, but instead his clothes, his hair, smelled of a minty, forest scent she'd couldn't fully place. Not as sharp as pine or with the depth of cedar. Not really the scent of an individual tree she could name. More the fresh, living scent a whole forest had.

She knew what she needed to tell him. She wasn't sure what difference it would make in this moment, but it was what he needed to hear. "I missed you while you were gone."

With a puff of a released breath against her hair, Farrendel relaxed. Just a fraction, but enough for her to feel the hint of a tremble in him.

As much as Essie wanted to stay like that, her head resting against his chest, her arms around him, this moment was for him, not for her. There would be other moments, ones when he was less hurting, when she could pause and enjoy.

She pulled back just enough to rest her hand on his chest over his heart where she'd drawn the elvish symbol at their elven wedding. She couldn't meet his gaze and instead focused on her hand pressed against the white of his shirt. "I don't know all your reasons for asking your family give you space after a battle like this, but I understand there are some parts of ourselves that we can't show even our families. But you don't have to hide anything from me. I don't fully understand all the implications of the elven marriage vows we spoke, but they are similar enough to the human ones that I know that in marriage our hearts are linked. That means when you are hurting, I'm hurting. When you need help, I'm here to help. If you want space, I'll give you space. But please know you don't have to be alone. I'm here for you."

Now she was the one holding still, holding her breath, waiting, wondering.

Farrendel remained still, almost frozen. Then his hand reached out and clasped her free one. He raised his silver-blue gaze to meet hers. "Do not leave."

The words were spoken as if they cost him dearly.

Essie glanced past his shoulder to the darkness of his room beyond. Did he mean stay here? In his room? Even if they did nothing besides talk, she wasn't sure she was ready for something that close and personal yet.

She gripped his hand to make sure he knew she wasn't contradicting what she'd just said and took a step away from him, back the way she'd come. "Why don't we go to the main room and just talk for a while?"

He gave her that tiny nod again, and something about that nod felt like the deepest sort of trust.

Essie led the way down the stairs to the main room, still clasping Farrendel's hand. The moment was déjà vu of their first night there, except this time it was Essie leading the way across the elven handrail-less stairs with sure steps.

If Essie had been in Winstead Palace, she would've sneaked into the kitchen to fetch him a hot drink. Her favorite hot chocolate, perhaps.

But elves built all their cook fires on the ground, and Essie had yet to see any magic used to heat food or drinks in the upper stories of the treetops. Instead, Essie let go of Farrendel's hand as the door to the main room closed behind them and headed for the cold cupboard, picking her way across the room in the dark. "Would you like a drink? Water? Juice?"

"Water?" The inflection in his voice was part question, part a plea.

After living here the past few days, Essie was familiar enough with the cupboards and room to fumble her way through finding the cups, fetching the jug of cold water from the chilled cupboard, and pouring a glass for Farrendel with only the stars above the dense foliage for light.

When she turned back to the room with the cup of water, it took her a moment to find Farrendel where he curled in the far corner on one of the overstuffed cushions on the floor with his back to the wall. She'd only spotted him because of the glint of starlight on his silver-blond hair.

She crossed the room and held out the cup. When he took it, she fetched two blankets from a nearby cupboard and settled onto a cushion next to him. Not close enough to be touching, but within easy handholding space if he would be all right with that.

Farrendel cradled the cup in both hands and sipped, as if he needed the water to steady whatever memories were shaking him inside.

Tucking one of the blankets around herself, she let him have these few moments of silence to piece himself together from the nightmares tormenting him.

He was waiting for her to ask. She could see it in his tense posture, the way his knees were drawn up as if to protect his heart even from her.

How did a family that loved him as much as Essie knew King Weylind, Melantha, and Jalissa did let Farrendel become this wounded? How could King Weylind possibly send Farrendel back into battle knowing how it tore

Farrendel inside?

Unless King Weylind didn't know? Was that why Farrendel demanded space from them after a battle? He let them think it was his way to process, and what he was really doing was hiding his breaking? And yet Farrendel went back into battle, became Laesornysh again and again. Was it because he felt it was better that he was the wounded, broken one than someone else?

Probably, but now wasn't the time to talk about it. She wasn't going to ask about the nightmares or make him talk about this when he was so clearly unready.

"I visited with your grandmother Leyleira while you were gone. I think she approves of you marrying me, though it's hard to tell." Essie rested her hand, palm up, in the space between them. Inviting him to hold her hand if he wanted to.

She wasn't going to mention the topic of her discussion with Leyleira. Now wasn't the time to tell Farrendel that she knew he was illegitimate.

He set the cup of water to the side, pulled the second blanket over his legs, and leaned his head against the wall, staring into the darkness instead of looking at her. After a moment, he inched his hand toward hers and tentatively clasped her hand. Not a two-finger, elven style hand-holding. But fingers clasped, palms together, human handhold.

When he finally spoke, his voice was low, his tone questioning rather than accusatory. "You were dining with my family."

Essie let out a breath in a small laugh. "Yes. I don't do well all by myself. I like to be around people."

"I did not think you would be brave enough to face them alone." Farrendel still wasn't looking at her, but some of the tension had eased from his shoulders.

"I decided I wasn't going to let them intimidate me. I'm never going to make a spot for myself beside you if I'm always cowering behind you. And it wasn't all bad. They mostly spoke in elvish and ignored me, though your grandmother and Jalissa occasionally made a point to include me." Probably best to steer the conversation away from his family. "I also spent time with Illyna. I think she's going to become a good friend."

"Good." Farrendel closed his eyes. Was that a tremble she could feel through his fingers? "You both could use a friend here."

As could he. She clasped his hand between both of hers. His fingers were cold, colder even than they'd been at their weddings.

Was this the time to bring up her idea? "I was thinking. In Escarland, a princess often does charity work. I'm not sure how it works here, but I think I would like to start a— I'm not sure what to call it—maybe foundation? It would be an organization to help the elves who fought in the wars, especially those who were wounded. We could start out by making a list of businesses, like Illyna's that are friendly to elves with visible scars. We could help them find jobs, those kinds of things. Do you think that would be something helpful here?"

Farrendel tilted his head toward her, finally meeting her gaze. "Yes. It may not be popular but it is needful."

And they could bring together damaged, hurting elves who needed to find others like them who would understand their nightmares and their struggles better than those who hadn't fought, who hadn't been injured, like they had.

Now wasn't the time for more of a discussion or planning. Farrendel was still trembling in the aftereffects of his nightmares, too damaged to properly process anything of what she was saying tonight.

Essie held his hand long into the night. Talking when he seemed like he wanted to talk. Staying silent when he seemed to need space. And thinking that, for all the cultural and magical differences, elves weren't all that different from humans after all.

CHAPTER THIRTEEN

Essie's eyes felt gritty as she blinked against the light shining on her face. She was curled on her side on one of the cushions in the corner of the main room, snuggled under a blanket.

Farrendel curled a foot away from her, still asleep as far as she could tell. His face was so very young in his sleep while his hair lay perfectly smooth over his cheek and shoulder, the tip of his ear visible.

For a moment, Essie had the nearly irresistible urge to touch his ear, and only the fact that her hand was still loosely held in Farrendel's between them stopped her.

Besides, she was in no hurry to wake him. After the rough night, he deserved his sleep. There was something soothingly peaceful about his even breathing, his expression stripped of the tense hardness he so often wore. As he normally woke well before her, she wouldn't see him like this often.

A knock came from the front door, jolting Essie. She suppressed a groan. Why was someone at their door at this hour? It wasn't exactly early anymore, but it was still morning. Had King Weylind sent a messenger to make sure Essie hadn't bothered Farrendel?

Essie began to lever herself to a sitting position, but Farrendel's hand tightened on hers. When she glanced down, he still had his eyes closed, but his body had that still, tense look of someone awake instead of relaxed in sleep.

"If you do not answer, they will leave their message or package by the door," Farrendel murmured.

Essie sank back to her side on her cushion and whispered, "I see. You have this whole hide away in your rooms thing down to an art form."

Not that she minded, at least, not this morning. She was rather content to hide away in his rooms with him.

After one more knock, there was silence. Essie waited, holding her breath. Her own tension nearly turned into giggles. One would think they were hiding from an enemy instead of some poor elf servant just doing his or her job.

Farrendel sighed and opened his eyes. "They are gone." He pushed himself into a sitting position.

Essie levered herself upright and hopped to her feet. "I'll fetch whatever the servant left if you'd like to start on breakfast."

She didn't wait for his reply but hurried to the door.

Even though Farrendel said the servant had left, Essie still took a moment to peek through one of the windows to make sure no one was around before she opened the door.

A canvas-wrapped package sat on the narrow porch in front of the door with several folded and sealed papers stacked on top. Essie picked up the whole bundle in both arms, shut the door behind her with a foot, and carried everything to the table, setting it down on one side to avoid the plates of cold venison and fruit Farrendel was setting out for their breakfast.

"This is a larger pile than I was expecting." Essie picked up the first of the sealed letters, this one a single sheet of paper. A single word was written on it in elvish. "I'm assuming this is yours."

As she held it out to him, she nearly dropped it as she caught sight of the thick letter beneath it with her name written in her mother's familiar handwriting. "A letter from my mother. Hopefully that means she got the one I sent with you before you left. I have a stack of letters and packages for her and Paige and my brothers, but with you gone, I didn't know how to send them."

Farrendel took the note from her, saving it from falling into a bowl of fruit. "We can see to sending your letter and package this afternoon. You can add a reply to her letter if you wish."

"Perfect." Essie glanced between the thick stack of

paper that her mother had sent to the package waiting to be unwrapped. The package wasn't from her mother. It had a note with elvish script pinned to the canvas.

As much as Essie wanted to sit and read her mother's letter right then and there, she would rather take the time to savor it, not read it while eating breakfast. With some effort, she set her mother's letter to the side. "I'll read it and answer it after breakfast. Who is the package for?"

Farrendel looked past the note he was reading to peer at the paper pinned to the package. "For you. It must be some of the dresses and tunics we ordered."

Already? That was fast service. But perhaps the elf who worked as the tailor and seamstress had the same problem as Illyna. The shop might not be as popular due to the elf's hobbling gait from a war wound.

Essie unpinned the canvas wrapping. It flopped open, and deep, royal blue fabric spilled onto the table and flowed over the edge. Essie picked up the dress almost reverently. "This is even more beautiful than I imagined when I picked out this fabric."

"It will look stunning on you." Farrendel's mouth tilted with the hint of a smile, something Essie wouldn't have guessed she'd see that morning after the rough night they'd had. His eyes still held a faint weariness, though as an elf, he didn't have so much as a wrinkle, never mind dark circles under his eyes. Still, she had the feeling he didn't normally wake rested and relaxed after a night like last night. He held up the note. "My brother offered to send Jalissa to save me from you today."

Farrendel was probably paraphrasing that to make it sound nicer than it probably was.

"Do you need saving from me?" Essie kept her smile in place, her tone light, as she carefully set the dress over the back of one of the chairs, then set the canvas package with the tunic, shirt, and pants that had been hidden beneath the dress on the chair as well to get it out of the way.

When she turned back to him, Farrendel's smile had faded into something serious. He'd gone still again. "No."

Who knew that one word could turn her insides so mushy? Essie slid into one of the chairs by the table and tapped her mother's letter. "My brother probably sent along a letter with my mother's, offering to rescue me from you. And I'm going to tell him that I don't need saving from you either. I think our brothers would get along if they just united in their shared, older sibling over-protectiveness."

Farrendel took the seat across from her, the almost smile back on his face.

They ate their breakfast in a companionable silence. Then, while Farrendel cleaned up the dishes, Essie curled in one of the chairs with her mother's letter, unable to resist a moment longer.

Reading her mother's letter was both wonderful and

heartaching at the same time. Missing her family was an ache so constant she almost didn't realize it was there until something like this prodded it into a painful stabbing.

They were all doing well. There hadn't been any more incidents at the border, and the reception to her marriage to Farrendel at home seemed to be favorable enough. The gossip was apparently painting her as the selfless, tragic princess sacrificing herself to the ruthless, heartless elves to secure peace.

And, yes, her brothers all included short letters, each of them giving some variation of the *if he has hurt you, I will march right over there and beat him up for you* threat. It was odd that having her brothers threaten to punch Farrendel brought a smile to her face, even though she didn't want them to get anywhere near punching him. It just showed how much they cared for her. She wouldn't trade that fierce love for anything, even if it meant missing them just as fiercely now.

"Is your family all right?"

Essie looked up to see Farrendel, his silver-blond hair wet and shining as it hung down his back, where he knelt in front of her. Not touching her, but close enough to almost seem like he was. His eyes searched her face, and that made her realize she had tears tracing their way down her cheek.

She swiped at her face. "They're fine. Just reading their

letters made me miss them. I was right. My brothers all wrote letters to threaten you and offer to save me if I needed them to."

For a moment, Farrendel remained frozen as he was, and she wasn't sure he was going to reply. Then he tipped his face to meet her gaze. "In six months, if the border with your people remains quiet, my brother will send an emissary. If I can be spared, maybe we can visit your family."

"I'd like that." She smiled, but she hadn't missed the way he'd worded it. She turned to fully face him, setting her letters aside. "How bad are things with the trolls?"

He dropped back from his crouch into a cross-legged position on the floor. That couldn't be a good sign, if he took the time to get comfortable before answering. "There have been more raids on our border by the trolls in this last year than there have been in the past decade. Last time they raided this much, it turned into an invasion."

An invasion. Essie swallowed. That explained why the elves were desperate enough to agree to a marriage alliance with her kingdom. They did not want to risk fighting a two-front war again. "If that happens, my brother might be persuaded to send help. Escarland doesn't want to see Tarenhiel overrun with trolls either, since if you fall, the trolls would be at our border next."

Farrendel shook his head. "I fear my people will not

seek aid from yours unless the situation was very dire indeed. By then, it would most likely be too late."

He was probably right. And it was doubtful her country would go to war to aid the elves unless the elves looked about ready to be overrun. Even then, many would advocate waiting for the elves to fall and then holding the trolls at the Escarlish border.

"If it looks like it's coming to that, we both can work on our brothers. That's what a marriage like ours is supposed to be for, politically anyway. I would rather not see either of our kingdoms fall to the trolls because our people are too stubborn to help each other." Stubborn pride only went so far. Surely common sense would win out eventually.

"It may not come to war. If the trolls have been scouting our defenses, they will have found we are just as strong as we were fifteen years ago. And I am stronger." Farrendel's voice had a fierce note to it, one that reminded her of that first morning here when she'd seen him pushing himself relentlessly through morning exercises.

She leaned forward to clasp his hands. "And you have me." She wasn't sure how much her presence helped, but she wasn't going to let herself be simply a burden.

Her words must have meant something to Farrendel because his hint of a smile flashed on his face for a moment. But when he met her gaze, his expression was serious once again. "Would you come with me to dinner with my family tonight?"

His question held more than just an invitation to dinner. After all, she had dined with his family for the past several nights, though this would be her first time at Farrendel's side. "You don't usually go to dinner with your family on a day like today, do you?"

He shook his head, and only when his fingers tightened around hers did she realize she was still holding his hands. "No."

Not only would attending together be a statement, but the fact that he was going at all would be a statement that something was different. That something was her. Was it a subtle way for him to tell King Weylind to back off? That Essie was good for Farrendel?

"Of course, I'll come." Essie let go of his hands and stood. "Though I should follow your example and wash now so my hair has time to dry before tonight. Should I wear the new dress? Or is that too flashy for a simple dinner with your family?"

Farrendel rose gracefully to his feet, and when he smiled, there was a glint to the expression. "Please do."

Essie smoothed her royal blue skirt as she stood in front of the mirror. The fabric was ethereally soft against her skin, floating about her ankles. The bodice was beaded with silver and embroidered with a navy blue thread in patterns of maple and oak leaves. The sleeves were simple down to her elbows before they flared in a gauzy, draping train. She would've thought having fabric fluttering down from her elbows would get in the way, but it seemed to stay trailing behind her as if hanging on a light breeze.

This was possibly even more beautiful than her re-done wedding dress. With her pale skin and red hair, the dark blue highlighted her features better than the white of the wedding dress, especially since she'd decided to wear her hair down. The elves seemed to favor leaving their hair loose and long, and the elven shampoo and conditioner were working their magic. Her hair flowed down her back in the hint of waves without so much as a hair frizzing out of place.

It was time to meet Farrendel. Essie swallowed down a churn of nerves. Why was she so nervous? She'd dined with his family before, though not with King Weylind in attendance. And not in an elven dress made specifically for her.

Would Farrendel think her beautiful in this dress? Essie ran her fingers over the skirt once again. She felt beautiful already. She didn't necessarily need Farrendel to appreciate her in it. But it would be nice.

She was stalling. She forced herself to turn away from

the mirror.

After navigating the stairs, she stepped into the main room. Farrendel was already there, wearing his silver circlet and dressed in a silver tunic over a midnight blue shirt the same color as the embroidery on her dress. The matching color scheme was so obvious, it had to have been done on purpose.

He glanced up as she entered the room. A hint of a smile curved his mouth, his silver-blue eyes warm. "You look beautiful."

"This dress is lovely. I can't thank you enough for purchasing it for me." Essie gave a half-twirl back and forth to send the skirt swishing around her ankles.

Farrendel stepped closer, holding something silver in his hands. He slipped it over her hair and settled it against her forehead. "You are a princess of the elves. And with this, no one who sees you will forget it."

She reached up and touched cool metal worked in what felt like maple, oak, and beech leaves. "Is this a matching circlet to yours?"

He gave her another one of his small smiles. "Yes. I started the jeweler working on it before I left and picked it up this afternoon after I sent your package and letters."

That was so adorably sweet of him. Essie clasped her hands in front of her to resist launching herself into a hug. "Thank you. I…" She couldn't even think of anything to say to convey how much she appreciated the gesture. "I will hold my head high when I wear it."

"I know." Farrendel took her hand. "Ready?"

She tipped her chin higher. "Yes."

They set out across the branches for the dining room. Even in her fancy dress, Essie didn't fear falling like she once had, thanks to all her practice walking across the branches. Farrendel's presence might have had something to do with her lack of fear.

As they approached the dining room, Essie's nerves returned, and she almost wished they were caused by walking across branches insanely high in the air. Just before the door, Farrendel pulled his hand from hers.

Essie swallowed, wishing they could have walked into the room hand-in-hand. But that would have been improper and wouldn't match the image they were showing before his family.

He, of course, would hold out his arm. Impersonal, but proper.

Instead of holding out his arm, he linked his two fingers with hers in the elf way of holding hands in public.

Essie held up their linked fingers. "Are you sure about this? You don't want to go with something more formal?"

"No." Farrendel's smile had that glint to it again. That one that was slightly dangerous.

The way he was acting, he seemed about ready to pick

a fight with his family if he had to. Essie gripped his fingers as he pushed the door to the dining room open. Hopefully it wouldn't come to that. She didn't want to be the reason there was a rift in his family. King Weylind, Melantha, and Jalissa would blame her if that happened.

With a deep breath, Essie entered the dining room at Farrendel's side.

CHAPTER FOURTEEN

arrendel's family was still talking in small groups, not yet seated around the table. At her and Farrendel's entrance, the conversations fell silent. Jalissa's eyes widened while Melantha's expression hardened. Brina and Ryfon glanced between King Weylind and Essie and Farrendel as if expecting something explosive to happen. His expression too blank to be readable, King Weylind froze where he was, Queen Rheva gaping as she stood next to him with a hand on his arm.

Leyleira, though, wore the touch of a smile. At least someone in Farrendel's family approved.

"I see we are on time." Farrendel drew Essie farther into the room, his stride graceful, yet somehow dangerous. More stalking than strolling.

Whatever King Weylind had written in that note, it made Farrendel *furious*. Or maybe he'd heard rumors of what they had been saying behind Essie's back. Either way, it might be up to Essie to defuse the situation.

Essie put on her brightest, most oblivious smile and patted Farrendel's arm with her free hand. "He was worried we would be late since he had to wait so long for me to get ready."

Farrendel glanced down at her, and she met his gaze, hoping she managed to convey that she didn't want him starting anything over her. Not here.

That seemed to ease some of the tension in Farrendel's shoulders, but not all of it. This was going to be one interesting dinner.

King Weylind made a small sound in the back of his throat that may have been the elf version of clearing his throat. He sank into his chair at the head of the table, and the others quickly headed for their seats as if the room would catch fire if they didn't sit fast enough.

Where would Essie sit? She suspected she had been sitting in Farrendel's seat the past few days, but with him here, she would be bumped down one more chair, placing her at the far end where it would be even harder for her to be included in conversations. Or she could sit across from him, but that would be just as isolating, sitting next to Brina, who had yet to say a word directly to Essie.

Farrendel solved the problem by steering her to the left side of the table and nudging her toward the seat next to

Jalissa. While Essie eased into the chair, Farrendel took the seat to her left, placing himself at the far end. If anyone wanted to include him in the conversation, they would have to lean around Essie to do it, making it hard to exclude her.

The way Farrendel's eyes narrowed and glinted, that was done on purpose.

As the servants set down the plates of salad before them, Melantha leaned forward to peer past Essie and spoke in elvish, ending with Farrendel's name.

Farrendel leaned closer to Essie and whispered in her ear. "She said she's glad to see me here tonight." He glanced back to his sister. "It has been too long since I came to dinner. But Essie encouraged me to come."

She smiled and glanced at Farrendel. "I have been enjoying these family dinners, and I'm sure I'll enjoy them even more with Farrendel here."

She'd managed to keep most of her sarcasm out of her voice, right?

Not enough, perhaps, because Farrendel's small returning smile had the hint of Laesornysh in him.

Now it was Farrendel's nephew Ryfon making a coughing noise. He glanced around at everyone staring at him before he ducked his head.

King Weylind said something in elvish before he began eating his salad. Essie dug in as well. No reason to waste a good salad because of the tension in the room.

Leyleira stabbed a bite of salad with her fork. "I, for one, am pleased that both of you returned from the border safe. I assume the troll threat there has been neutralized?"

Beside Essie, Farrendel stiffened, though not enough that anyone but Essie would notice from the far side of the table.

King Weylind's gaze flicked to Farrendel before resting on Leyleira. "Yes."

It was interesting that all of them continued to speak in her language. Perhaps to humor Farrendel.

She reached for Farrendel's hand under the table. The topic of the conversation couldn't be comfortable for him. "I'm glad to have Farrendel back. We had far too little time together before he was called away. I enjoyed our tour of Estyra." Essie glanced over at Farrendel's niece and nephew. "Anyone have any suggestions for other places Farrendel should show me?"

Jalissa set down her fork, glancing around the table before she turned to Essie. "Have you seen the palace library yet?"

"I found it when I was exploring the castle, but I couldn't read most of the titles. I would love to explore it with someone who speaks elvish." Essie felt a mostly genuine smile tug at her face. If they could hit on a topic where they could all relax, maybe they could manage to have a normal conversation and enjoy this meal. "If there is a book there to help me learn elvish, that would be even better."

Melantha sniffed. "I am sure there are some primers for children stuffed in a corner."

If she wanted that statement to sound condescending, she didn't manage it in more than tone.

Brina glanced up from her salad. She was young, probably a few decades younger than both Farrendel and her brother Ryfon. "We will be traveling to Lethorel in two months. That is always exciting."

"Lethorel?" Essie glanced around the table.

Melantha scowled and jabbed at her salad as if she were trying to torture it.

"It is a summer palace for the royal family." Farrendel seemed to have relaxed with the new topic.

"We travel there each summer to stay for two weeks." Jalissa too relaxed with this change in topic.

"What is it like?" Essie smiled at Jalissa and at Brina.

That was all the encouragement that was needed to send the conversation into a description of Lethorel, which was apparently a large tree at the edge of a crystal-clear lake. That soon turned into stories about past adventures and summers spent there. The conversation eventually switched to elvish, but Farrendel kept Essie in it by translating for her.

By the time dinner was finished, Farrendel had relaxed enough to smile, and his smiles seemed to encourage the rest of his family to smile. And look at Essie differently. Melantha still didn't seem to like her, but Jalissa and King Weylind eyed her with something like speculation.

When Essie and Farrendel arrived back in their main room that evening, Essie touched his arm. "Are you going to be all right tonight?"

Farrendel stilled, his eyes growing distant. "Yes. I do not think I will have any nightmares tonight."

"If you do, don't hesitate to wake me, all right?" Essie reached out, then halted. She wasn't sure if she'd been about to touch his arm or his cheek or hug him. Something was crackling between them, and whatever it was, she wasn't sure either of them was ready for it.

He tipped his head in a slight nod, and that was all she waited for before she turned and headed for her room.

CHAPTER FIFTEEN

S tifling a yawn from her lack of sleep, Essie sipped the sweet juice in her glass as she worked her way through the crowd. Elves filled the open space in the forest below the lift from Farrendel's rooms. A much larger turnout than Essie had been expecting, considering this was the first event she was hosting for elves wounded in the wars.

Either Farrendel's reputation as Laesornysh was a draw or Illyna had far more contacts than Essie had expected.

She paused next to a male elf leaning on a crutch. She smiled and spoke in her shaky elvish, "Glad you could come."

The male elf looked at her, expressionless. The elf version of blinking in confusion.

Farrendel appeared at Essie's elbow. Glancing at him, she switched to Escarlish. "What did I say wrong?"

His mouth tilted. "Your Escarlish accent is thick."

She winced. "How is it supposed to sound?"

He said the greeting, and she repeated it several times until it sounded right to him. By that time, both Farrendel and the other elf had smiles that were the restrained, elf version of uproarious laughter.

No matter. That was her role. Bring humor into Farrendel's life.

She chatted with the male elf for a few more minutes with Farrendel helping when she didn't know an elvish word or her accent made her words intelligible. At least she had little trouble understanding the spoken elvish conversations around her. The past month, her elvish had improved by leaps and bounds. Every time she turned around, she picked up another word, another phrase.

It was odd. She'd never considered herself good with languages. Not like her brother Edmund. It had taken her years of work to teach herself to read elvish as well as she did. It almost seemed like some sort of magic.

But that was ridiculous, wasn't it? Just because elves had magic shampoo and conditioner, magic trains, magic hot water systems, didn't mean their magic would rub off into her learning their language faster.

As the male elf limped away with his crutch to look over the lists of elves looking to hire employees, Illyna joined Farrendel and Essie and spoke in elvish, "This has been quite the success."

"It seems to be, at least." Essie replied in Escarlish and watched the crowd of elves mingling. There seemed to be a lot of smiles and chatting. But would tonight accomplish its purpose? Would the elves looking for jobs find places to hire them? And businesses that didn't scorn them?

Illyna held out her hand and her stump. "Even if it accomplishes nothing else, it has brought a bunch of us together for the first time since the war. We have been able to talk about our challenges more tonight than we have in years."

Essie glanced at Farrendel. He was half-turned away from them, having been caught in a conversation with another male elf, this one with a scar running across his face and damaging one of his eyes. Essie had yet to hear Farrendel speak of his challenges, even to these elves. But, perhaps, as their prince, he couldn't admit to his own struggles.

Essie desperately wanted to ask if any of the elves here had advice for dealing with nightmares. In the weeks since he'd returned from turning back the trolls' raid at the border, the nightmares had tapered off. Until another raid had sent him back to the border, and the cycle began again. He'd only just returned yesterday from turning back yet another raid. Hence their exhaustion after a sleepless night.

She didn't know how to help. She hadn't even dared ask what he dreamed about when the nightmares plagued him. What tortures had the trolls inflicted on him fifteen years ago? Was it the torture he dreamed about? The battles he'd fought? The enemies he'd killed?

At least they had less than a month until they left for Lethorel. By the way he'd talked about the place, surely it would give him enough peace and quiet to relax. To sleep without nightmares for two whole weeks at a stretch.

That was something to look forward to.

Illyna bumped Essie's arm, drawing her attention. Illyna's eyes had a sparkle, her mouth a wider smile than Essie had seen yet. "I received an order from Escarland today. From that merchant you recommended. The order was so large, I am paying Fydella to help me box up the items and haul them to the border exchange." Illyna tipped her head toward another female elf warrior.

"I'm so glad it's working." Essie scanned the crowd. "Do you know of any other elves here who would have products they would like to sell in Escarland?"

Illyna's smile blossomed wider. "Several. Let me introduce you."

Essie spent the rest of the evening in a whirl of speaking to various elves and taking notes. She would have to send another letter to her brothers so they could help set up the trade on the Escarlish side. Averett would have administrative officials to help implement it. Julien would work with the army for securing the trade across the river. And Edmund would make sure the merchants Averett recommended were honest and not about to cheat the elves. These elves were trusting Essie rather blindly to set up this trade. The last thing any of them needed was to start an international incident because one of the Escarlish merchants decided to get greedy.

By the time the event ended, Essie could barely keep her eyes open as she leaned against one of the support posts in the lift. Through her half-lidded eyes, she peeked at Farrendel as he pulled the rope, raising the lift. Hopefully he remained nightmare free tonight.

After all the talk of past wars and battles, a nightmare-free night was probably too much to hope for.

She woke to the sound of Farrendel's muffled screams wafting on the night breeze. Yawning, Essie rubbed her eyes and stumbled out of bed. She took a few moments to wake up before she braved the stairs down to the main room and back up to Farrendel's room.

Farrendel's door swung open before she had a chance to knock. He propped himself against the doorframe, head hanging. "Sorry."

"It's all right." Essie stifled another yawn. One late night she could handle. Two in a row was starting to catch up with her. She took Farrendel's hand and navigated the stairs to the main room. "Come on. If this is going to be a habit, I'm going to have to write my mother to send the supplies for hot chocolate. Have you ever had hot chocolate? It's the perfect drink for late nights when you're troubled. We'll just have to figure out a way to heat milk and chocolate here. Our magicians in Escarland might be able to come up with a magical device to heat things without fire."

Farrendel settled onto his favorite cushion in the corner. "I would like to try this hot chocolate of yours."

"It's the best." Essie sank onto the cushion next to him. Would Farrendel flinch away if she leaned against his shoulder? Handholding had become almost second nature now. He reached for her hand nearly as often as she reached for his.

But leaning against him would be another level of invading his personal space. Would he be all right with it?

As much as she wanted to be there for him as she had the night before, her eyes ached. She needed to lean against him or the wall or something. She yawned and inched closer to Farrendel. When he didn't shift away from her, she rested her head against his shoulder. It wasn't the most comfortable shoulder to lean against. He was far too bony. But she was too tired to care. "I'll try to stay awake if you want me to..." Her words ended in another yawn.

"Rest." Farrendel clasped her hand. After a moment, he leaned his head on top of hers. "*Linshi*."

The elvish word for *thank you*.

"No problem." Essie let herself drift back to sleep.

CHAPTER SIXTEEN

Essie tried to be more regal and composed on this train ride than she'd been on the one into Estyra. But as the train carried them deeper into the elven forests, she couldn't help but crane her neck to peer out the windows at the view.

This time, Farrendel sat beside her with Brina and Ryfon, his niece and nephew on his other side. Jalissa, King Weylind, and Queen Rheva had claimed the bench across from them. Melantha and Leyleira had remained behind in Estyra to keep things running smoothly.

"How long until we get there?" Essie peered out the window yet again. She probably sounded just like a child, but she didn't care.

Farrendel's mouth curved enough to count as a real, full smile. Had Essie ever seen him so relaxed? "We will arrive in Arorien, a small town, this evening. Then we will ride to Lethorel by horseback the next morning." He tensed and sat straighter. "Can you ride? I did not think to ask."

"Yes, of course, I ride. It is one of the skills considered proper for a lady of the Escarlish court." Essie grinned and plopped down on her seat facing the interior of the train once again. "I also know archery. It was all the rage for the court ladies a few years ago."

Jalissa sat forward, her dark brown eyes fixed on Essie with more interest than Essie had seen on her. "Are you any good?"

Essie squirmed in her seat. "I was all right. I'm better with a rifle, but I'm assuming you probably don't have any here. I'd love to brush up on my archery, even if my skills can't compare with your elf archers."

Jalissa smiled. "We will have to test that. I love archery, and there are several spare bows at Lethorel. I believe Farrendel's old bow is still there."

Farrendel's shoulders lifted in an elven version of a shrug. "I was never any good. I always preferred my swords. Besides, it is not really my bow. I just was the last to have it handed down to me."

The elven royalty used hand-me-down bows? Essie had to suppress a snort. It was just the sort of practicality she loved about living here.

"It sounds like a lot of fun." Essie rested her palms on the pad of the bench beneath her, one of her hands less than an inch from Farrendel's leg. These next two weeks might be just what she needed to fit in with this family. "This place sounds really special to all of you. I gathered that when we talked about it at dinner, but all of you are happier the closer we get."

Farrendel stilled. "I spent much of my childhood there."

He was tense. As if waiting for her to ask why.

Except that she knew why. It would have been a difficult childhood for him, bearing the scorn of the elven court for being illegitimate. It would have been easier to hide him at Lethorel, both to keep the proof of King Lorsan's mistake out of the public eye all the time and to spare Farrendel from some of their cruelty.

Did Farrendel's father raise Farrendel there? Had the other family members been there? Or had Farrendel been alone, the illegitimate son shuffled off to be raised by servants?

Jalissa was watching Essie. Did she know Leyleira had told Essie the great family scandal? Or was she, like Farrendel, waiting for Essie to ask the hard questions and probe for the truth?

"My family has a similar summer cottage. My mother would take us there as often as she could when we were growing up." Essie let herself smile at the memories. "It is hard enough growing up under the scrutiny of the court all the time. At that cottage, we had a chance to be children. I imagine Lethorel must be like that for you, though you weren't all children at the same time the way me and my brothers were. One of the few memories I have of my father is at that cottage."

Farrendel was staring down at the floor. "Yes, Lethorel is like that for us."

What would it have been like for Farrendel growing up? Was Lethorel where he felt truly a part of this family in a way he hadn't in Estyra? Until he'd proved his worth to the elven court by becoming Laesornysh, their renowned warrior, Lethorel was probably the only place where he could relax without the sneers.

"Father was able to love all of us best at Lethorel. Some of my best memories of us as a family are there." Jalissa was looking at Farrendel as she said it, as if wanting to gauge his reaction more than Essie's.

It must be difficult to have a family strung out over so many hundreds of years with the mix of scandal and tragedy they had. All of Jalissa's memories of her family with her mother wouldn't include Farrendel. In some ways, he was everything that had gone wrong with their family. The queen's death. Their father's grief. An illegitimate brother who was the constant proof and reminder of all of it.

Or was Farrendel the silver lining in that tragedy? The

person who had pulled all of them, especially the late king, out of grief and gave them a reason to feel like a family again, even if that family would be forever aching from the loved ones lost.

Essie certainly didn't question that King Weylind, Melantha, and Jalissa loved Farrendel as a brother.

Farrendel turned away to stare out the window, looking like he wanted to draw up his knees as a wall as he did when he suffered nightmares.

Essie didn't care if the elves frowned on public displays of affection. She scooted closer to him and leaned her head against his shoulder, curling her legs onto the train bench beside her. "I think I'm going to take a nap."

Farrendel was rigid beneath her. But he was warm, and Essie squirmed and shifted until she found a spot against his bony shoulder and stiff muscles that was almost comfortable.

This close, she could smell the minty scent of his clothes and the fresh, woodsy smell of the shampoo and conditioner he used on his hair. Strands of his hair brushed against her face, and it took more self-control than she'd admit to keep from winding a lock through her fingers.

Really, it was almost laughable. Her younger self would've been rolling her eyes at how attractive she found Farrendel's long hair. Must be the magical elven conditioner.

After several minutes, Farrendel relaxed beneath her and shifted so that she was better settled against him. That suited her just fine. She'd used the nap thing as an excuse to be close to him, but as his warmth seeped into her, the idea of a nap sounded better and better. She might regret it later when she wouldn't be able to sleep that night because she'd napped during the day, but no matter. It meant she would be wide awake to take in Arorien and explore the elven inn. Besides, she had a lot of sleep to catch up on anyways.

She let herself drift, feeling like she was wrapped in warmth, her muscles relaxed. Her breathing slowed until she was in that hazy place where her body was asleep and her mind was only half-awake.

"Is she asleep?" King Weylind's voice buzzed through the haze in Essie's mind. Thanks to her improving elvish, Essie could understand him.

She probably should tell them she was still awake, but her body was already asleep, and the impulse just rattled around in her head without making her mouth so much as twitch.

"Yes." Farrendel replied, also in elvish. The word rumbled beneath Essie's ear, far deeper in his chest than it sounded out loud.

"Do you … for her, shashon?" Jalissa spoke, her words low. Shashon. Brother.

What was that word was in the middle? The one Essie hadn't learned yet. Love would make sense, but didn't fit the elvish grammar. Perhaps the word was care. That would fit. It seemed rather important, and Essie struggled to keep herself relaxed and not tense toward wakefulness.

She probably should do the decent thing and let them know she was still awake. Eavesdropping never ended well, right?

But she didn't have the self-control to resist at the moment. Besides, she might end up only understanding about half the conversation.

Farrendel remained still, his heartbeat a steady rhythm under Essie's ear. He was silent so long Essie started drifting off again, though his voice roused her back to her semi-sleeping state. "Yes." Another pause before he spoke again, his voice low but closer to Essie's ear as if he was looking down at her. "She does not mind my ..."

His what? Essie had learned enough elvish to follow along, mostly. But she kept missing the most important part of this conversation.

What would Farrendel think Essie didn't mind about him? His nightmares? His army friends?

No, his scars. That had to be it. That was the moment where she had begun to make progress with him. It was the moment he'd begun to care.

Jalissa's sigh was so loud Essie didn't even have to

strain to hear it. "We do not mind your scars either."

"Not like her. She…" Farrendel trailed off, as if he couldn't put what he was thinking into words. "They do not bother her."

"Of course, they bother me. You are my little brother. I held you as an infant. I dried your tears when you were a child." Jalissa's voice tightened and rose. "It hurts to see my little brother hurt."

"I know." Farrendel's voice was quiet.

"That is why I do not want to see you hurt by her. I want you to be happy."

"She makes me happy." Farrendel's tone held a warmth to it, and if Essie hadn't been so comfortable and interested in the conversation, she might have gripped his hand. Or maybe even indulged in hugging him.

"Does she care for you?" Jalissa's voice had an intense tone.

"It has only been two and a half months." Farrendel had that slightly dangerous note to his voice again, as if offended that Jalissa wasn't giving Essie time.

Yet Farrendel had no problem in saying he cared for Essie, even though it hadn't been that long.

Perhaps care was the right word. Yes, Essie cared for Farrendel, a caring that would surely deepen into love.

Didn't Farrendel know she cared? What else could he think all the late nights staying up with him after his nightmares and the handholding and the snuggling meant?

"That did not stop you from caring."

Essie could feel herself drifting deeper into sleep, rocked by the steady movement of the nearly silent train and the warmth of Farrendel against her.

But, before she slipped all the way into sleep, Farrendel's breath shivered along Essie's hair. "I think she does."

Essie woke with a start. Her head still rested against Farrendel's shoulder, though her hand had somehow found its way onto Farrendel's chest, her fingers clasping his tunic. She wanted to pretend she was still asleep, but her start had been a little too obvious.

With a sigh, she reluctantly pried her fingers from Farrendel's tunic, scrubbed at her face, and pushed herself upright. She wasn't about to glance across the way toward Farrendel's family. She probably looked a sight. Her own fault for napping in front of them.

Farrendel was looking at her, his face blank. Probably doing his whole wait-for-her-to-speak-first thing hoping she'd spout something humorous.

"I slept well, thanks for asking." Essie smiled and peered over her shoulder out the window. "How long did I sleep?"

"A couple of hours." Farrendel shifted his arm.

Essie winced. "Your arm fell asleep, didn't it? I'm so sorry. You could've moved. Or woke me. I wouldn't have minded."

He shrugged. "I do not mind either."

After another hour, the small town of Arorien came into sight out of the forest. Much like Estyra, the rails skirted the edge of the town with the platform on the far side. Also like Estyra, the town was made of booths tucked against the trees with an upper layer of shops and living quarters in the trees. Unlike Estyra, there was only a single, winding street and far fewer elves bustling around.

The elf equivalent of the town mayor met them on the platform. Essie understood some of his welcome speech, but it seemed he used many large words that Essie had yet to learn. As she stood next to Farrendel on the platform, she caught the mayor and several of the other elves in town glancing at her.

It was hard for her to tell if the glances were disgusted or curious or something in between.

This was the first time Essie had traveled with the royal family. The first time the wider elf population would meet her. She needed to hold her chin high and make a good impression.

After a few more minutes, the mayor gestured to a few of the male elves standing nearby. The elves gathered the luggage, and King Weylind led the way down the street.

He lifted his hand in an elven wave to some of the bystanders who were doing their genteel waving. Apparently even country elves in a small town didn't go in for large displays of enthusiasm, even when their king was stopping for a visit.

Jalissa's mouth tilted in a small smile as she too waved, occasionally stopping and conversing with someone she probably knew from past trips to Lethorel.

Farrendel twined his fingers with Essie's once again, choosing to hold her hand rather than hold out his arm.

And it struck her then just how much Farrendel had given up to marry her. He could have married an upstanding elf. Maybe even elf nobility, which would have helped in erasing the scandal of his birth and legitimizing a place for him in society.

Instead he caused another scandal and married her. Yes, it was for peace between their countries. Yes, it was sanctioned by his brother, the king.

But it was an action that would remind everyone of the scandal already surrounding him. Make him even more of an outcast than he already was.

Was there anything Essie could do to help him?

Not much besides do her best to earn the respect of the elves who took the time to know her. And for those who didn't, she would hold her chin high and give them very little ammunition to work with.

Farrendel glanced at her, and she gave him a nod back. She was ready for this.

As they set out after King Weylind and Jalissa, Essie caught the moment the smiles of the townsfolk froze. She hadn't even realized there had been a buzz of conversation, a floating laughter, a festival hum to the air until it died.

Farrendel's fingers tightened on hers, his muscles going taut. Maybe she was ready to face this, but she wasn't sure Farrendel was. He was the type who would rather hide from this sort of scrutiny than face it head on the way they were now.

Essie refused to cower beneath the stares turning into glares. She had been raised to be a princess, and sometimes that meant not being popular to stand for what was right. To do what was best for the kingdom even when it would get herself publicly vilified.

She kept her smile in place and waved as Jalissa had. Regal. Restrained. She glided forward, and Farrendel fell into step with her after a hesitation so small it would've been hard to notice except under intense scrutiny.

Which, of course, was exactly what they were under at the moment.

They had only gone a few yards from the train platform when someone in the crowd shouted something Essie couldn't understand.

Probably just as well she couldn't understand it since Farrendel stiffened next to her. A hint of a crackle filled the air.

Essie turned to Farrendel and placed her free hand on his chest. "I don't know what they just said, but I think it's best if we just walk away."

The crackle left the air, and Farrendel gave her a small nod. They resumed walking, following King Weylind, Queen Rheva, Brina, Ryfon, and Jalissa, pretending not to hear the way the townsfolk turned silent as she and Farrendel passed by.

Thankfully, the inn wasn't far from the train platform, and the elf man and woman who ran the inn welcomed all of them—including Farrendel and Essie—inside without their smiles falling from their faces. As they were the ones getting paid for the royal family's stay in Arorien, they had a vested interest in remaining pleasant, no matter their personal feelings regarding Farrendel's human bride.

In short order, they were all shown to rooms. As with the palace, the inn's rooms were individual rooms built in various locations along a tree's spreading branches.

Essie soon found herself alone with Farrendel in what she guessed was the farthest room in the inn. It would've been more awkward, except that a quick glance around the room showed it had four elven beds grown into the walls with windows above them, each with a curtain that could be drawn to give the sleeper privacy. Like the inns in Escarland, these rooms were designed to house an entire elf family traveling together or multiple individuals if the inn was particularly crowded.

"Are you all right with this?"

Essie turned to find Farrendel still standing in the doorway, the door wide open behind him as if he wanted to give her the option to bolt if she wanted to.

She grinned. "Yes, this will work perfectly. I was expecting a room with only one bed, and we'd have the whole who-gets-the-bed-and-who-sleeps-on-the-floor discussion. Now we just have to decide if we pick two of the beds next to each other or beds as far away from each other as possible."

Farrendel stared back at her. Probably waiting for her to continue rambling on.

"Fine. I'll at least choose my bed, and you can pick whichever one you want." Essie pointed at the bed on the west side of the room. "I'm going to pick that one. I don't want the sun to wake me up right away in the morning. What is Lethorel going to be like? Are we going to share a room there or will there be several rooms?"

Farrendel stepped inside the room and closed the door behind him with a soft click. "In Lethorel, my room has several small sleeping quarters attached to it."

"I see. That will be perfect." Essie located her luggage

—a single canvas tote with her name embroidered on the top flap. "It turns out I am very awake now thanks to my nap. What are we going to do this evening?"

"We have supper downstairs as soon as you are ready. Then it is up to you."

"We could come back here and work on my elvish." Essie stepped closer to Farrendel.

Should she admit to him that she overheard him talking with his family earlier? How much did she tell him?

"Farrendel?" Essie reached out and lightly rested her hand on his arm. His muscles tensed beneath her fingers, but he didn't pull away. She struggled to find the words, and the moment stretched longer. "This truly doesn't bother me. I think..." Why was it so hard for her to get the words out? "I care about you. I want us to eventually get to the point where this isn't awkward. Where..."

She couldn't finish. Her face was heating up even just thinking about it. They weren't there yet. Neither of them could even say love. Falling in love, maybe. In love, not yet.

Farrendel closed the distance between them and wrapped his arms around her. Essie held still, holding her breath as if she feared scaring him off. This was the first time he'd initiated a hug.

When he didn't back away, she leaned against him,

wrapping her arms around him. His back was stiff and strong beneath her hands, the fabric of his tunic soft against her palms. Giving in to temptation, she trailed her fingers through the ends of his hair. Yes, it was just as soft and silky as she had been imagining.

The ends of her hair shifted, and tingles shot through her scalp and down her back.

Maybe, eventually, this whole husband and wife thing would work out after all. Once she and Farrendel got to that stage in their relationship.

Farrendel stepped back first, though he kept his hands lightly resting on her shoulders. He glanced at her but dropped his gaze almost immediately. "You do not know everything yet."

Should she tell him she knew he was illegitimate? Essie held her breath, letting the thought sink in, trying to figure out what her gut was telling her to do. Somehow that wasn't a conversation she wanted to have right now. This moment had been sweet. Something she wanted to cherish. She didn't want to ruin it with a troubling conversation that wouldn't be easy on either of them.

Would he think she had been lying to him if she didn't tell him she knew the truth? Or would he appreciate her waiting for him to bring up the topic when he was ready?

This was a subject that should wait until Farrendel was ready, and she wouldn't know he was ready until he was the one who mentioned it.

"I know there are things about you I don't know yet. But I'm all right with that, and I'm willing to wait until you are ready to tell me. Whatever you have to tell me won't change what I'm beginning to feel about you." Essie decided to be daring and touched the scar on his cheek. "You don't know everything about me yet either. Not that I can think of any deep dark secrets at the moment. I tend to just say everything I'm thinking and feeling without holding all that much back. But I'm sure I can think of something you don't know about me yet if I think about it hard enough."

Farrendel's mouth tipped in a slight smile. And that smile did something funny to Essie's heart. She would keep blabbing the first thing that came to mind for the rest of her life if it meant she could keep seeing that smile.

CHAPTER SEVENTEEN

Essie perched on the small mare she had been given to ride. Ashenifela was a pretty brown mare with a white stripe down the center of her forehead and the softest muzzle. Her name meant *Dances with the Fair Wind,* and Essie thought it perfect. She itched to urge the mare into a full gallop and see how well she lived up to her name, but the narrow path through the trees gave no room for a run, bordered as it was by thick undergrowth on both sides.

They had been riding for about two hours now. Long enough that she was probably going to be sore for the next few days, but Essie didn't care. Being out in the vast forest with the fresh air filling her from head to toe reminded her of how invigorating such a country estate was. In the last few years, there had been little time for relaxation at their summer cottage, and Essie hadn't even realized until this moment how much she'd missed that freedom.

Ahead of them, the forest opened up, and Essie had to blink at the brilliance of the sunlight, more sunlight than she'd seen since coming to the dense forest. As her eyes adjusted, she took in the scene spreading before her.

A small lake formed a teardrop shape with the creek dumping into it on the thin side and the rounded end bordered by a stretch pebbled beach. Up the bank a truly massive willow tree draped flowing branches over the pebbles and patches of grass below. Lethorel was tucked among the whispery branches, and Essie couldn't imagine a more picturesque—and romantic—setting.

Farrendel glanced over at her, and his smile was already twitching his face. Almost twinkling in his eyes.

She grinned back at him. "Can we race around the lake? Ashenifela is itching for a run."

As an answer, Farrendel urged his dark brown gelding into a gallop. His silver-blond hair streamed behind him, and it would be almost worth it to lose to watch the way his hair floated gracefully on the breeze.

Almost.

She leaned low over Ashenifela's neck and urged her into a full tilt run. The mare glided over the gravel path, her hooves skimming over the ground. The wind tugged at Essie's hair, running fingers over her scalp.

She nudged the mare into more speed. The mare responded, and together she and Essie were flying.

They rounded the bend around the lake, and Essie was now level with Farrendel. She glanced over at him and couldn't contain a laugh.

They flashed into the green yard in front of the willow tree. Both of them reined in their horses, and they came to a skidding, prancing halt.

Essie patted the mare's neck. Ashenifela tossed her head and blew out a snort, as if the run had been far too short. Essie couldn't help but agree. That was one thing the elves lacked in their dense forest. What she wouldn't give to take Ashenifela to the open, grassy hills back in Escarland. Ashenifela would truly be able to stretch her legs and fly there.

Maybe someday she and Farrendel would be able to visit, and she could take Ashenifela along.

Essie dismounted and walked Ashenifela in a circle to let her cool down. Not that it was necessary after such a short run, but it kept Essie busy as the rest of the Farrendel's family, the few servants they had with them, and the ten guards caught up.

One of the servants took the reins from Farrendel, then held out a hand to Essie. Essie placed Ashenifela's reins in the servant's hand. She watched as the servant led the horses away, spotting the small stable grown out of a thicket of trees. At least she would be able to find Ashenifela if she wanted to go for a ride.

"You like that horse."

She jumped and turned to Farrendel. With his soft footsteps, she hadn't heard him join her. "Yes."

"Then she is yours." Farrendel held out his hand. "Would you like to see our rooms?"

Essie clasped his fingers with hers in the proper elf handholding since his family was watching. "Yes, please."

Farrendel led her to a gate-like door, opened it, and together they climbed the spiraling staircase grown into the willow tree. At the top where the biggest limbs branched out from the main trunk, a dining room had been grown into place, much like in Estyra. Walking around the dining room, Farrendel led the way onto one of the branches.

After living in Estyra for the past few months, Essie's stomach only gave a small flip as they stepped onto the two-foot-wide branch. It was still far too narrow for comfort, and she was glad she had Farrendel's hand to steady herself.

The farther they walked from the main trunk, more branches and twigs trailed around them until they were brushing them aside as they passed. The wispy, trailing leaves fluttered in a light breeze filled with the clear scent of the lake, damp earth, and a green, warm scent that could only be the willow tree surrounding them.

It was magical. And put thoughts into her head that

she wasn't sure she and Farrendel were ready for yet. But maybe they could get comfortable heading in that direction. Perhaps even share a first kiss. This seemed like the kind of place for kissing.

Farrendel pushed aside a particularly dense curtain of willow twigs and leaves and there before them was a cottage grown from the limb itself with twining branches forming walls and a roof.

Essie nearly stumbled, and thankfully Farrendel was steady on the branch. He glanced back at her, and she smiled. "It's beautiful."

Farrendel's smile bloomed, more relaxed than she'd ever seen. This place must be truly special to him. A place that felt more like home even than Estyra.

The cottage had a small porch just across the front. Leaves trailed from the porch posts, posts that were living branches. Essie ran her fingers over one of the leaves as she crossed the porch.

Farrendel opened the door and led the way inside. They stepped into a small sitting room, only big enough for a couple of chairs and a small countertop with cupboards along one wall. Two doors on the far side filled the entire wall across from them.

Essie waved at the doors across the way. "Is your room on the right and mine on the left like at home or do we switch it up here?"

Farrendel stared at her with some unreadable expression in his silver-blue eyes.

Essie waited, but Farrendel didn't say anything. He didn't look away either. She cocked her head. "What? Is something wrong?"

Farrendel looked away, his hair falling like a curtain to hide his expression. "You called Estyra home."

She had, hadn't she? It had seemed so natural. When had she started thinking of Estyra as home instead of Aldon?

No, not really instead of. In some ways, Aldon with her childhood room in Winstead Palace would always be home.

But home didn't have to be only one place at a time. It could be Winstead Palace in Aldon and Ellonahshinel in Estyra.

"Of course, I did. It's home." Essie squeezed his hand. "I mean it. I love Estyra. I love our rooms there. I love so much of my new life."

Farrendel's smile twitched onto his face. He gestured at the doors. "You can take your pick if you would like."

Essie shook her head. "I know you. You like your routines and habits. Your room is usually the one on the right, isn't it?"

Farrendel gave a small snorting sound. Was that a laugh? "Yes, it is."

"Then I'll take the room on the left." Essie let go of Farrendel's hand and headed for the door. Pushing it open, she stepped inside and glanced around. The room was smaller than her one in Estyra, but in some ways that made it cozier. The bed was against the far wall under the window. Branches formed shelves for her clothes while a small mirror was set into the wall. "It's adorable."

Cozy. At Estyra, their rooms were on completely separate tree branches. Here, only a wall would separate them.

Progress, perhaps?

After a restful night, Essie stretched as the morning sunlight filtered through her window, then suppressed a groan. She was just as sore as she'd feared. All that riding yesterday had stiffened her muscles.

A faint thumping came from outside. Essie pushed herself on her elbow to peer out the window.

Farrendel was in the middle of his morning workout routine, dashing along one of the branches. He was far enough away that he wouldn't see inside her windows.

She leaned against the windowsill and rested her chin on her arms. She held her breath as Farrendel somersaulted in the air and landed on a branch that looked far too small for doing maneuvers like that. He spun on a heel, his arms out as if swinging a pair of swords. The early morning sunlight streaming through the dancing strands of willow branches glinted across his sweat-slicked muscles and the scars cutting across his skin.

After a moment, she forced herself to turn away from the window. She found her lightest weight shirt and pants and dressed. She didn't put on a tunic or a belt over it. Instead, she left her room, crossed the main room, and found her way onto the network of branches surrounding the cottage. It took her a few minutes to traverse the far too skinny branches until she reached the far side.

Farrendel had left his shirt hanging on a branch, and Essie lowered herself into a sitting position next to it.

Farrendel performed several more spins and flips before he dashed toward her, flipped one more time, and landed a few feet away, his hair floating around him.

She grinned and clambered to her feet. "Impressive as always."

Farrendel shifted, ducking his head. Were the tips of his ears growing pink? He made a sound in the back of his throat, like he was clearing it. "I usually swim in the mornings afterwards."

"I figured as much. My brothers would never pass up a perfectly good lake after getting all hot and sweaty. Why do you think I'm dressed for swimming?" Essie waved down at herself. When Farrendel reached past her for his shirt, she halted him. "You don't need that. You're fine.

Back in Escarland, all the guys swim with their shirts off. It's time you elves learned to be a little more daring. Now, what's the fastest way down to the lake?"

The smile that creased Farrendel's face was almost mischievous. He held out a hand. When she took it, he led her onto one of the branches that spread over the lake. Reaching up, he disentangled a rope.

Essie looked from him to the rope. "You have got to be fooling me."

Farrendel's smile grew a hint wider. If he smiled any wider, his teeth might even show. He gripped the rope and launched himself from the branch. He arced down from the willow tree and flew over the water. At the apex of the swing, he let go, flipped in the air, and dove into the water with barely a splash.

The rope swung back toward her, and Essie snagged it.

This was crazy. It was an awfully long way down to the lake, and she wasn't nearly as graceful or coordinated as Farrendel.

She could hear her brothers' ragging on her for being scared. Gripping the rope tighter, she drew in a deep breath and stepped from the branch.

Her breath caught as she swung toward the ground at a speed that was exhilarating. She let out a whooping shriek. As she reached the end of the rope, her weight tugged on her arms, but she hung on. The pebbled beach flashed below her, then water was beneath her.

At the moment she felt herself go weightless once again, she let go of the rope, tucked into a ball, and pinched her nose. After two heartbeats of falling, she hit the water with a huge splash, one that would have made her brothers proud.

The cold lake water closed around her as she plunged deep. Uncurling, she pushed herself to the surface.

An arm wrapped under her shoulders and yanked her upward. Her head broke the surface, and she swiped the water from her face. When she opened her eyes, she was face to face with Farrendel.

He wasn't smiling as she expected, but his eyes were wide. Almost scared. He swiped a lock of her dripping hair from her face. "Are you injured? That was a large splash."

Essie couldn't help the giggles that burst from her. It hadn't occurred to her that Farrendel would worry when she didn't perform the same graceful dive he had. "I'm fine. Truly. We humans are uncoordinated, so we came up with a few other ways to enter the water besides diving. That particular move is called a *cannonball*. My brothers and I would try for the biggest splash. That one would've gotten a cheer."

Farrendel's shoulders relaxed. "You did it on purpose."

"Yes. I'm sorry. I didn't realize I'd scare you." Essie shook her head. Every time she thought she was getting the hang of elven culture, she realized she still had a lot to learn.

Time to get that smile back on his face. It was either that or she was going to be tempted to kiss him with him this close. She pushed away and waved her hand across the lake's surface, sending a spray of water into Farrendel's face.

Farrendel started and blinked at her as if he couldn't believe she'd just done that.

She grinned. "That's another human tradition. Water fight."

Cocking his head, Farrendel flicked the water. Only a few drops spattered Essie's face.

She snorted. "I don't think you get the point of this." She splashed him again.

This time when he splashed her back, the splash actually soaked her face. She grinned and let out a laugh as the water fight began in earnest.

After several minutes, Essie staggered out of the water and collapsed on the pebbles of the beach, laughing too hard to catch her breath or care that the pebbles dug into her shoulder. Had she laughed this hard since coming to Tarenhiel?

Farrendel sank onto the ground next to her, his long

hair plastered against his back and a shade darker than it usually was. His smile was the widest she had ever seen. Big enough that it might even count as a real smile.

Essie caught her breath and pushed herself onto an elbow. "I can see why you like it here so much. It's easy to relax."

"Yes." Farrendel leaned back on his hands. He was more relaxed than she'd ever seen him with his scars visible as they were when he wasn't wearing a shirt. Maybe she'd finally convinced him that his scars truly didn't bother her.

She ached to ask him about them. But she didn't want to break this moment.

Footsteps crunched on the pebbles behind them. Farrendel stiffened, his fingers clenching as if he wanted to reach for the shirt he'd left by their rooms in the tree.

Essie turned. King Weylind stood a few feet away, arms crossed. Essie spotted a flicker in his eyes as his gaze focused on Farrendel's scars. What that flicker meant, Essie couldn't be sure. Was King Weylind disgusted by them? Or remembering how Farrendel got them? If Essie remembered right, King Weylind helped rescue Farrendel from the trolls. Perhaps it was guilt more than disgust in his eyes.

And something in his expression said whatever he had to say was bad news.

Farrendel climbed to his feet and crossed his arms over his chest. Not in a defiant way. More like he was trying to hide behind the small safety his arms provided.

Essie stood and rested a hand on Farrendel's arm. Hopefully it helped him know she was there, no matter what King Weylind had to say.

King Weylind held a small piece of paper. "There was another troll raid on the border."

Farrendel stiffened, hardened, as if a part of him was dying inside yet again. "Do they need me at the border?"

"No, not at this time. The trolls disappeared after the raid." King Weylind shook his head. "But it may come to that once we have more information."

CHAPTER EIGHTEEN

"Here is Farrendel's old bow." Jalissa held out a small recurve bow made from a silver-gray wood.

"It's beautiful." Essie took it and ran her fingers over the smooth curve of the bow's limbs. She approached the bins of arrows, neatly arranged by size, and picked out one that she believed was the right size. Nocking it to the bow, she drew back, testing the draw weight of the bow and measuring the length of the arrow. Yes, it was the correct length. She eased the bow back to neutral position. "Where is the range?"

"This way." Jalissa grabbed a handful of arrows and led the way out of the small storage shed.

Essie collected several of the arrows of the right length and followed Jalissa. At the far side of the shed, a servant was hauling a bundle of a hay with a target on it out into the forest. When it was about seventy-five yards out, the servant halted and set the target up.

"We will start with an easy distance." Jalissa nocked an arrow. She raised the bow, aimed, and released so quickly it was a blur of movement. The arrow slammed into the bullseye.

Essie breathed out something that was part amazement, part a laugh. "Good shot. Don't expect the same out of me. I'm out of practice, and I was never that good. Not elf good, anyway."

Jalissa's face took on a small smile. "Are you stalling?"

"Maybe." Essie nocked an arrow and raised the bow. She aimed, let out half a breath, and in that steadiness of her held breath, she released. Her arrow thunked into the circle surrounding the bullseye.

Back in Escarland, it would've been a great shot. Here in Tarenhiel, it looked paltry compared to Jalissa's ease.

Essie grimaced. "At least I was close. I was worried I would miss the target altogether and really embarrass myself."

"A troll is a big target. You would still hit somewhere in the chest. You would not kill him but maybe slow him down." Jalissa knocked, aimed, and released another arrow. It slammed into the target so close to the first Essie wasn't even sure how both of the arrows managed to fit in the space.

Essie swallowed. This past week at Lethoral had been pleasant, but it had been tempered with increasing reports of troll raids at the border. Any moment, Essie expected a message to come over the network of roots that served like telegraph lines, calling for Farrendel to come to the border.

Both Farrendel and King Weylind had grown increasingly tense. Even now, Farrendel was scouting the forest around Lethoral, instead of relaxing as he had on the first day.

He'd told her to relax. Not to worry. As if she could, with him tense as a bowstring.

She picked out another arrow and made her shot. This one thudded into one of the outer rings. She winced. Even worse. At least Farrendel wasn't here watching her embarrass herself with her archery skills.

As Jalissa reached for another arrow, Farrendel dashed from the forest, his twin swords strapped to his back and his hair flying behind him. He skidded to a halt next to them. "Get inside. Now." He didn't wait for them to follow his orders but raced past them.

Jalissa grabbed her bundle of arrows and ran toward the shed. Essie scooped up her own handful of arrows and followed Jalissa. Inside the shed, Jalissa snagged armloads of arrows. Essie quickly joined her, grabbing as many arrows as she could carry.

"We need to go." Jalissa gripped her bow and bundles of arrows in both arms. She led the way from the shed and raced for the stairs to Lethorel.

Essie followed, struggling to keep up with her shorter legs while carrying the armload of arrows. As she reached the base of the stairs, the ten guards deployed in front of Lethorel. Essie huffed as she ran up the stairs—the far too steep and small steps without handrails. But she couldn't think of that now.

As she reached the top platform, branches sprang across the opening of the stairs, blocking it off.

What was going on? Were they under attack? Lethorel wasn't anywhere near the border, even if it was closer than Estyra. Surely the trolls hadn't gotten this far into Tarenhiel?

Essie found Jalissa kneeling beside one of the windows overlooking the forest. When Essie peered out the window, she could just make out the line of guards standing below with King Weylind in their center. Where was Farrendel?

Jalissa nocked an arrow to her bow but didn't draw it.

Essie also nocked an arrow, her heart pounding in her throat. "What's going on?"

That's when she heard it. A howling, growling sound rose from deeper in the forest, followed by a crashing of under-growth.

Jalissa remained tense as she stared out the window. "Trolls."

Essie swallowed and let out a long breath, trying to

keep her heart from pounding. "How did they get this far from the border?"

"We do not know." Jalissa's knuckles whitened on her bow.

This wasn't good.

The howling sound grew louder. Gray-white shapes moved between the trees. In a moment, a troll stepped around a tree. He was dressed in gray clothing only slightly darker than his grayish skin. His dark hair was cropped short over ears that had less of a point than elven ears, but more tapered than human ears. Two more trolls stepped up on either side of him. They focused on the line of elves standing in front of Lethorel, raised their weapons, and let loose with their undulating howl again.

Goosebumps raised on Essie's arms. She'd never seen trolls before. Tarenhiel always stood between her kingdom and the raiding trolls. And, for years, she and everyone else in her kingdom hadn't given that much thought. The elves were their enemies, and they didn't care if the elves and trolls fought as long as it didn't bother Escarland.

What happened if the elves were overrun? The elves were mighty warriors, especially with their magic. But they were not numerous, even though they lived so long. Elf couples tended to only have a few children for all the hundreds of years they lived. And the wars with both the trolls and Escarland had depleted their numbers. What would another war do?

These trolls could be at her people's doorstep next. And that was something Essie couldn't let happen.

More trolls appeared from the forest. Ten. Twenty. Thirty.

The elves had ten guards. King Weylind. Farrendel. A few servants. Jalissa and Essie. That was it. Against thirty trolls.

Essie flexed her fingers on the bow in her hand. Her palms were sweaty. Her tongue stuck to the roof of her mouth. Was this what fear felt like? She'd always wondered what her father had felt in those last few minutes walking into battle. Was he scared thinking this might be the end? Did he have time in his final moments to realize he was about to die? Or had it been over too fast for him to know?

"Do not worry." Jalissa glanced at Essie. "Farrendel can handle them."

Farrendel? By himself?

Essie drew in a deep breath and peeked out the window once again. Her heart flipped into her stomach as she spotted Farrendel striding forward, all alone.

He wasn't running, but there was something in the way he walked. He was stalking forward, like a cat hunting its prey.

The trolls rushed forward, brandishing their weapons and howling their war cries.

"Why isn't anyone else going to help Farrendel? He's Laesornysh, I know but..." Essie stared at Farrendel, standing there alone as the trolls rushed forward.

"Farrendel needs room to fight." Jalissa still didn't draw the bow back, even though the first of the trolls was now within range.

In a blur of movement, Farrendel drew both of his swords. A crackle filled the air, and a blue light coursed down the sword blades.

Essie gasped at the raw power filling the air, so thick it filled her lungs each time she breathed in.

Farrendel surged forward. His swords blurred as he sliced through the first two trolls. As he did, a surge of power sizzled and blue bolts struck three more trolls. Even as those five trolls toppled to the ground, Farrendel launched himself off one of the falling bodies, spun in the air, stabbed two more trolls, flipped, and took two more trolls down.

Essie could only gape as the power around Farrendel continued to build.

Not Farrendel. Laesornysh. Death on the wind. Now Essie truly understood what that meant. He was terrifying. Power crackled around him, destroying any of the trolls that came too close. That explained why no one, not even his allies, could get close, not even to protect his back.

One of the trolls raised a musket and fired, releasing a cloud of powder smoke. Essie couldn't see the bullet, but something sparked in Farrendel's magic. As if his magic had incinerated the bullet before it could get to him.

Several of the trolls circled around Farrendel. Jalissa raised her bow and released. One of the trolls fell, an arrow between his shoulder blades. Two other trolls also fell to arrows, and Essie leaned to see the guards and King Weylind below. Two of the guards held bows and were reaching for more arrows.

Should she also shoot? She didn't trust her skills enough to shoot anywhere near Farrendel. But she also didn't like the helplessness of sitting there doing nothing while Farrendel fought. Then again, King Weylind and his guards were standing back and doing nothing but making sure none of the trolls got past Farrendel.

Now if Essie had a rifle in her hands, then she might be able to do something.

Not that anything needed to be done. Only three trolls remained, and all of them pressed forward, raising muskets and firing at Farrendel, even though they had to know this was a losing battle. Why didn't they surrender? Or run?

But they kept fighting. Even as an arrow slammed into one and Farrendel's sizzling power blasted another.

Farrendel drove his sword into the chest of the last remaining troll. The troll fell, leaving Farrendel standing, blood spattered and alone, in the center of a ring of dead bodies.

Jalissa relaxed and set the arrow aside. "It is over."

Essie glanced over the windowsill. Farrendel had lowered his swords, but he was still standing there, head bowed. And Essie wasn't so sure.

As soon as the barrier was taken down, Essie rushed down the stairs. Five of the guards were moving among the trolls while the other five were still standing guard. King Weylind was pacing a few yards away from the lake. Farrendel was nowhere in sight.

Essie marched to King Weylind. "Where's Farrendel?"

King Weylind tilted his head toward the lake, the area under Essie and Farrendel's room that was obscured by a stand of underbrush. As Essie started in that direction, King Weylind moved to block her path. "You cannot see him right now. He wants space after a battle."

Essie crossed her arms. Once again, Farrendel's siblings were playing hard and stubborn with her. And she wasn't in the mood for it. "Look. I know you just want to protect Farrendel. And I know you watched Farrendel grow up and all that. But I'm his wife. I know him. Please accept that. Now I'm going to see my husband, understand?"

King Weylind didn't move. "Do not startle him. I do not want to deal with the consequences if he accidentally kills you."

She nearly said something bold like *he would never hurt me.* But she wasn't sure that was true. It wasn't that she was afraid of Farrendel. But, after that battle...

She'd promised him she'd stand by him. That she wouldn't flinch away from his scars or his nightmares or anything about who he was. She wasn't going to turn away now.

She dipped her head in a small nod. "I will be careful."

King Weylind stepped aside. "Very well. When Farrendel is ready, please let him know we need to talk."

Essie couldn't read the expression on his face. She wasn't sure if she'd convinced him or if he figured she wouldn't be able to do much harm, puny human that she was. Whatever his reasons, Essie didn't care. She hurried around him.

At the stand of underbrush, she slowed her pace. "Farrendel? It's me. Essie."

"Leave." Farrendel's voice had a growl. A dangerous sort of growl that should've made her turn around and follow the command.

"Farrendel, I'm not leaving you." Essie walked around the bushes. Slowly, but keeping her footsteps loud so she didn't startle him. After that display of his magic, she didn't want to spook him while battle was still coursing through his body.

On the other side, Farrendel knelt beside the lake, his blood-spattered shirt clenched in his fists. He was still as a statue, not looking at her. "Leave. Please."

That please stopped her. Should she leave as he was asking her to? "I will go if you truly want me to. But please know you don't have to be alone. I'm here for you."

He was still, as if frozen there with his fists in the shallows and blood still smeared across his face and speckled in his hair. Then a shudder trembled down his back. He hunched over the water, his hands shaking, as he scrubbed his shirt over his arms.

Essie crept closer and knelt on the pebbles next to him. She simply sat there. Words now would make things worse.

Farrendel scrubbed at his arm with his shirt, rubbing until his skin grew red and raw.

Essie rested her hand on his, halting his frantic movements.

His silver-blue eyes lifted to hers, but something in his expression was wild. Shaking. "I can't...can't get clean." His breaths came faster, shuddering through his whole body.

"I know. I know." Essie eased his fingers from his shirt. "Let me help."

When he remained still, she lifted his dripping shirt and wiped the spatters of blood from his face. She started on the blood on his jaw, moving up to his cheek and then his ear. She had to wet his shirt several times to continue dabbing away the blood, but he stayed still beneath her fingers. The longer she worked, the more his shaking subsided.

When he met her gaze again, the wildness had left his expression, though he had a hint of wariness about him. He reached up and rested his fingers over her hand where she had been dabbing at a blood smear across his neck. "I have been dreading the day you would see my magic. I did not know how you would react. My magic is not..." He trailed off, as if he wasn't sure what to call it. "Most have magic that grows and creates. Mine destroys."

One more thing to make Farrendel feel different. As if being the illegitimate prince wasn't bad enough. As if pushing himself to earn his place wasn't enough pressure. He also had this powerful, destructive magic that would seem out of place among the rest of the elves.

"Your magic protects. There is no shame in that." Essie held his gaze and released his wet shirt so she could swipe her thumb across his cheek. "I care about you, Farrendel Laesornysh. All of you. Your magic and all."

"You do not know everything about me." Farrendel hung his head. "I..." His words faltered. Would he tell her the truth of his birth now?

But he remained silent, as if he couldn't figure out what to say. It was probably too much too fast after the troll attack.

Even if it was time. Right now, he needed to know she wouldn't turn away from him. Not because of his magic. Not because of his illegitimate birth.

"I know." Essie touched his cheek again.

"You know?" Farrendel stiffened, but his gaze lifted to hers, searching her face. "That I'm a..." He spat out a word in elvish, one Essie was guessing was a derogatory term.

How many times had he had that word spat at him while he was just a child? Yes, his father had done wrong. His mother had done wrong. But none of the blame lay on Farrendel. He should not bear the punishment for his parents' mistakes.

"Your grandmother told me. On my third day here." Essie held his gaze. This moment felt fragile. As if one move the wrong way could shatter everything they'd built.

Farrendel's gaze slipped away from hers, his shoulders slumping. "I am sorry."

"Why are you sorry?" Essie cradled his face in both of her hands. Even when she tipped his face up, he still wouldn't look at her. She traced her thumb over the scars on his cheek. "It's not your fault, Farrendel. None of the mistakes are yours. You can't help how you were born."

"I am still tainted." Farrendel held up his hands. Blood still crusted underneath his fingernails and in the creases of his palms.

"You are your father's son, no matter how it happened. He acknowledged you and raised you as one of the family, as you deserve to be. That makes you a prince of the elves." Essie eased closer. She needed Farrendel to listen. "No matter your magic. No matter your birth. No matter what anyone says. You are not tainted."

With her hands on his cheeks, she felt his muscles relax.

Farrendel took her hand and squeezed her fingers. "*Linshi.*"

"Of course." She reluctantly withdrew her hands. "Your brother said to talk to him as soon as you were ready. He sounded serious. Well, more serious than usual."

Farrendel nodded, picked up his sopping shirt, and eased to his feet. He eyed his shirt, blood spattered and dripping wet, as if he was trying to decide if he should put it on to hide his scars. After a moment, he wrung it out but didn't put it on. Instead, he gathered his tunic, belt, and swords and straightened his shoulders as if finishing pulling himself together.

Essie fell into step with Farrendel as he strode around the bushes to where King Weylind still waited, pacing.

As soon as he glanced in their direction, King Weylind stopped pacing. Something changed in his expression, though Essie couldn't exactly say what it was. Either way, he still looked grim.

They had been attacked by thirty trolls, but a tightening in her gut told her it had only been the beginning.

CHAPTER NINETEEN

F arrendel faced his brother. "There is more to this attack."

Essie tucked herself close to Farrendel, not wanting to be excluded from whatever King Weylind had to say.

King Weylind's gaze flicked to Essie, and his jaw tightened, but he didn't try to order her to leave. "This attack should have been larger."

Essie glanced to Farrendel. What was she missing?

Farrendel met her gaze. "A patrol stumbled across evidence that a large group of trolls had killed the border guards and disappeared deep into the trees. Their numbers were suspected to be over a hundred. We did not think they would reach this far into Tarenhiel."

"And we were attacked by only thirty." Essie shifted even closer to Farrendel.

That meant there were roughly seventy to a hundred trolls wandering around Tarenhiel and no one knew where they were.

Why had these thirty trolls attacked here? It could have been random. Yet, they would have passed many villages to get here.

But the trolls had headed straight for Lethorel. That meant they knew where it was and that most of the elven royal family was here, only lightly guarded. Yet how would they know that information?

"If they had over a hundred, why did they attack with only thirty? Surely they know thirty wasn't enough with Farrendel here?" Essie glanced from King Weylind to Farrendel. The two of them had probably already processed all of the implications, but she wasn't trained for war. Nor had her kingdom fought the trolls the way the elves had. "Why did they keep fighting when it was obvious they were about to be wiped out?"

Farrendel's shoulders slumped, and he glanced at the dead bodies soaking the grass with blood. "This attack was most likely meant to flush us from Lethorel into a trap on the trail. These trolls knew they were going to die."

"And yet they still attacked?" Essie couldn't wrap her mind around it. "I didn't think the trolls were that ...fanatic."

"They are not." King Weylind shook his head, his gaze also straying to the dead trolls. "But they value honor. Perhaps these trolls had done something to disgrace

ELVEN ALLIANCE BOOK ONE

themselves and their family. A death in battle would be the easiest way to redeem that honor."

Essie shivered. That wasn't a culture she could fully understand. Maybe because it wasn't her culture, but suicide by forcing Farrendel to kill them didn't seem all that honorable.

"If we are ambushed on the road, I may not have the space to use my magic properly." Farrendel shook his head, his face and muscles hard. He was all Laesornysh at that moment. All warrior and steel, contemplating the best way to deal swift death to his enemies.

King Weylind's eyes were distant as he gazed over what had been the peaceful glade around Lethorel, the grass now stained with blood and covered with bodies. "Yet we cannot remain here when an invasion might be happening. Tarenhiel needs its king and foremost warrior. We must return to Estyra and deal with this threat, but...the roots seem to have been cut."

If the roots connecting Lethorel to Arorien had been sliced, then the elves were cut off. They couldn't ask for more guards to defend them. They couldn't discover the situation outside of Lethorel.

What was the trolls' plan? If this was some prelude to another war, then Farrendel had to be a target. They would struggle to win a war against the elves unless they eliminated Farrendel first. Killing all but two members of the royal family would be a bonus.

It might be safer to wait here at Lethorel, but King Weylind was right. A full-scale invasion could be happening for all they knew.

Farrendel glanced at Essie, some of his hardness cracking.

They would have to risk the road back to Estyra, even if it meant the non-warriors among them, Queen Rheva, Brina, Ryfon, Jalissa, the servants, and Essie, would be put at risk.

She might not be the warrior Farrendel was, but she would not be completely helpless in this fight. Neither would Jalissa, nor any of the other elves who could handle a bow and arrows, even if they had never done so in battle before.

Essie raised her chin and faced King Weylind and Farrendel. "I assume we are leaving as soon as possible. And leaving everything non-essential behind." When King Weylind tipped his head in a nod, Essie faced Farrendel. "I'll grab you a fresh shirt from our room. You might as well stay in that tunic and pants. They're probably going to get more blood spattered before the day is out. If you could gather the muskets and ammunition from the dead trolls, I'll pick out the best one or two guns and as much ammunition as our pack horse can carry. If we're going to have a major fight on our hands, I'll do better with the musket than a bow and arrow, and it would be best to save the arrows for those who can use them."

Farrendel nodded, pivoted, and headed for the dead bodies, strapping on his swords as he went.

King Weylind eyed her up and down then gave a sharp nod before turning away, probably to organize the others. Essie hoped that meant he was all right with the idea of placing a weapon like a gun in her hands.

In half an hour, they were on the trail back to Arorien, all their luggage left behind at Lethorel. Even the dead bodies of the trolls had been left where they lay. They would be taken care of later, once King Weylind had a chance to send a well-guarded burial detail back here. If he got a chance. If they survived.

Essie had the best of the muskets resting across her lap, her right hand steadying it as she guided the horse with her left. While the musket was outdated, it was at least breach-loading and the trolls had a decent supply of the cartridges. It would've been a great deal harder to load and fire rapidly if they'd had the even older, muzzle-loading style of musket.

Though, that meant the trolls they had yet to face also had more breach-loading muskets. The trolls they'd already faced had about fifteen guns for the thirty of them. If the rest of the trolls had that many guns, they would have nearly fifty.

Unless they had more guns. If they each had a gun...Essie swallowed. Her single musket would be a poor match against a hundred muskets firing back at them. Even with Jalissa, Queen Rheva, Prince Ryfon, and four of the servants also now armed with bows and arrows, they had a total of eighteen archers. And if things came to hand to hand combat, they had only King Weylind, Prince Ryfon, and the ten guards.

And Farrendel. How many trolls could Farrendel take on his own? He'd made taking on those thirty trolls look easy. Jalissa, King Weylind, and the guards had shot a few more to feel like they were helping. But that had been in an open glade where Farrendel could use his power most effectively. Hemmed in by trees and needing to protect the others at his back...not even Farrendel was making any guesses on how that would go.

This was a chance. A chance they would get through. A chance they could all be killed.

Essie flexed her fingers on the musket, glancing around at the trees as they cantered past. They were pushing the horses, cantering and trotting at a steady pace that the horses should be able to maintain for a while at least.

The pack horse behind Essie kept pace with Ashenifela, tied as the pack horse's lead was to Essie's saddle. The pack horse held nothing but Essie's extra ammunition and a second musket. In the event battle broke out, keeping a hold of that pack horse was Essie's priority.

She glanced ahead, catching a glimpse of Farrendel's silver hair between the heads of the others ahead of her. Farrendel was leading, his senses attuned for any sign of a troll ambush. King Weylind guarded their rear while the rest of the elven guards were scattered in the middle. Before they'd left Lethorel, King Weylind had outlined what he wanted all of them to do in those first seconds of the ambush when falling into a tight, fighting formation as quickly as possible could mean the difference between dying and surviving.

Essie tried to swallow, but her mouth was achingly dry, her tongue sticking to the roof of her mouth. Her palm was so sweaty she feared Ashenifela's reins would slip from her fingers.

If she'd thought those moments huddled next to Jalissa in Lethorel had been bad, this was far worse. Then, at least, she'd had the safety of height and Lethorel's walls.

Now there was nothing around her but open sky and trees, and those same trees could be hiding the enemy.

She wasn't wired to be a warrior. More than anything, she wanted to get to Arorien, board the train, and relax on a peaceful trip into Estyra. Would she even be able to raise the musket and pull the trigger if it came to that? Could she take a life, even the life of someone attacking her and the family she'd married into?

With everything in her, she didn't want to find out. A hard knot in her stomach told her she wouldn't have a choice.

Farrendel held his hand up. Essie scrambled to rein in Ashenifela as they went from a canter to a skidding halt.

"Down!" Farrendel shouted even as he vaulted from his horse and urged it to lie down crossways across the path.

Something zipped overhead, and a bolt of Farrendel's magic shot out and burst in the air above them, destroying a bullet and leaving behind the acrid scent of sulfur and overheated metal.

Howls rose from the forest ahead of them. This close, Essie could make out the form of words in the chanting and howling. She didn't know the trolls' language to understand what they chanted as they marched to battle, but it was a reminder that these were people just as much as humans or elves, with their own code of honor and orders that spurred them into this battle.

That's what made battle so terrible.

Essie's heart lurched into her throat, her heartbeat thundering in her ears until it drowned out the howls of the approaching trolls. Her breath caught in her throat, her body frozen there in the saddle.

Ahead of her, the guards, servants, and Jalissa threw themselves from their saddles, urging their horses down, and yanking arrows from their quivers. Over their heads, Essie spotted Farrendel. His magic crackled, his hair floating with the energy surging around him. He walked forward, his swords drawn, prepared to take on the entire pack of trolls.

She couldn't let him down. And freezing like this wasn't helping anyone.

Essie threw herself from the saddle. Ashenifela remained steady, but the pack horse was shifting, tossing its head. Essie tried to get the pack horse to calm enough to lie down, but the horse only danced more.

She didn't have time to wrestle with the horse. She was a larger target standing as she was, even if she currently had the bodies of the pack horse and Ashenifela protecting her.

As quickly as she could, she unbuckled the pack and let it fall to the ground. Then she unclipped the lead from the pack horse's halter, slapped the horse's rump, and let the horse gallop off down the trail, dodging the others already huddled behind their horses.

Hefting the pack with one hand, her arm and shoulder muscles burning at the weight, she grabbed Ashenifela's halter and hurried forward. The guards, servants, and

Jalissa, who had been ahead of Essie in their traveling line, had already gotten their horses on the ground, forming the front side of a circle. Even one of the guards and Queen Rheva were already there, having passed Essie while she'd been wrestling with the pack horse.

Jalissa pressed her hands to the ground. Prince Ryfon joined her. Around the front of the circle of horses, saplings sprouted from the earth, twining together in a wall.

Reaching the circle, Essie positioned Ashenifela in the next open spot next to one of the guards and dragged down on the mare's halter. Ashenifela laid down without a protest, even if her ears were twitching, her nostrils flaring. Dropping the heavy pack, Essie threw herself to the ground behind the mare, rested the musket on the horse's shoulder, and sighted along the barrel, though she didn't yet have a shot.

The first of the trolls had reached Farrendel, and he sliced through them. His magic spread like blue lighting in shimmering, crackling bolts. Flares popped in a constant barrage along the bolts of power as his magic stopped and incinerated the bullets raining toward him. Not a single stray bullet made it past him, keeping Essie and the others sheltered long enough for the rest of the group to finish forming the circle with their horses.

More of the elves pressed their hands to the ground.

The wall of saplings thickened and strengthened. It was now waist high at the front, while before Essie it was barely a foot tall.

The air choked with the stench of gunpowder and blood and a biting, metallic smell that coated Essie's tongue with the taste of lighting strikes.

The trolls had probably been planning to surround them before launching the ambush, but Farrendel's alertness had forced them to charge from the front. The trolls would try to flank Farrendel and get past him to reach the elven king and the rest of them huddled back here.

Essie searched for a shot, but she still couldn't get a clear line of sight past Farrendel's magic blasting through the air. It was just as likely to take out her bullet as it tried to whip past him as it would stop the trolls' bullets.

The sapling wall in front of Essie grew another foot. It left an opening around the barrel of her gun big enough for her to see through.

Princess Brina belly-crawled until she lay next to Essie. "Show me how to load your musket."

Essie glanced over her shoulder at the elf princess. She was seventy years old, which made her roughly fourteen or fifteen. Far too young to be caught in a fight like this.

"Please." Brina worked the second musket free of the pack on the ground. "I have not the aptitude for the bow nor has my magic developed, but I want to help."

Essie could understand that. It was bad enough hiding behind her mare's warm, breathing body and a flimsy wall of saplings while those trolls howled only a few yards away when she had a weapon in her hands. It would be worse to be helpless.

Farrendel's power crackled, tearing through trolls and trees, blasting over their small circle to keep them safe and sheltered. Farrendel himself was a blur, his swords and hair whipping around him as he tore into the trolls, leaving bodies scattered on the ground in his wake.

If he'd been terrifying back at Lethorel, here he was...Essie couldn't even come up with a word to describe him. She hadn't even realized he'd held back before, and now the full extent of his power and skills were unleashed.

They had a few moments. Long enough for her to show Brina how to load a musket. Thankfully, these were breach-loading weapons with the newer metal shell casings on the cartridges. She wouldn't have trusted an inexperienced hand to load muzzle-loading weapons with the old paper cartridges where the chances of doing it improperly were high and the consequences could be a weapon exploding in their hands.

Essie lay on her back below the shelter Ashenifela provided and showed Brina the lever that cracked the gun in half where the barrel met the stock, how to slide the cartridge into place, and then snap the barrel back, making sure it was secured once again.

Rolling to her stomach, Essie rested her musket across her horse's back again. Somehow, explaining how to load the gun to Brina had steadied Essie's hands and cleared her head, even if her heart still pounded wildly. Perhaps that was the key to surviving battle. Don't think about it. Don't feel. Don't worry about dying. Simply go through the familiar motions trained into one's muscles and just exist until the moment was over.

The trolls had begun to spread out, trying to get past Farrendel's killing swords and fury of magic. Essie would've expected Farrendel to be tiring after all that expenditure of magic and physical strength, but, if anything, the power surging from him kept growing. Was he even in control of it anymore? It seemed impossible that one person, even an elf, could control something that powerfully destructive.

To the far left of the trolls' line, a root snaked out and grabbed a troll's ankle, yanking him down, tree roots crawling over him.

A cold wind blew over them, holding a hint of ice and snow. Essie sucked in a breath, her grip tightening on the gun. It was mid-summer. The air shouldn't feel this cold.

Rocks burst from the ground and hurled toward the wall of saplings protecting them, smashing through several sections. Wood splintered. One of the horses whinnied shrilly while an elf cried out.

The wind built, cold and sharp. Frost formed along the barrel of Essie's gun.

Was this the trolls' magic? For some reason, she hadn't expected them to fight back with magic as well. Though, she should have realized they would. Her musket seemed all too small compared to the forces of ice and rocks and growing things ripping the forest apart around them.

Farrendel's magic blasted a hot breeze across them, sweeping both the icy wind and a spray of rocks away from the palisade the elves had grown.

A guard to Essie's right and King Weylind to her left both popped to their knees and released arrows through gaps left in the sapling wall, taking out two of the trolls on the fringes. Farrendel's magic protected them from any return shots, but Essie tightened her fingers on her musket anyway.

She had an advantage the elves didn't. They had to reveal themselves, unprotected above their horses' backs and the saplings, when they wanted to shoot while Essie could shoot on her stomach behind Ashenifela, only a small sliver of her head peeking over the mare's back. Not that Essie wanted to get shot there since being shot in the forehead would be a fatal, if quick death. But she presented a far smaller target than the elves did.

More trolls spread out, both to the right and left of Farrendel, coming nearly level with Essie's position halfway around the circle. Strands of Farrendel's magic lashed back, taking out the bullets, but surely there would come a moment when the trolls were out of reach of his magic.

Rocks pummeled the saplings only a few feet away. An elf cried out, and Queen Rheva crawled toward him, placing her hand over the wound.

More of the elves within the circle popped to their knees, released, and dove back down for cover, doing it at random intervals as far as Essie could tell.

Essie held her fire. As long as the trolls' bullets couldn't reach them, she'd let the elves handle it. Her chance would come once the trolls fired back unhindered.

Sunlight glinted on the weapons the trolls facing them carried. She focused on one, watched as the troll raised the gun to his shoulder. It was hard to tell at that angle, but it didn't match the musket Essie held in her hands. This reminded her more of...but it couldn't be. Those guns were a new invention. The trolls couldn't possibly have gotten a hold of any.

The troll fired the gun and—impossibly—levered a piece of the action and fired again without reloading. A bolt of Farrendel's magic exploded both bullets in the air, but Essie's stomach turned to ice anyway.

Somehow, these trolls had gotten their hands on some of the new, rapid-fire carbines the gun manufacturer in Escarland had just shown Averett earlier that year. They had just been put into production. Averett had forbidden them to be traded with other countries, wanting to keep such technology for Escarland as long as possible.

And yet here they were, the trolls levering five shots at a time before needing to reload.

How had the trolls gotten these weapons? Did her country have a traitor? More like, a whole gang of traitors to pull off something like this.

What would it mean for the tenuous peace between Tarenhiel and Escarland? Once the elves figured out the origin of these weapons, would they assume her country and her family had traded the carbines to the trolls on purpose?

It would mean war. A war between the two countries and two peoples Essie called home.

She had to survive today and stop whatever this was. She would not let all the good her marriage had done to build peace be torn apart so easily.

The war howls of the trolls turned into a gruff, rhythmic chanting. Above the crackling zing of Farrendel's magic, there was the faintest creaking sound.

On the path in front of them, four trolls pushed a large gun mounted on two wagon wheels. At this distance, Essie couldn't see the individual barrels, but she could see the snaking line of ammunition gripped by one of the trolls and the distinctive crank on the side of the gun.

A repeater gun. Another of the weapons so recently invented and perfected in Escarland. It should not be here.

Yet, here it was.

"Get ready, Brina." Essie murmured, not taking her eyes off the repeater gun. She couldn't fire yet, not with Farrendel standing between her and the gun, his magic shielding him in humming, jagged lines.

Farrendel took two running steps toward the repeater gun, his magic lashing out ahead of him.

But he was too late. The trolls cranked the repeater gun. Bullets spat from it in a continuous stream, all directed straight at Farrendel. At the same time, all the trolls spun, faced Farrendel, and also concentrated their fire directly at him. The icy wind and stones bombarded the shield of his magic.

It was a killing field directed at Farrendel from three sides.

His magic shrank to protect him, flares bursting so constantly Essie couldn't see Farrendel inside the tornado of his magic. The repeater gun hammered, and the explosions of Farrendel's magic boomed. Essie's ears rang.

Essie pointed her gun at one of the trolls in front of her, vulnerable to her fire now that Farrendel's magic wasn't between them. She tightened her finger on the trigger, aiming at his chest. She couldn't think of it as taking a life. She couldn't feel at all.

She squeezed the trigger. The musket bucked into her shoulder, and the acrid smell of gunpowder sliced into her nose.

The troll crumpled to the ground.

She held her breath for a heartbeat, waiting for some lurch in her chest. Some visceral or emotional reaction.

There was none. It had no place for it here. Here there was only noise and numbness and Brina beside her holding out the second, loaded musket.

Essie took the other gun, handed over the one she'd just fired, and picked another target. Aimed, concentrating only on the square of dark brown shirt where she'd send the bullet without looking at the troll's face.

But as her finger tightened, a cry of pain cut through the thunder. Farrendel's magic blew outward in a wave before it winked out, nothing but a breeze against Essie's hair and a prickle against her skin.

Farrendel collapsed to his knees, three spots of blood growing on his middle and lower back.

CHAPTER TWENTY

It was not a conscious decision. Essie snapped her gun around, aimed, and squeezed the trigger. The troll cranking the repeater gun staggered, blood blossoming at his shoulder.

One of the elf guards got to his knees to shoot but toppled as gunfire erupted around them again, this time aimed back at them. Farrendel's magic didn't protect them this time. Something zipped overhead, so fast the noise only registered after it was past. Dirt flew as bullets struck. A horse whinnied in pain.

More roots burst from the ground, but ice coated them before they could wrap around any of the trolls.

Only Essie could effectively fire back. Any elf that attempted to shoot now would take his life in his hands.

Essie reached blindly for the second musket. Her hand connected with wood and steel, and she yanked it from Brina's grip, aiming as soon as the gun's butt settled against her shoulder. One of the other trolls by the repeater gun was reaching for the hand crank. This time, her bullet struck him in his chest. When he went down, he stayed down.

She held out the empty gun. It was taken from her grip, and the other gun smacked into her palm so quickly air had barely brushed against her hand before it was filled again.

As Essie aimed for one of the two remaining trolls by the repeater gun, Farrendel staggered to his feet. Essie fired, and the third troll fell before Farrendel launched himself forward, both swords taking the last troll in the chest.

Farrendel's magic sparked to life, but it was only a few shivering bolts taking out the stray bullets still flying in his direction.

Essie swapped guns again, fired, repeated, taking down the trolls closest to Farrendel.

Without Farrendel's magic suppressing their fire and the elves' arrows to deter them, the trolls were charging forward. Twenty feet away. Fifteen feet. Sunlight glinted on drawn swords and raised guns for one last volley.

Essie swallowed and raised the musket again. They were going to be overwhelmed. Nothing but a mere ten feet stood between her and a troll raising a large war ax as he charged. She fired, and the troll stumbled, but the trolls behind him pushed forward.

She probably should keep her gaze fixed on the advancing trolls. But if these were her last moments, she didn't want her last memories to be just of charging enemies. As she swapped guns yet again, she glanced toward Farrendel.

He was stumbling toward the charging trolls, facing her now so that she could see the blood soaking the front of his tunic in a way the troll blood splattered across him didn't. As if sensing her gaze, he looked up, his silver-blue eyes meeting hers.

It sent a jolt through her, making her wish for all sorts of impossible things. If only she'd used the word love that morning instead of taking the coward's way out and saying care. What would it have been like to kiss him?

She should've kissed him. She'd thought she'd gone into this battle with no regrets, but battles had a way of bringing out all kinds of regrets she hadn't known were buried in her chest.

But she also could see the things she didn't regret. She didn't regret marrying Farrendel or letting herself fall for him or coming to love his kingdom. She didn't regret the moments that had led here, to this battle, beyond the fact that the massacre here would probably start a war between both kingdoms she loved.

Hopefully Farrendel could read her regrets and her

love in her eyes. Separated as they were on the battlefield, they wouldn't even get a moment for a semi-romantic goodbye.

Something hardened in his expression, and he took one, shaking step forward before going down to one knee. Magic built around him, crackling stronger and stronger until a hum filled the air. His skin glowed faintly blue, his hair swirling as if it lifted on a breeze.

Farrendel's magic blasted outward in lightning-like streaks of pure power. The force of it pressed Essie against the dirt, her chest squeezing so tightly she couldn't breathe. In front of her, Ashenifela squirmed, a frightened squeak of sound blowing from her nostrils for the first time the whole battle. But even the mare was pinned to the ground under the weight of the power hurling through the air.

This magic held such a wild, raw fury that it tore the air apart. Something exploded with a boom that shuddered through the ground. The trees around them groaned as if they too were in pain under the onslaught.

Then it all went still, the power sizzling into the sky before dissipating, leaving behind the smell of lightning and burned flesh.

All the trolls lay in dead heaps on the ground. Ash and gun smoke drifted.

Farrendel met Essie's gaze again before his body went

limp and sagged to the ground.

"Farrendel!" His name tore against her throat, raw from gunpowder and magic. She jumped to her feet, leapt over Ashenifela, and scrambled over the remnants of the sapling palisade, her musket thunking on the ground as she dropped it.

She probably should look to make sure all the trolls were dead before she charged across the open. She should wait until King Weylind gave the signal that everything was safe.

But she was dashing across the battlefield, dodging fallen trolls and slipping on loam slick with blood. Her vision had narrowed to the ground immediately in front of her feet and Farrendel's body lying there, bloody and still.

Essie crashed to her knees next to him, pressing her hands against his stomach as if her two small hands would be enough to halt the bleeding. There was so much blood she couldn't tell where the wounds were to apply pressure.

He was alive, his chest rising and falling.

He was dying. Tremors coursed through him. Blood flecked his lips with each exhale.

She pressed one of her bloody hands against his chest. She was begging and babbling and crying so hard she wasn't even sure what she was saying besides the ringing of his name over and over in her ears.

He couldn't die. He mustn't die. Not like this. Not now. Not Farrendel.

His eyes flickered open, and he reached one shaking hand toward her. "Essie..." Her name was a breath gurgling between his lips.

She gripped his hand and hugged their clasped hands to her heart. "Don't die. Please don't die. I love you, Farrendel. I can't..."

She couldn't get the words out. The light in his eyes was fading, his grip on her hand slackening.

No. He couldn't die. Not like this. Not in some troll ambush. Not when they were so close to being able to say they were well and truly in love.

She tightened her grip on his hand, her other palm over his heart. "Did you hear me, Farrendel? I love you. You can't die now. You have to live. We're supposed to have a love like Daesyn and Inara. Of one heart. That's what we vowed. This isn't how it is supposed to end."

Something tugged deep inside her chest, like it had during their vows in the elven wedding ceremony, but deeper. Stronger.

Essie gasped as pain tore through her middle, and her head spun with the effort it took to simply draw in a breath. Her heart beat hard and painful inside her chest.

Jalissa sank to her knees next to Essie. She glanced

from Farrendel to Essie and back, her eyes widening. She placed a hand on Essie's shoulder. "Whatever you do, do not let go of his hand. Not unless you cannot take in another breath."

What was happening? What was this? Essie fought, dragging another gasp into her chest.

Jalissa glanced up, and only then did Essie register King Weylind standing on her other side, looking down at her and Farrendel with a stricken expression. Jalissa's grip tightened on Essie's shoulder, as if through that contact she could give Essie strength to draw in another breath.

Queen Rheva rushed up and knelt next to Jalissa. She spoke in elvish, but Essie couldn't seem to concentrate enough to understand what she was saying.

Essie blinked, but black spots were dancing across her vision. Each breath was hard, as if the weight of a boulder pressed down on her chest.

Queen Rheva rested a hand on Farrendel's forehead.

Pain flared inside Essie, white and crackling. There was a cry of pain. Hers or Farrendel's or both, she didn't know.

She was sinking, blackness hovering, the only sensation besides pain and pressure was the feel of Farrendel's warm hand still gripped in both of hers.

She was on the ground. Damp, cool earth pressed against her cheek, the sensation soothing. Until that moment she hadn't realized how hot she was. Burning. Sweating.

Hands lifted her. Fabric replaced the earth against her cheek. She didn't have the strength to open her eyes. It took all her will to drag in yet another breath and hold on to Farrendel's hand.

He was next to her. Her body bumped against his as the fabric beneath her moved and swayed. Voices in elvish spoke somewhere in the haze above her, but she couldn't decipher the words.

Breathe. In. Chest aching, throat burning. Out.

It might have been minutes later. Hours later. Days later. They were jostled and transferred to something softer, steadier than before. More voices. More pain flaring before something soothing and cool washed through her.

And with that, she lost her grip on her last thread of consciousness.

CHAPTER TWENTY-ONE

Some part of her seemed to have a memory of a soothing rocking motion. Whatever it had been, it had stopped, though she couldn't say if the motion had stopped hours or minutes ago.

Essie blinked, bringing a silver, arching ceiling into focus. Trees filled the bank of windows across from her.

She was in an elven train car, though the train around her remained still. Were they parked at a platform? Had they made it all the way back to Estyra? How long had she been out?

This wasn't one of the seating cars she'd ridden in before. The mattress beneath her was soft while blankets were piled over her, as if she'd been tucked in and cared for while she slept.

She started to push the blankets away but halted. Her right hand was free, but her left hand...

She turned her head. Farrendel lay on his back next to

her, still asleep, his chest rising and falling with gentle, steady breaths. The blanket had fallen down, revealing his bare chest and stomach covered with bandages. Someone must have taken the time to wash the blood from his skin and face, though a few flakes still clung to his hairline and dusted his hair as it spread across the pillow.

Whatever was in that elven shampoo and conditioner, it apparently could keep his hair tangle free even through an entire battle. It still looked nice, even with the dried blood. Hers was probably a tangled, frizzing mess. The ends of her hair were flopped over Farrendel's in between their pillows, hers a burnished red against his silver-blond.

She was still gripping his hand like she feared he'd die the moment she let go. Something in her chest still felt connected to him, but breathing was easier. What had happened back there on the battlefield?

They were both still alive. That was the main thing.

She eased onto her side so that she faced Farrendel. He didn't stir, his face tipped partially away from her, giving her a good look at his pointed ear.

He was still asleep, and her fingers were itching with curiosity. Essie reached out and ran her fingers through Farrendel's hair. The strands slid across her fingers, not a tangle or split end. Maybe it wasn't the conditioner. Elves had magic hair. That was simply the only explanation.

His breathing remained steady. He didn't stir at her

touch on his hair. It made her feel daring.

She traced her finger over his ear. It didn't feel all that different than a human's ear, warm when she'd been expecting it to be cool, but pointed instead of rounded.

"Why are you touching my ear?" Farrendel's voice was groggy, and he remained perfectly still, his words the only indication he was awake.

Essie snatched her hand back. This was awkward. There really wasn't any good way to reclaim her dignity. Not after he'd woken to her fondling his ear. Ugh, that was embarrassing. "I...um...your ear is pointed. I've been curious ever since I married you and...sorry."

He turned his face toward her, his eyelids drooping sleepily. "Do all humans find pointed ears attractive?"

"I don't know. Maybe. I do, apparently." She curled her fingers, resisting the urge to run her fingers through his hair again. She never would've pegged herself as the type to be attracted to men with pointed ears and hair longer and silkier and better styled than her own, but there was just something about elves...

Or maybe it was just Farrendel. She loved him from his looks and his scars to his quiet, almost shy demeanor that hid his thoughtfully caring heart. She even loved his fierce, terrible magic and the protectiveness that went along with it.

When she was with him, she felt so completely free to

be herself, a freedom she never would've guessed she'd find in the reputedly staid and stuffy elven court. He never told her to stop chattering, quiet down, hush, remember to act like a demure princess. Even her mother and brothers had at times admonished her for speaking too much or too loudly. They'd done it out of love, but it had still chafed.

But Farrendel didn't tell her to stop talking. He told her to talk more, to talk freely. To spout out the first thing that came to mind because he found that trait endearing instead of annoying.

Somehow, his encouragement to talk made her want to listen. To stop talking occasionally so that he would have a chance to.

And he had. Her lack of judgment had given him the freedom to speak. She could hardly remember the way he'd been when she'd married him, barely speaking to her at all besides a word here or there.

Farrendel struggled onto his elbows as if he was trying to push himself upright. He grimaced, sucking a sharp breath between his teeth, and collapsed onto the pillow, pressing a hand against his bandaged stomach.

Essie shoved onto her elbow. "Do you need me to get you anything? A drink? Painkiller? I don't know where anyone is, but I'm sure someone is around who can fetch the physician. Or healer I guess you call them." She shoved aside the blanket, letting go of his hand.

He gripped her forearm. "No, please stay."

She halted. "Are you sure?"

"Yes. I am fine." His eyes were clearer, less sleepy than they'd been a moment ago. Now that he was lying back down, he didn't seem to be in terrible pain. "I am used to being healed more than this when I wake up. It is fine."

Essie eased herself down next to him, though she remained propped on one elbow to keep a better eye on his expression. "All right. But the moment you look like the pain is getting to you, I'm going to find the healer."

If she could find someone. She still didn't know why they were stopped, where they were, or why they seemed to be left so alone. Not that she minded the privacy, but she would've thought Jalissa and King Weylind would hover with how hurt Farrendel had been and still was.

Farrendel reached for her hand. "You saved my life."

"I did? I kind of thought you saved mine. That last blast of your magic was incredible." Essie ran her thumb over the back of Farrendel's hand. "I thought we were all going to die there. But I guess I did save you when I shot the trolls by the repeater gun. None of the elves could shoot back without exposing themselves to fire."

Farrendel reached his free hand up and touched her cheek. "How are you doing? It was your first battle."

How was she doing? Essie shifted closer to Farrendel. "Honestly, I haven't thought about it much. I woke up only a few minutes before you did, and on the battlefield when you were hit, I just did what I had to do."

"If it hits you later or you have nightmares, I will be here." Farrendel's thumb was soft and gentle as he stroked her cheek.

"I know." Their faces were only a few inches apart now. Essie's breath hitched in her throat, and her heart was pounding. A different sort of pounding than it had been doing during the battle. She ran her fingers through Farrendel's hair. "When I thought we were all going to die, I regretted that I'd never kissed you. I know you elves aren't ones to kiss before you truly love someone and all that, but I—"

Farrendel tugged her down, and her words died against his mouth.

If she'd given it much thought and had expectations about her first kiss with Farrendel, she would've guessed his kiss would be as restrained and quiet as he was.

But something sparked deep inside her chest. His kiss was more like his magic. Crackling. Reckless.

He tugged her closer, a hand on her waist, the other hand cradling the side of her head. She smiled against his mouth as his thumb skimmed her ear. He'd been as curious as she was about their different ear shapes, even if he was a lot more subtle about it.

This kiss was spark and fire. Lightning and magic.

She eased back, her breath coming fast.

The hitch in Farrendel's gasps was probably from the kiss, but the ragged edge was his pain. His hand left her waist, and he pressed against the bandages around his stomach.

"Sorry. You're in pain." Essie put a few more inches between them, but she didn't pull away that far. "Maybe we should hold off on kissing until you're finished healing."

The corners of Farrendel's mouth tipped up. "Depends on how long the healer takes to finish healing me."

Essie let out a small laugh. "I like kissing you too."

They remained still and silent, simply relaxed in the moment. It was comfortable here with Farrendel. Essie could get used to waking curled up next to him.

Was this what love felt like? Yes, it could be fiery and passionate. But it was also this. Warmth and comfort. A quiet sort of trust that didn't need to be spoken.

Farrendel's breathing steadied into something more relaxed, less pained. The tilt of his smile faded from his expression. "When I said you saved my life, I did not only mean when you shot those trolls. I was dying, and you did not let go. We elves call that *elishina*. Heart-bonded."

"*Elishina*? What do you mean? How did I save you then? I'm not even sure what happened." Essie tugged her pillow closer to him and lay back down. Her shoulder and elbow were getting sore from propping herself up.

"Do you remember in our wedding ceremony when we pledged that our hearts would be as one?" Farrendel shifted, winced, and glanced toward her before focusing on the ceiling.

Essie nodded. "There was this zing of magic, at least I think that's what it was."

"When we elves marry, we become very literally and magically bonded. Sometimes, the bond is so deep that if one is injured, the other's heart can literally keep beating for both of them." Farrendel remained staring upward, but his hand squeezed hers. "I was not sure it would happen with us. The only human and elf pair to experience it was Daesyn and Inara, and even then, it was the elf's heart beating for the human's."

Essie propped herself on her elbow again. "So when I gripped your hand and it felt like I was struggling to breathe, it was because I was breathing for you?"

"Sort of. More like as long as you were breathing, I would stay breathing, and as long as your heart was beating, mine would be too." His expression sobered, and he pushed a strand of hair from her face. "You could have died if the strain of keeping me alive had been too much. Before I met you, I never would have expected a human's heart could sustain an elf's that way."

Essie shook her head, something of a smile tugging at her mouth. Even after all this time, she was still reminded of how little the elves understood humans. "We humans may be reckless and make a lot of mistakes, but when we love, we love fiercely. Our lives are too short to afford to do anything less."

"We elves could probably learn something from you about making each day count." Farrendel didn't smile as he cupped her cheek. "I hoped on the day I married you that we would form a heart-bond. But I did not expect, if it would happen, that it would occur this soon. We had not even kissed before the battle."

"Maybe we hadn't kissed, but both of us have been choosing to love each other from the day we married." Essie wanted to kiss him again, but that would distract them, and this heart-to-heart conversation was something they needed. "Love is a choice, and it's one we have been making all along. That probably counts a whole lot more for a heart-bond than kissing does, even if I'm discovering I really like kissing you."

A smile briefly flickered on Farrendel's face before it faded. "Will it bother you if your life is longer than what is expected for a human?"

He was talking cryptically. Essie huffed and flopped back down next to him. "What do you mean? This has something to do with Daesyn and Inara again, doesn't it?

I think it's high time I heard that whole story."

Farrendel twined his fingers with hers. "Inara was a princess of the elves, and Daesyn was a human woodsman. They met and fell in love. Daesyn helped the elven king, Inara's father, push the trolls back into the northern realms, and he was wounded in the last, great battle. Inara's heart-bond with him kept him alive until the healers could save him. Their heart-bond was so strong that Daesyn lived to nearly five hundred years old. Inara died shortly after he did, young for an elf. The stories say she gave her years to him, and that's how he lived for so long."

Essie stared at the ceiling, trying to absorb what Farrendel was telling her. Was there a possibility she would live to be several hundred years old? She would outlive her family. Her brothers. Her mother.

But she would have Farrendel. She would see her brothers' children and grandchildren grow up and grow old.

If she and Farrendel had children, she would be able to see them grow to maturity. Maybe even marry. If she lived only a normal human's lifetime, she would never see her half-elf children reach their adulthood.

"This is why your family was so concerned about you falling in love with me. They feared that either we wouldn't form a heart-bond and your heart would be broken when I died in only a short time compared to an elf's years or we would form this special bond and you would end up dying young. They don't want to lose you."

"No, they do not. But, Essie," Farrendel pushed himself onto an elbow, only a tightening of his jaw to betray his pain. His hair fell in a curtain around his shoulders. "I would gladly give up a few hundred years if it meant that the years I did have were spent with you."

That was the most adorable, swoon-worthy, romantic thing anyone had ever said to her. Essie leaned closer so their faces were only inches apart. "And I would happily live to be five hundred if I'm with you."

This time, he was the one to close the distance, burying his fingers in her hair. At least the elven conditioner had been doing its job, and her hair was the silkiest, non-frizziest it had ever been, even after going through a battle.

Not that she cared what her hair looked like at that moment. Heart-bond, indeed.

Farrendel drew back, just enough to murmur, "I think I am in love with you."

"I should hope so. I know I'm in love with you." Essie thought about continuing kissing him, but his breathing was growing ragged again. She toyed with a strand of his hair. "There isn't a guarantee that whatever heart-bond we have will give me a longer life, is there? We know there is one, thanks to me saving your life, but if I'm understanding this right, then we still don't know if that means your magic will give me a longer life."

"No, it does not. We may not know for years, not until you stop aging like you normally would." Farrendel's eyes held a sadness. As if it was too much to contemplate that she might die after only a few decades together.

Seventy years. It was a lifetime for Essie. It was hard to wrap her mind around the thought that, to Farrendel, seventy years would seem like only the beginning. If she had only a normal, human lifetime, Farrendel would be left mourning her longer than he'd been married to her.

But if his magic gave her a longer life? What would it be like to live for centuries? There was no guarantee that it would happen, but if the whole heart-bond thing was any indication, then they had a better chance than most human-elf couples.

A knock sounded on the door to their train car. Essie had just enough to time to lurch back, putting a few more inches of space between her and Farrendel before the door opened, and Jalissa stepped inside.

Her gaze flicked from Essie to Farrendel and back. Essie didn't want to know what Jalissa was thinking. The way Essie and Farrendel were facing each other, it wasn't too hard to guess they had been kissing, even if they had been some space between them now.

Jalissa's mouth twitched. "Good. You are both awake."

Essie sat all the way upright. "Where is everyone? Are we in Estyra? Why are we still on the train?"

Jalissa paused for a moment, as if she wasn't sure which of those questions to answer first. "We arrived in Estyra an hour ago, but we did not want to move Farrendel until after the healer finished."

Farrendel eased himself back onto the pillow, grimacing and pressing a hand to his stomach. Blood now spotted the bandages.

Essie rested a hand on Farrendel's shoulder. He hadn't even moved that much, and it had caused his wounds to bleed again. How badly was he still hurt? "Why wasn't he healed all the way? I don't know much about elf magic and healing, but…"

She wasn't even sure what she'd been trying to ask with the end of that question.

Jalissa stepped closer, her gaze focused on the blood dotting Farrendel's bandages. "It was because of the *elishina*."

When Jalissa hesitated, Essie nodded. "Farrendel explained about the heart-bond thing and how I accidentally kept him alive. But what does that have to do with healing him?"

"When Rheva and the healer in Arorien started to heal Farrendel, it put an additional strain on your body. We feared that if the full healing was completed, the strain would kill you, and we did not think that Farrendel would want us to heal him at your expense."

"No." Farrendel shook his head.

"Exactly. We did only what was necessary, and our healer has been waiting for you both to wake up to finish. With Farrendel awake, the healing will not put a strain on you." Jalissa turned back to the door. "I will fetch him."

"Jalissa." Farrendel's voice held a taut note to it. "Has Weylind called a Council yet?"

Jalissa didn't look at them as she answered. "Weylind left shortly after we arrived to arrange a meeting of the Council. I believe it started a few minutes ago."

The Tarenhieli Council. It was the governing body that made the big decisions for the elves. As far as Essie knew, it wasn't called often.

Was it called because of the trolls' raid so deep into Tarenhiel? Because the attack was targeted to wipe out King Weylind and Farrendel all at once?

Or…Essie swung her feet to the floor. "I have to stop the Council. Or talk to them. They're discussing the weapons that the trolls had in that second attack, aren't they? I can't let them decide to go to war because someone is making it look like Escarland had something to do with it. My brother would never give guns to the trolls. Never."

Farrendel shoved onto his elbows. "I will stand with you."

The blood on his bandages was getting worse. Essie pressed a hand to Farrendel's shoulder. "Don't get up. You aren't going anywhere until after you're healed."

Jalissa paused in the doorway. "I will return with the healer, then you can both clean up to face the Council."

Farrendel relaxed back onto the pillow, his skin a pale gray.

"The pain is getting worse, isn't it?" Essie took one of his hands. "Are you sure you want to go with me before the Council? I know it will be mostly my word that my brother didn't have anything to do with it."

"I will be fine once I am healed." Farrendel squeezed her hand. "I will be at your side when you face the Council. They can be...hard-headed."

There was something in Farrendel's voice. He didn't like the Council that much. The Council probably didn't like him all that much either. If they were as stuffy as they sounded, the late king's illegitimate son wouldn't be their favorite person, especially since the royal family had fully embraced Farrendel's place as one of them.

Jalissa returned, followed by a male elf with long, light brown hair. The male elf—the healer Essie assumed— shook his head and said something in elvish. Essie only understood a few of the words, but she understood the sentiment. Farrendel had been moving about far too much for someone in his condition.

"I need to be healed quickly." Farrendel said in elvish, something in his expression going hard.

The healer frowned. Farrendel held the healer's gaze. After a moment, the healer sighed and tipped his head in the elves' small nod.

Essie squeezed Farrendel's hand. Why would a fast healing make the healer frown?

Farrendel tugged his hand free from Essie's. "I do not think we should be touching during the healing. He is going to do the healing fast instead of gently. I do not want you to feel it through the heart-bond."

Was that possible? Essie still felt connected to Farrendel, but not the way she had before.

Farrendel turned back to the healer and nodded. The healer produced a small shears and cut through the bandages around Farrendel's torso. As he peeled them back, Essie could see the three bullet wounds, still raw, gaping, and oozing blood.

The healer placed his hand over the wounds. A green light burst around the wounds, flaring bright enough Essie had to look away, squinting.

Farrendel squeezed his eyes shut, making a small, muffled sound in the back of his throat as if he'd swallowed back a cry of pain.

Then it was over. Three scars were all that remained of the bullet wounds.

Farrendel pushed into a sitting position, hunching over as if he was still in some kind of pain.

The healer glanced from Farrendel to Essie, and when he spoke, it was in Escarlish. "You will be sore for a few days after such a..." the healer paused as if searching for the correct word, "forced healing."

Farrendel nodded and pushed to his feet. *"Linshi."*

The healer gave a nod to Farrendel, Jalissa, and even Essie before he stepped from the room. Essie wasn't sure what she had done to earn the healer's respect. Was it because of the heart-bond between her and Farrendel? Had the healer been able to sense it?

Essie glanced from herself, still wearing the bloodstained tunic and pants from the battle, to Farrendel, shirtless and bedraggled, or as much as an elf could look bedraggled, with blood dried hard and crusty on his pants and still flaked in his hair. "We have to hurry if we want to change before facing the Council. I don't think we'll make a good impression at the moment."

Farrendel's expression twitched with something of a grimace. If he was as sore as the healer had hinted, he probably wasn't up to hurrying.

Jalissa gave a smile, though her eyes were steely. "I sent a servant to fetch your clothes and crowns while you slept. I expected you would wish to speak before the Council." She took Essie's arm and guided her from the room. "We will show them you are a princess of the elves, Elspetha Shynafir."

Shynafir? Essie blinked at Jalissa, before turning to Farrendel. The *a* at the end of her name turning Elspeth into the elvish Elspetha didn't surprise her. But until now, the elves had just given her the title of princess. She hadn't earned a title-last name the way Farrendel had with Laesornysh.

Farrendel smiled. A large, teeth showing smile. "Shynafir means Fierce Heart."

Fierce heart. She didn't need to be known for heroic deeds or great battles. It was not a bad thing if, when the history books remembered her, all they said about her was that she loved fiercely.

She had come here determined to love Farrendel, love the elves, and love this new home of hers. If she managed to bring peace between her kingdom and the elves, it would be because she loved both of her homes and peoples so fiercely that she could stand between them, one foot in both worlds.

It was time to show the Tarenhieli Council just how fierce she could be.

CHAPTER TWENTY-TWO

E ssie glided at Farrendel's side, her head held high and her hand lightly resting on his forearm. They were dressed as they had been for that first dinner together with his family.

Farrendel wore the silver tunic only a shade lighter than his hair, his silver crown resting on his brow. She wore the royal blue dress, its skirt fluttering elegantly around her as she moved, while a matching crown to Farrendel's glittered against her hair.

Considering they'd had only a few minutes and no time for proper showers, they'd both managed to clean up rather well. A wet washcloth could do wonders for scrubbing flakes of blood away from hairlines and skin. No one on the Council would come close enough to notice if they both smelled faintly of blood and sweat.

Jalissa trailed a few steps behind them, dressed in a deep red dress and wearing a thin silver circlet. At least

Essie had won over one of Farrendel's family members. Perhaps more. Leyleira had been supportive from the start. Princess Brina had helped tremendously during the battle.

But King Weylind? Essie wasn't sure where she stood with him. He didn't seem to hate her. He never would have approved of the marriage alliance between her and Farrendel if he had. But he didn't seem to approve of her either.

Essie and Farrendel climbed the last of the stairs and reached the landing before the large hall where their elven wedding had been held. Today, the doors were shut and two elves in leather tunics embossed in gold stood in front of the doors. With the leather tunics and their helmets on, Essie couldn't tell if the guards were male or female.

Farrendel faced them with all the dangerous hardness that made him so feared as Laesornysh. When he spoke in elvish, his tone was icy. "Farrendel Laesornysh and Elspetha Shynafir to speak before the Council."

The guard on the right moved a fraction to face them. "The Council is not expecting you."

A female guard then, based on the voice. Essie didn't let herself blink at the cold words. Was Farrendel's brother trying to prevent her from defending Averett before the Council? Surely not. King Weylind had allowed Farrendel to marry a human for the sake of peace. He wouldn't throw that away.

Perhaps he merely hadn't expected Essie and

Farrendel to wake in time.

Farrendel stared at the guard. "They will wish to see us."

It was a command. The female guard gave a small nod, then stepped inside, closing the door behind her.

The minutes seemed to drag as they stood there, facing the door in complete silence while the other guard stared off into space as if they weren't there.

Finally, the female guard returned and opened the door for them. "The Council will see you."

Farrendel stalked inside, and Essie did her best to glide like an elf princess at his side. Inside the room, thrones filled the dais where she and Farrendel had stood during their wedding. King Weylind sat in the largest, center throne, wearing a spiked, gold crown.

Queen Rheva was on his right with Leyleira to her right while Prince Ryfon was seated on King Weylind's left with Princess Brina and Melantha next to him. There was an empty throne next to Melantha and next to Leyleira. Empty places for Jalissa and for Farrendel, probably. None for Essie.

Out of the corner of her eye, she spotted Jalissa slipping past them and gliding along the edge of the room. Probably headed to claim her place.

But Farrendel remained by Essie, and she got the sense that he would stay there with her as long as it took for them to add another throne at his side.

On either side of the room, tiers of benches had been set up, filled with both male and female elves, all dressed in finery. Unlike the Parliament in Escarland where the lords and delegates rarely used the seats because they were so busy shouting and shaking their fists at each other, the elves sat in neat, orderly places along the benches, the hush over the room complete.

On a table in the center of the room lay one of the lever action carbines the trolls had used in the attack, its stock still a spattered with blood.

The female guard stepped forward and announced them in elvish, and Essie had to suppress a smile at hearing the guard use her new title.

The elves in the stands stirred but remained hushed. Across the large room, King Weylind's face was made of stone for how hard and expressionless it was.

Was he convinced that her brother had something to do with this? Was he angry at Farrendel for standing at her side even now?

Yet how could King Weylind question that Farrendel loved her and she loved him in return after the whole heart-bond thing that had kept Farrendel alive?

King Weylind's dark, cold eyes rested on her. "Elspeth of Escarland, please identify the gun on that table."

She refused to flinch at his hard tone. He hadn't even

named her as Farrendel's wife, much less given her the title Shynafir.

Underneath her hand, she felt Farrendel stiffen. She squeezed his forearm and gave him a slight shake of her head. They had agreed that Farrendel would only step in when it was absolutely necessary. He was at her side to show his support, but this was her brother she had to defend.

After a heartbeat of glaring at his brother, Farrendel led Essie forward and halted in front of the table that held the gun. Essie let go of Farrendel's arm so she could turn the gun over as she inspected it. She made sure it stayed in contact with the table. She didn't want the elves to get jumpy thinking she was trying to use the weapon against them.

Both the gun's stock and the barrel had the stamped mark of one of the largest gun manufacturers in Escarland. A figure of an eagle clutching a sword in its talons had been carved into both sides of the stock. She studied the figure closely, but it was too perfect, too precise, to be anything but the real thing.

Not only was this one of the new types of guns manufactured only in Escarland, but it was a gun purchased by Escarland's army and marked by the king's symbol.

An icy feeling settled into her stomach. Could her brother have—

No. She refused to even think it. No wonder King Weylind and the elves on the Council were so convinced Averett must have knowingly traded guns to the trolls. The evidence looked convincing.

Essie swallowed and faced King Weylind. "It's an Escarlish army carbine. But—"

"Explain to me how Escarlish army weapons came to be in the hands of trolls intent on assassinating me and my family." King Weylind's voice slashed into the room.

It took everything in Essie not to flinch. She drew in a deep breath, looking at the other members of Farrendel's family. Jalissa had taken the chair next to Melantha, and her eyes were slightly wide, as if even she was questioning her new friend-ship with Essie. Melantha was glaring, as usual. Queen Rheva and Prince Ryfon were just as expressionless as King Weylind. Princess Brina glanced between her father and Essie as if she too were confused by her father's harsh tone.

Leyleira met Essie's gaze, her eyes soft, and she tipped her chin up. As if reminding Essie to hold her head high and proud before the assembled elves. She must not flinch away, no matter how harsh King Weylind's words sounded.

Farrendel's presence was warm and solid next to her, a faint crackle humming around him as if he was just barely keeping himself in check.

Essie met King Weylind's gaze and refused to look away no matter how hard and dark his eyes were. "*Daresheni*," she began, using the elf honorific, "My brother King Averett of Escarland, had nothing to do with trading these weapons to the trolls."

"Then is your brother such a weak king that something as momentous as this could occur behind his back?"

She bit back her first instinctual reply. King Weylind was trying to get a rise out of her. "As you have also experienced recent trouble with a traitor who must have given the location of Lethorel to the trolls, my brother is not the only one with forces in his kingdom working behind his back. I can assure you, once my brother is alerted to this issue, he will take swift action to correct it."

One of the male elves on the benches to the right stood. Unlike King Weylind, he spoke in elvish, as if he didn't care if Essie understood his question clearly or not. Thankfully, Essie knew enough elvish by now to figure out the gist of his question was "Why should we believe your assurance?"

Essie continued to face King Weylind as she spoke. It was important to convince the Council, but in the end, they were little more than advisors with some pull in the government. King Weylind was the real authority here. "I can give you several reasons for why I know my brother did not give these weapons to the trolls. First, my brother loves me. He would never aid an ambush that would endanger me. As the witnesses to the ambush on the royal family can attest, I was in just as much danger as everyone else there."

A female elf stood this time. "We have only your word that he loves you. He may not have known the trolls planned to use the weapons to ambush the royal family. It is well known that your father died fighting us. Your brother has little reason to love Tarenhiel."

"The people of Escarland may have little love for the elves thanks to the war years ago, but they also have no love for the trolls. King Averett understands that, if Tarenhiel should fall to the trolls, it would be only a matter of time before the trolls turned to Escarland." Essie pointed at the gun on the table. "Besides, this gun represents the latest in Escarland's technology. A kingdom does not arm a potential enemy with the weapons that enemy could use to destroy them. Perhaps someone could argue for giving the trolls outdated, muzzle-loading guns. But brand-new weapons? No, that is the work of a small group of traitors unsanctioned by Escarland's king and government."

"If I should believe you, where does that leave me?" King Weylind's gaze didn't soften, but at least his tone wasn't quite as harsh. "Your brother promised that marrying my brother to you would eliminate issues like this. Those promises have failed."

"No, they haven't. This is exactly the situation for

which a marriage alliance is designed." Essie reached out, and she could feel Farrendel link his two fingers with hers in the elven way of holding hands. "Before, when an issue like this would arise, you had no ally to speak for you before Escarland's court. But I am your ally. I am a princess of both Tarenhiel and Escarland. I can speak for you before my brother, and he will listen to me."

Essie glanced around the room. The elves' expressions seemed to be softening. Maybe. "In the end, a war between our two peoples benefits neither of us. The only one who benefits is the trolls who will have their enemies and their enemies' potential ally weakened. I don't believe it is a coincidence that the trolls began raiding Tarenhiel again shortly after my marriage to Farrendel. The trolls would have much to fear if my marriage led to a stronger alliance between our kingdoms."

King Weylind's gaze sharpened, though not with anger. "Could your brother be persuaded to fight alongside Tarenhiel against the trolls?"

"With a compelling enough reason, he might. As I stated, Escarland has no love for the trolls." It would be a hard sell. Averett might be for it, but Parliament would balk at helping the elves with a war that didn't pose an immediate threat to Escarland. But if it could be proved that the trolls had something to do with getting their hands on Escarland's army guns and thus meddled in

Escarland's affairs, Parliament and Averett might be convinced to act before it was too late.

The hush in the room hurt Essie's ears. She wasn't sure if the humming she heard was Farrendel's magic or her own ears making up a sound because the room was too quiet.

One of the older male elves on the back row of one of the benches stood up. The lines of silver in his dark brown hair were stark against the youthfulness of most in the room. Surprisingly, he spoke in Escarlish. "As has been stated, the evidence for Escarlish involvement in this attack is circumstantial. I counsel that we do not take any rash actions and wait to see if this marriage alliance will indeed work as promised. We should spend our resources on strengthening our own borders and discovering how the trolls were able to plan such an ambush before we start a war that may not be warranted with Escarland."

His speech had some of the elves around the room nodding. Was it a sign the favor was turning?

There was more discussion, and most of it was in elvish using longer words Essie had yet to learn. But the air of anger and hardness seemed to be fading from the room.

"Very well." King Weylind spoke in elvish, but Essie could interpret the first couple of words anyway. Whatever else he said, she only picked out bits and pieces.

His words had the Council calmly filing from their benches and exiting the room.

Once they were gone, King Weylind stood and strode down from the dais. He halted before Farrendel and gripped his shoulders. "You are well?"

The question had an intensity to it, and Essie remembered the stricken look on King Weylind's face when he'd seen Farrendel's wounds after the battle. Whatever King Weylind thought about her, she couldn't fault his brotherly care for Farrendel.

"Yes." Farrendel gripped King Weylind's upper arms in return before releasing him. "Thanks to Essie."

King Weylind turned to Essie and lightly rested his hands on her upper arms. The elvish version of a hug. "You have my thanks, *isciena*."

Sister. Farrendel had explained one of the times he was teaching Essie elvish that they didn't have a word for sister-in-law. The marriage bond was considered so complete that a sister-in-law was just as much a sister as a biological one.

But this was the first time King Weylind had claimed her as such. For much of the time since she'd married Farrendel, his family had struggled to know how to treat her. If they saw her as Farrendel's wife truly, then she was their sister and should be treated as fully one of the family.

It had been rough, but she couldn't blame them for

their hesitation. Her brothers were probably going to act similarly if she and Farrendel ever had a chance to visit her family.

The warmth in King Weylind's gaze was a stark contrast to the iciness of a few moments ago. The hardness had been an act for the Council, no doubt. It had forced Essie to prove without a doubt that Escarland wasn't to blame for this. If King Weylind had acted supportive of her, it would've looked like he was being swayed simply because of the family relationship.

King Weylind glanced over his shoulder at the rest of the family, who were standing as if waiting for some signal. "Let us take this discussion to the dining room."

Farrendel held out his arm, and Essie rested her hand on his forearm again. As the others filed past them on the way to the dining room, he leaned closer. "You did well."

His words warmed her deep inside her chest. Somehow, she had been convincing enough to talk the elves down from the brink of war. "Thanks for standing with me. It helped to know you were beside me."

That was his place now. Beside her. As it was her place beside him. Together they linked their two peoples. Hopefully that would be enough to stop one war from breaking out and maybe end another.

After the short walk from the hall to the dining room, Essie and Farrendel claimed their usual seats while King

Weylind asked the servant to bring in some cold meats and cheeses. Essie's stomach rumbled, loud enough Farrendel glanced at her. When was the last time either of them ate? Sometime in the morning at Lethorel. Before the battle. Before passing out for hours on end. It was amazing either of them were functioning at the moment.

Once the food arrived, there was a quiet moment as everyone began nibbling—or in Essie's case, wolfing—down the venison sausage and mild cheese.

King Weylind studied Essie, and she quickly swallowed a bite. He seemed about to say something, and she didn't want to answer when her mouth was full.

"It seems I will need to send a diplomat to your brother's court sooner than I had expected. Elspetha, I believe it would be best if you were a part of the diplomatic party." King Weylind's gaze didn't waver from her, as if searching for some reaction.

She grinned. She would see her family again, hug Mother, tell her brothers about life in Estyra, and do her best to convince all of them that she was blissfully happy. "Yes, that would be best. Averett will listen to me, even if he will be wary for some trick on your part."

Farrendel's hand found hers beneath the table and clasped her fingers. He glanced from her to King Weylind, something in his expression torn and resigned at the same time. "I would like to go with Essie. But after that attack, I know I am needed here."

Essie squeezed his fingers in return. Selfishly, she wanted him with her. Her family would have a chance to get to know him. Not to mention, they would have an easier time believing she was happy if they could see her and Farrendel together.

But he was Laesornysh. After that ambush so deep in Tarenhiel, the elves would need their deadliest warrior at the border protecting them.

King Weylind's gaze was calculating as he focused on Essie and Farrendel. "The trolls will take a few weeks to plan a new attack since their ambush failed, and they will assume you have been sent to the border. I believe our case will be better presented before Escarland's king if both you and Elspetha are there together. Jalissa, I would like you to go as well as the official ambassador."

Essie cleared her throat. "I believe the official reason for our trip should be establishing trade between our kingdoms, along with a personal visit to my family. My brother can know the full truth, of course, but I don't think it would be wise for everyone in Escarland to realize just how precarious our situation with the trolls is."

For a moment, both Farrendel and King Weylind just looked at her. Farrendel's mouth curved with the hint of a smile.

That's when it hit her what she'd said. *Our* situation

with the trolls. Like she was claiming the elves as her people and Estyra as her home.

Well, she had. They were her people. This was her home. And she wasn't about to let it get overrun with empire-building trolls.

Darkness had long since descended by the time Essie and Farrendel strolled home through the treetops of Ellonahshinel. Far below, the lights of Estyra glittered, pinpricks in the darkness.

Home. Essie breathed deeply of the fresh scent of sky and tree, her footsteps sure and steady along the winding branches. As they approached the main room nestled in the treetops, something deep inside her relaxed, her chest filled with warmth.

This was home. Oddly, something in her ached at leaving it again so soon, even to see her family.

Two days. That's how long it would take to send messages across the border and arrange her visit. And that's assuming Averett put things in motion quickly on his end. He might hesitate once he learned she was bringing a contingent of elves along with her.

As they stepped inside the main room, Essie started for the doors on the far side but halted. Farrendel had stopped just inside the door, giving her that uncertain look that made her heart go all melty and gentle.

She returned to his side and wrapped her arms around him. It felt so right being close to him like this. "What's wrong?"

"You will be going home." Farrendel remained still, not reaching for her in return.

"I am home. Right here. Right now. Yes, I'm going to be visiting my mother and brothers. Winstead Palace will always be one place I call home. But this place is also my home now." Essie paused, trying to picture Farrendel in Winstead Palace with all its stone walls and floors barely softened with tapestries, woodwork, and rugs. "Honestly, I don't think you're going to like Winstead Palace that much. And my brothers are probably going to be hard on you. Sorry about that in advance. But you'll win them over eventually, or as much as any man I married could win them over. I'll always be their little sister and they will always be protective. I have a feeling you understand that."

Farrendel huffed a breath that might have been an elf version of a laugh. His hands lightly rested on her waist. "You have convinced my family. I will do my best to convince yours."

"I know." Essie stepped closer to him, threading her fingers into the silken strands of his hair. How she loved elven conditioner.

He cupped her cheek with a gentle hand. "Please stay. Tonight."

"Nightmares?" It wouldn't be surprising. She probably would have a few nightmares of her own. With everything that had happened since the battle, she hadn't had a chance to process that fight.

"Yes." Farrendel's eyes searched Essie's face. Maybe he could read the traces the battle had left there.

For now, she had tonight. She stood on her tiptoes and kissed him.

He returned her kiss, his fingers easing into her hair, sending tingles down her back.

There would be no wounds to cut this kiss short. No conversations that needed to be finished. War was coming. There were traitors in both his kingdom and hers. Whatever else the future would hold, she wanted to face it with no regrets.

Time was precious. Maybe it was a human way of thinking about it, but Farrendel was no more guaranteed a long life than she was. Warrior that he was, he would be right there in the center of the battlefield when this war came.

They had two days. Essie didn't plan to waste a single moment.

Don't Miss the Next Adventure!
WAR BOUND

Marriage to an elf is complicated …especially bringing him home to meet the family.

Princess Elspeth of Escarland married the elf prince and achieved peace between the elves and her human people. But after a recent ambush by the trolls, it is clear the trolls are trying to start a war between the elves and humans once again. To keep their peoples at peace, Essie and Farrendel travel to meet Essie's family and negotiate peace.

Yet in Escarland, not everyone is happy with peace. Traitors lurk in both Escarland and Tarenhiel, and it will be up to Essie and Farrendel to flush them out. The consequences of failure might be more personal and deadly than they fear.

COMING SOON!

Also Available from Tara Grayce
LOST IN AVERELL

Average high school student by day, princess by night.

Amy lives both in our world and in the fantasy world of Averell, struggling to balance homework and her duties as a fairytale princess negotiating the intricacies of unicorn -dragon politics.

When her high school crush stumbles through the portal to Averell in her family's basement, she sets out with her shape-shifting unicorn best friend to find him before he dies or sparks a war.

AVAILABLE NOW!

Free Book!

If you sign up for my newsletter, you'll receive a free novella, *Torn Curtains: A Regency Beauty and the Beast Retelling*.

In a magical version of Regency England, scandals abound, especially the magical kind.

Rosalie Klampton is the daughter of a naval admiral. Her father has never been right after his head wound during the battle of Trafalgar, and only Rosie's determination has kept her family together and out of the poor house.

When her father tears down the ugly rose draperies in the country house owned by the elusive earl of Warnwick, Rosie finds herself in service to the earl. He has his own problems, mainly the spell turning him into a beast, the fact that all the magical scholars in England haven't figured out a way to break the spell, and the scandal being a beast has caused.

It will be up to Rosie to help Lord Warnwick navigate the social Season and evade whoever put the spell on him in the first place. Between the scandals and the French spies, working for an earl-turned-beast may be the least of Rosie's worries.

ACKNOWLEDGEMENTS

Thanks so much for reading *Fierce Heart*! I hope Essie's and Farrendel's story touched your heart and brought a smile. If you loved the book, please consider leaving a review on Amazon or Goodreads. Reviews help your fellow readers find books that they will love.

Thank you to everyone who made this release possible! To my writer friends, especially Molly, Morgan, Sarah, Sierra, and Savannah for sharing my excitement for this book. To my dad for loving this book even if it is a romance. To my sisters-in-law Alyssa and Abby for adoring Essie and Farrendel. To my friends Jill and Paula and Bri for loving this book. To my proofreaders Tom, for reading this even if it is a kissing book, Mindy, and Heather, thanks so much for stepping up and getting this done on short notice!

If you want to learn about all my upcoming releases, get great book recommendations, and see a behind-the-scenes glimpse into the writing process, follow my blog at www.taragrayce.com.